THE OUTCAST

AND OTHER DARK TALES

THE OUTCAST

and Other Dark Tales by E.F. Benson

edited by

MIKE ASHLEY

This collection first published in 2020 by
The British Library
96 Euston Road
London NW1 2DB

Dates attributed to each story relate to first publication.

Cataloguing in Publication Data

A catalogue record for this publication is
available from the British Library

ISBN 978 0 7123 5386 1
e-ISBN 978 0 7123 6755 4

Frontispiece illustration: Standing Stone; Wingletang, Scilly Isles.
Photo Fay Godwin © The British Library Board.

Cover design by Mauricio Villamayor with illustration by Sandra Gómez.

Text design and typesetting by Tetragon, London
Printed in England by CPI Group (UK) Ltd, Croydon, CR0 4YY

CONTENTS

INTRODUCTION

THE TRUE GOLDEN AGE OF THE GHOST STORY IS NOT THE High Victorian era, as we may first think. That is the period in which the ghost story was developed, its key features explored and the atmospheric imagery scratched out on the sands of imagination. We owe much to those early writers—Bulwer Lytton, Mary Molesworth, Charlotte Riddell, Sheridan Le Fanu and many more.

But it was their successors who added their own dimension of fear to those images and moods, allowing the ghost story to blossom. From the 1890s and early 1900s the ghost story matured into its full bloom in the 1920s. This was the era of M. R. James, Arthur Machen, Algernon Blackwood, Violet Hunt, Henry James and, of course, E. F. Benson. S. T. Joshi in his definitive study of weird fiction, *Unutterable Horror*, believes that, next to M. R. James, Benson was 'probably the greatest writer of pure ghost stories during this period.'

If anyone was responsible for bringing the ghost story into the twentieth century it was Benson. He enjoyed finding thrills and horrors amongst new inventions such as cars, telephones and the wireless. One can but wonder what horrors he would have evoked with the computer. Although he was as adept at the haunted house story as anyone, he liked to add a new dimension, sometimes light-hearted but more often menacingly sinister. Not for him the flimsy spectre of draperies when instead he could have a phantom with its throat cut; not for him a ghost emerging in the darkness when one can be as frightening in broad daylight. And not for him the restfulness of the grave when the earth itself won't accept the dead. Benson delighted in twisting every idea and image and exploring the unexpected.

During his life Benson put together four collections of his weird tales, *The Room in the Tower* (1912), *Visible and Invisible* (1923), *Spook Stories* (1928) and *More Spook Stories* (1934) but he had been writing such stories since 1896 and continued almost to his death in 1940, so there were many that remained uncollected until Benson expert Jack Adrian brought these together in *The Flint Knife* in 1988. Others still occasionally surface. I included 'The Woman in the Veil' in the British Library anthology *Glimpses of the Unknown* and this volume includes a further previously unreprinted story 'Billy Comes Through'.

Since Benson's death there have been several compilations of his work, but these concentrate mostly on either his best known and most reprinted stories like 'Mrs Amworth', 'Caterpillars' and 'Negotium Perambulans…' or on assembling material from the four standard collections. The lesser known material often gets forgotten.

For this volume I have reassessed all of Benson's output concentrating on those darker stories rather than the more light-hearted tales, and looking for those lesser known stories which demonstrate his ability in creating atmosphere, often with an unusual setting or motif. In addition to the unreprinted 'Billy Comes Through', I've gone back to Benson's earliest collection, the unusual *Six Common Things*, which was full of dark tales but which tends to be overlooked when considering Benson's work.

Yet here you can find ideas and plots that revealed the birth of the more sinister side to Benson's writings which later reviewers forgot.

The stories are presented in chronological order (with one exception) and include an account by Benson of a personal experience he had at his home in Rye along with the story that it inspired. This selection therefore covers the range of Benson's tales of the weird from over forty years with stories that may come fresh to many.

There is, though, something we have to consider about Benson. He may be regarded as one of the best purveyors of ghostly fiction for the first third of the twentieth century, yet he is a complete contradiction. He had earned his reputation as a sharp satirist of Victorian High Society starting in 1893 with the publication of *Dodo*, and was known ever after as 'the author of *Dodo*'. He was a keen sportsman, an expert skater and cricketer who would later write books on the subject. So, when he turned to his novel of the macabre, *The Luck of the Vails*, in 1901, reviewers did not know what to make of it. 'He is about the last novelist whom we should have expected to try on the mantle left by Wilkie Collins,' wrote the reviewer in *The Graphic*, whilst the *Pall Mall Gazette* caustically remarked that writing this novel was 'a rather unwise thing to do.' Yet by the time his ghost-story collections started to appear reviewers had changed their minds, commenting that his stories were 'strikingly original' (*The Scotsman*) and 'brilliantly conceived' (*Irish Society*). Just how did Benson the satirist and Benson the cynic become Benson the master of the ghost story? Therein lies much that will add a further dimension to the stories included here.

BENSON'S GHOSTS

Edward Frederic Benson, always known as Fred to friends and family, was born into a privileged, though not prosperous, well-connected family but one that was also disturbingly dysfunctional. At the time that Fred was born, in July 1867, his father, Edward White Benson, was Master of Wellington College in Berkshire. From there he became Chancellor of Lincoln Cathedral in 1872, before becoming the first Bishop of Truro in 1877 and finally being ordained Archbishop of Canterbury in 1883. He died in 1896 aged 67.

Fred's mother Mary, usually called Minnie, was the sister of philosopher Henry Sidgwick. She was only eighteen when she married White Benson in 1859, he was twenty-nine. They had become acquainted when she was only eleven, and he had recorded in his diary at that time that 'some day dear little Minnie might become my wife.' Within twelve years of their marriage she had given birth to six children. Her life was not her own, not at any time from her eleventh birthday till her husband died forty-four years later. During her adult life apart from being a wife and mother, housekeeper and hostess, she served diligently supporting her husband in his work despite his dominating character and his flares of temper. The Prime Minister, William Gladstone, who was a friend of the family, had mischievously called her 'the cleverest woman in Europe'. Certainly, she had far more to offer than she was ever allowed to give, and at times this led to frustration and mood swings. In fact, depression was almost endemic in both the Sidgwick and Benson families and became a feature of all the children except Fred—or rather he seemed the least affected.

Fred had five siblings. The eldest Martin was almost certainly the most gifted and expected to go far in the world but tragedy struck in February 1878 when he died suddenly of tubercular meningitis, aged only seventeen. Fred, who was ten at the time, had held Martin in awe, and though his brother's death did not immediately affect him, he noticed its affect on his parents and how the loss seemed to drive a wedge in their relationship.

The second eldest child was Arthur who whilst not quite as brilliant as Martin nevertheless became a redoubtable scholar but was somehow remote from the rest of the family. Arthur was never happier than when ensconced in the halls of academe but that did not stop him having severe bouts of depression. He would today be diagnosed as having bipolar disorder, or what was once called manic depression, and yet, it was he who, in 1902, wrote the lyrics for 'Land of Hope and Glory' to Edward Elgar's *Pomp and Circumstance March No. 1*. It seems ironic that such a popular and uplifting song should have been written by someone who, for years, was 'gashed with periods of helpless misery' as Fred put it.

The third child was Mary Eleanor, known as Nellie, who was the most carefree and joyous of the children and seemed the most generous. After studying at Oxford, she moved to London to work with the poor in Lambeth as a volunteer social worker. Alas she died of diphtheria in 1890 just days after her twenty-seventh birthday. Perhaps the most rounded of all the children she had become a shining light around which the family bonded and her death left the family bereft, even more so than Martin's. 'With her death some unrecapturable magic was lost,' wrote Fred.

The fourth child was Margaret, or Maggie, just two years older than Fred and for some years his closest companion. She was highly intellectually gifted but suffered from frail physical health. For a change of climate she accompanied Fred to Greece and Egypt, joining him in his archaeological work and though untrained she became a renowned Egyptologist. She was granted the concession in 1895 to excavate the Temple of Mut at Karnak and in 1899 produced her account of the excavation with her companion Janet Gourlay. Maggie also worked relentlessly in the promotion of women's rights and opportunities to study as well as furthering her own theological studies. This relentless drive was a symptom of her own mental imbalance which also manifested in a savage temper (inherited from her father) and bouts of jealousy. After her father's death in 1896 the family had taken in Lucy Tait, the daughter of the previous archbishop, and before long Maggie became jealous of her mother's affections for Lucy. Lucy contributed to the family income and helped buy the lease to Tremans, at Horstead Keynes in Sussex in 1899. Maggie's emotions ebbed and flowed and for a while she seemed happier, but in 1907 her inner turmoil erupted. She began to self-harm and one night was overwhelmed by what Fred called a 'homicidal mania'. That has led people to believe that Maggie attacked either her mother or Lucy with a kitchen knife. But Fred was not present and it may be that Maggie was trying to kill herself. The full story has never been revealed. Maggie was certified (what we now call 'sectioned') and removed to an asylum. Fred remained a loyal friend until her final days and his help led to a degree of recovery such that she was released from the asylum to a nursing home in Wimbledon.

After Fred, the youngest child was Robert, always known by his second name, Hugh. He was petulant and selfish and seemed to take a delight in being at odds with the family. He was almost certainly spoiled by the family's devoted nurse, Beth, who regarded Hugh as her favourite. Hugh's opposition came to an extreme in 1903 when he converted to Roman Catholicism. Having got his way, Hugh became even more sanctimonious, though he was popular as a priest and preacher. There was always a feeling that he had never really grown up. He wrote prolifically until his death brought on by a feverish workload and a weak heart. He had a fear that he might become catatonic and implored his brother Arthur to make sure he was dead before he was buried. He wanted his tomb to be easily accessible and the coffin have a lid that could easily be opened, and also that before his burial he should be bled to ensure he was dead. Arthur obliged.

All three surviving brothers wrote voluminously, including ghost stories. Arthur's tended to be more antiquarian and scholarly, as you'd expect, with most collected in *The Hill of Trouble* (1903) and *The Isles of Sunset* (1905). Hugh's were, not surprisingly, more doctrinal and apostolic, collected in *The Light Invisible* (1903) and *The Mirror of Shalott* (1907), though Hugh also wrote several cautionary novels such as the apocalyptic *Lord of the World* (1907) and its partner novel *The Dawn of All* (1911) and the anti-spiritualist *The Necromancers* (1909). Hugh never seemed happier than when he was preaching, and especially when imposing his views upon others.

This, then, was Fred's family. He survived when all others passed away. After Martin's death in 1878, Nellie's in 1890 and his father's in 1896, Fred said farewell to Hugh in 1914, Maggie in 1916, his mother in 1918 and finally Arthur in 1925. Fred's strength lay in his remarkable resilience and his sense of humour. He was very thick-skinned, with little concern for how the world regarded him, and could somehow find humour in the most dire of situations. He also buried himself in his work, and though he was always the first to respond to any family emergency, his ability to not only write, but to work on several projects at once, kept his mind and intellect alert and vibrant. He wrote, compiled or collaborated on over a hundred books.

He was, of course, surrounded by incident. His entire family, sometimes disguised, provided sufficient material for background for his books, mostly his society novels but occasionally his ghost stories. In all the stories included here you will find references, often oblique, to disturbing families and events, such as in 'The Passenger', 'By the Sluice', and 'The Corner House'. There is also a beautiful evocation of childhood memories in 'Pirates'.

Fred must have been fascinated with ghosts, or at least the spiritual world, since his childhood. His father had co-founded a Ghost Society at Trinity College, Cambridge, in 1851 for the serious study of psychic and spiritual phenomena. The Society continued long after Edward Benson left Cambridge and a later member included Henry Sidgwick, one of Fred's mother's brothers. Sidgwick became co-founder of the Society for Psychical Research in 1882, serving as its first president. By then Fred's father had distanced himself from the study of ghosts, but Fred remained fascinated, later attending seances. In his book of reminiscences, *As We Were*, Fred tells a story, recorded by his father, about his grandfather's youth in Yorkshire where he was raised by a chemist, Dr Sollitt, who was also a practising astrologer and a dabbler in black arts. One day Sollitt endeavoured to summon the powers of darkness and was so frightened by the results that he took refuge in the local church.

Fred's mother also seems to have inherited the psychic abilities of the Sidgwick's. G. K. Chesterton once remarked that 'Mrs Benson not only seemed to know everyone who had ever seen a ghost, but every ghost as well.'

When at King's College, Cambridge, Benson came under the influence of M. R. James, who then served as Dean. They were both members of the Chit-Chat club, an informal literary society where, each Saturday, they gathered together and took it in turns to relate some subject or story. M. R. James began to tell one of his ghost stories each Christmas Eve. Fred's brother Arthur continued this tradition when he was a Master at Eton College and Fred sometimes attended these winter's tales. Fred later adapted one of the stories for his novel *The Luck of the Vails* (1901) a melodramatic account of a family goblet which is variously lost and found, but each time it is found brings with it a curse.

Clearly there was much in Fred's family background and upbringing to provide material for all his writings. Not that it seemed at the outset that he would become a writer. He was an active sportsman and mountaineer, climbing the Jungfrau in 1889. He gained an honorary degree in archaeology and won a grant to excavate the Roman walls in Chester in 1891. From 1892 to 1895 he worked at the British Archaeological School in Athens, and spent the winters working for the Egyptian Exploration Fund where Maggie joined him.

While at Cambridge Fred had started work on the novel *Dodo* for his own amusement with no real idea of what he wanted to do. After a while he ran out of steam, but he later returned to the story, with his enthusiasm rekindled, and completed the draft. Unbeknown to Fred his mother sent this scrappy draft to Henry

James who admonished Fred on his lack of style. Undeterred Fred worked on it again, this time sending another draft to Lucas Malet, the daughter of Charles Kingsley. Her comments were more incisive than James's had been and gave Fred the focus to revise and even extend the story and he sent the finished manuscript to the publisher Methuen at the end of 1892. Methuen accepted it immediately and it was published in May 1893.

Benson was then in Greece and had thought no more about the book so was astounded when he returned to discover that it had become a bestseller. Everyone was talking about it. It ran through twelve editions before the end of 1893 and was never out of print throughout his life. The book has no real plot, and maybe that works in its favour. The eponymous Dodo, or Dorothea Vane to give her full and very apt name, was a creature of London Society who uses her charms, beauty and wiles to her own benefit. It was rumoured at the time that Benson had modelled Dodo on Margot Tennant, later Margot Asquith, Countess of Oxford. Benson denied this, but the belief has remained.

It has never been clear how a twenty-six year old produced such a scandalous and successful novel, but it established his name, though it took him years to live up to it again. The next few books that followed, including *The Rubicon* and *The Judgment Books*, were dismal failures, but critical approval returned with *The Vintage* (1898), set during the Greek War of Independence, and its sequel *The Capsina* (1899). Readers wanted another *Dodo*, but Benson chose to write whatever appealed to him. He did, though, return to other satires of society, notably *Scarlet and Hyssop* (1902), and thereafter Fred was able to write enough that satisfied his critics and readers alike to sustain his reputation.

Between these novels, Fred turned to writing short stories, a fair percentage of which were either pure supernatural or simply odd. His second book, *Six Common Things* (1893) is a mixture of stories some, like 'Poor Miss Huntingford' satirising society, but others, like 'A Winter Morning', which is reprinted here, being uncommonly dark and morbid. The stories suggest that Benson was using fiction as therapy for some of the bleakness around him, not least the death of Martin, and though many of his later stories were also sombre and melancholy, none was as dark as those in this book.

Dodo had been Benson's key to the literary world and magazines welcomed him. He appeared regularly and soon notched up his first ghost story, 'Dummy on a Dahabeah' (included here), which was syndicated in newspapers during May and June 1896. It is set in Egypt, where Benson was most active at that time. He chose not to include that story in any of his later collections, though he did reprint his next weird tale, 'At Abdul Ali's Grave', published in 1899, in his first such collection, *The Room in the Tower* (1912). For years, though, Benson's output of short fiction was predominantly humorous or society stories. His production of weird tales averaged only one or two a year and did not start to rise significantly until after the First World War. This may partly have been because of his family commitment which were not released until after his mother's death in 1918, but it may also have been because Benson had not had much success with his novels which featured the weird.

The first of these had been the ill-fated *The Judgment Books* (1895) which took more than a lead out of the pages of Oscar Wilde's *The Picture of Dorian Gray* (1890). In Benson's version an artist produces a self-portrait but as he progresses he believes his personality is being absorbed by the picture leaving him nothing but a shell, whilst the picture takes on an image that is repellent. Was Benson feeling guilty, wondering if he was not the person he thought he was, or was he simply reproducing the mood that was prevalent in his family at that time?

After *The Luck of the Vails*, which proved popular with the public but was again critically mauled, Benson's next novel of the weird was *The Image in the Sand* (1905), which is set in Egypt and incorporates elements of his earlier story 'At Abdul Ali's Grave'. It tells of a man desperate to make contact with the spirit of his wife who has been dead for sixteen years. The novel includes all the paraphernalia of the occult and spirit possession and the critics recognised the powerful atmosphere that Benson created, yet still felt that the author was settling for mediocre potboilers rather than producing the good work of which he was capable.

Critics begrudgingly admitted that his next novel, *The Angel of Pain* (1906), expanded from his story 'The Man Who Went Too Far', was 'acceptable' and met literary standards, but the public adored it. The first printing sold out on the day of release. In this book Benson created a world which readers easily recognised, pitting a successful businessman against an artist for the love of a woman. The loser returns to the simplicity of Nature and it is there that the supernatural intrudes in the form of the god Pan.

It was with the success of *The Angel of Pain* that Benson risked writing more short stories of the supernatural leading to his first collection, *The Room in the Tower*, but it was thirteen years before Benson wrote another novel of the weird, leaving aside his children's fantasy *David Blaize and the Blue Door* (1918). *Across the Stream*

(1919) explores Benson's views of spiritualism and the extent to which trying to communicate with the dead is really opening a path to demonic powers rather than the spirits of the dead.

It was soon after this novel that Benson wrote *Queen Lucia* (1920) the first of what would become his series featuring the social rivalry of leading individuals in the town of Tilling, a thinly disguised Rye in Sussex. Benson had moved to Rye in 1919, after the death of his mother, and settled in Lamb House, which had been the home of Henry James. It came complete with its own ghost in the garden, which inspired Benson's story 'The Flint Knife'.

Following the success of *Queen Lucia* came *Miss Mapp* in 1922 and the two primary characters thereafter vied with each other through three more extremely successful books. At this same time Benson brought Dodo back in *Dodo Wonders* (1921) and turned to writing a number of popular non-fiction books about historical characters ranging from Sir Francis Drake to Charlotte Bronte plus several books of reminiscences. His production rate was phenomenal, often two or three books a year. He also served as Mayor of Rye from 1934 to 1937. Yet throughout the 1920s and into the 1930s Fred wrote more ghost stories than at any other time, and continued to produce the occasional supernatural novel, the last being the rather salacious *Raven's Brood* in 1934. This suggests that by the 1920s Fred had found increasing pleasure in turning to the ghost story and earning a second, or really a third reputation.

Edward Frederic Benson died of cancer on 29 February 1940 aged 72. His last book, *Final Edition*, was at the presses as he was buried in Rye cemetery.

Quality is not often equated with quantity, and Fred would have been the first to admit that many of his books were below par and forgettable, but that does not apply to his ghost stories. There are a few that are too formulaic, and Fred did occasionally use the same idea once or twice too often, but he also rang the changes and strove for originality. As the following stories show, E. F. Benson was a ghost-story writer of considerable talent, and his work will be read and enjoyed for many years to come.

MIKE ASHLEY

DUMMY ON A DAHABEAH

I HAD BEEN AWAKE SOME TIME, WEDGED TIGHT IN MY BERTH, with a knee against the wall and a foot against the iron rail, which prevented my falling bodily on the floor, listening lazily to the drumming of the screw. We had passed through very rough weather the day before, and the boat was still rolling heavily. From time to time I could see the horizon, bearing Crete on its rim, swing into sight across the glass of the porthole, and now and then a great blue transparency of wave would fling itself against the window, darkening the cabin for a moment. Then the boat righted itself, and the bright reflection of the water cast on the roof scudded along again till another big wave took us in hand. But it was a glorious morning, and though I would willingly have prolonged those delicious moments which lie on the borderland between sleeping and waking, I felt it my duty to wake Tom. He stretched himself lazily and sat up.

'It is good to be at sea,' he said. 'When do we get in to Alexandria?'

'About one.'

'Well, it's time to get up. Shall I get up first or you? How this old tub is rolling! There's not room for us both to dress together.'

'You,' said I promptly.

Tom rang the bell and ordered his bath.

'Hot and salt,' said he.

He staggered into his dressing-gown, plunged at his slippers, and sidled out of the cabin. I found to my disgust that I was too much awake to continue not thinking, and read the directions for putting on the lifebelt, according to the principles of the P and O. Drowning was a horrible death! People who had been nearly drowned were supposed to say that it was delightful, like going slowly to sleep. Well, perhaps it was better than some deaths. And then, by a natural transition, my thoughts wandered to where I was going, and what I was going to do.

Tom and I were on our way to join Harry Brookfield. Six months ago he had lost his wife. She had been dressing for a ball in London and her dress caught fire. She died in a few hours.

Since then he had been abroad, and this winter he was in Egypt. He had written to me saying that he was going up the Nile in a dahabeah for a few months, and would Tom and I join him. And, we for our vices and virtues, being people of leisure, said we would. Harry had been in Cairo for a few days already, and we hoped to join him there in the evening.

But the rough weather detained us, and we did not get into Alexandria till after the express for Cairo had left. Alexandria is not a particularly attractive place, but it has the smell of the south about it, and to me no place is without merit provided it smells of the south.

After dinner we sat in the open garden of the Hotel Abbat and smoked. Smoking begets silence, and silence thought, and thought speech; and after a little while Tom began to speak of a thing which had several times been in the background of my mind since the receipt of the letter which asked us to come to Egypt.

'It's odd Harry coming out to Egypt again, isn't it?' he said.

'Why?' I asked, because I knew and did not wish to say.

'His wife, you know. He spent his honeymoon on a dahabeah up the Nile.'

'Yes, and on the same dahabeah as that on which we are going now.'

'Have you seen him since—since it happened?'

'Yes, I met him in Florence in November, and he came with me from there to Athens before you came out.'

'How does he bear it?'

'He never mentions her name, and tries never to think of her,' I said.

'That makes it all the odder, his taking his dahabeah.'

'Yes, unless he has succeeded in never thinking of her.'

Harry met us next day at Cairo station, and we were both, I think, surprised to see him looking so extremely well and prosperous. Great sorrow—and his sorrow had been very great—usually leaves some trace behind, often some little nervous trick of manner, or, more generally, when the mind is unoccupied, a haunted, anxious look. But he was, in every respect, his old cheery self. The traditional English plan of travelling in order to forget, which reverses the '*coelum non animum*' proverb, had evidently vindicated itself in his case.

'Delighted to see you,' he said. 'Tom, you are growing fat. You shall sit in the sun till you are as dry as a grasshopper. As for you,' he went on, turning to me, 'you simply look absurdly well. People like you have got no business to spend a winter in Egypt. We'll go straight to the dahabeah. She's ready, and we can start in an hour. Cairo is hateful—cram full of the refuse of English-speaking people. One always sees on Shepheard's veranda some eight or ten of the people one hoped never to see again.'

And before three o'clock we were off.

At this point in my story I must give a word of warning. I make no defence for what I am going to tell you, except the very unsatisfactory and unconvincing one that I declare that what I record as happening to me is true. Tom Soden is also willing to declare that what is recorded of him is true. Harry Brookfield died last year, and I can no longer make him a witness. But many people who, before his death, played whist with him and Tom will tell you that they have often heard him say to Tom, 'Why can't you play your hand as you played your dummy's up the Nile?' And when he asked this question Tom not unfrequently would turn rather pale and ask for a whisky and soda.

That is all my defence.

We started with a good north wind which took us quickly along, the great sail stretched taut and firm, and the water rising from the forefoot in a thin feather. That evening we got to Memphis, and as the moon was full we took donkeys and rode out to Sakharah, on the edge of the desert. There is an Arab proverb, 'He who smells the desert once, smells it when he dies,' and sometimes in London, which smells quite different, I have felt, on hot June evenings, when the air seemed to be dying with the want of breath, that I should be almost willing to die if I could smell the desert once more. The truth is that the desert alone, of all things created, does not smell at all, and our sense of smell, the most delicate and keen sense we possess, finds it infinitely restful to draw in warm, unused air that smells of nothing at all. Perhaps that is what the Arab proverb means. The moon was at its full;

Jupiter, blazing low on the horizon, cast a shadow of its own; the seven Pleiades, distinct and unblurred, hung high, freed of their silver net; and low in the north the Great Bear swung slowly to its setting, upside down. To the west, the desert stretched away, silent and sombre, across a continent.

Even Tom, who is not given to have 'feelings,' felt its spell.

'I should like,' he said, 'to walk straight into it for ever, if only it was always moonlight.'

The false dawn was already beginning to glow faintly in the east when we got back to the dahabeah, and a couple of hours after we had gone to bed we weighed anchor, and still followed by the north wind slid on our course.

For several days we had a delicious, uneventful life, reading not at all, talking not much, only sitting in the sun and charging our bodies with stores of superfluous health. But towards the end of the week Harry began to get rather restless, and it occurred by degrees to all of us that we might perhaps do well to employ ourselves, however lazily, while we sat in the sun. The wind still held good, and it was a pity to stop the boat and go shooting, for the best shooting ground lay farther up the river, and in all human probability, we should have plenty of days on which we could not move, so that it was best to go on while we could. And one afternoon, while we were dozing after lunch, Tom said lazily:

'Why not play cards?'

Brookfield jumped up at once.

'The very thing,' he said. 'Have any of you fellows got cards? We'll play whist with dummy. Whist is the only game one doesn't get tired of. Three years ago we used even to play double—' and he stopped suddenly.

Brookfield was among the best whist players in England, but, as far as I can remember, his wife used to play even better than he. He, I know, always used to consider that she was the better player of the two. Personally, I play moderately well, but I have none of those instantaneous intuitions which mark a first-rate player's intuitions, which he will probably be able to justify by rule if he thinks, but which seem to dictate to him directly. Tom contrasted finely with Brookfield. He often had extraordinary promptings in his mind to play absolutely fatal cards, and his justification for following such promptings was a thing to make angels weep.

That night, after dinner, and for twenty-five successive nights, we played together, and sometimes also in the afternoon. On each occasion we cut for playing with dummy, and on each occasion, oddly enough, the cards determined that Tom should do so. We meant to write to the press about it till more extraordinary events put it out of our minds.

On the whole this was the best arrangement, for Brookfield would not have cared for the game if he had played with Tom, and as it is a slight advantage to play with dummy, it was better that Tom should do so than he. We played small points—a shilling, I think—and we played the same all the time.

For the first few nights, as was natural, Tom lost steadily, but slowly, for the cards favoured him. He played his usual inconsequent game, if possible leading a singleton, starting a rough at once, and after making a few tricks having his trumps cleared out by a couple of rounds, and losing the majority of the remaining tricks.

But on the fourth or the fifth night he quite suddenly played a game correctly, or, to be accurate, he made his dummy play correctly. I had dealt and his dummy was to lead. Dummy's hand contained four trumps, six spades, two diamonds, and one heart, and Tom's horny fist was, as usual, stretched across the table to pick up the heart. But instead of playing it he suddenly changed his mind and led a small trump, holding queen, ten, and two small ones. He himself took the first trick with the king and led them back. He hesitated a moment before playing dummy's card, but eventually played the ten, not the queen, and Brookfield took it with the ace. A round of diamonds fell to dummy, and he led the queen of trumps, capturing my knave. In other words, Tom, the illiterate, uneducated Tom, had executed a successful finesse—a simple one, it is true, but a correct and justifiable one.

Dummy was now left with the thirteenth trump. He established his spades after two rounds, lost one trick in hearts, roughed the next round with his remaining trump, and made four tricks in spades. Tom was already, then, up, and thus got out. Though dummy's hand was a good one, Tom himself held no cards except the king of trumps, and the only way to get out was to play the hand exactly as dummy had played it.

Now, it was a simple enough hand to play for anyone who knew anything about whist, but you must remember that Tom knew nothing about whist. That he had generalised from watching our play was almost impossible, for he had invariably nailed his colours to the single one lead before that, and indeed the last time he had done so he had scored heavily, for both Harry and I happened to be very weak in common suits, and had been unable to get the lead till the single rough had developed into a double.

Harry gathered up the cards and made them while Tom dealt for dummy.

'You played that hand correctly,' he said. 'Why didn't you lead dummy's single card as usual?'

'Well, you fellows always tell me it's wrong,' he said, 'and it seemed hard luck on dummy to make him play badly. Ace of hearts,' he added, turning up the trump card. Oddly enough, the next deal very closely resembled the last, but Tom held the sort of hand which dummy held before. He got the lead in the third round and led his single card, spoiled his triumph by roughing, let us in on clubs, and lost the odd.

Harry gathered up the cards with a laugh.

'So you've gone back to the old tactics,' he said.

'You had too many clubs, and, besides, the trumps went badly for us,' said Tom, meaning, I suppose, that he had only one club and had used his trumps to rough.

'The trumps lay just as they lay before when you scored off us by finessing,' said Harry. 'You could have done exactly the same thing again.'

'What's finessing?' asked Tom.

Harry stared.

'You finessed when you made dummy play the ten of trumps instead of the queen, two rounds ago.'

'Did I?' said Tom. 'It must have been a mistake. Don't argue, Harry. Whose deal?'

There were two candles on the table where we were playing, and a big lamp on the dining-table. Once or twice Tom looked up quickly, as if something had startled him, and then got up and moved the lamp away. All evening he seemed rather on edge, and when a moth flew in at the open window, and immolated itself in the candle, he started to his feet, dropping his hand. He continued to play with his usual cheerful disregard of anything but the current trick.

We played that night for about two hours, and though nothing interrupted the monotonous imbecility of Tom's play, I noticed several times that he played dummy's hand rather well. But about eleven he said he was sleepy, and yawned his way to bed, while Harry and I went on deck to smoke the last cigarette of the day.

We had stopped for the night just below a small Arab village. A late rising moon showed the mud huts huddled together on the bank, a few palm trees cutting the sky with their incisive fronds, and on either side the long line of the desert. It was very hot, and now and then a truffle of wind blew across the stream; a dry, scorching wind, without health in it. A dog sat on the edge of the river, howling lugubriously. The moon was so bright that one could hardly resist the illusion that its light was hot, and, indeed, Harry moved his chair into the shade, with a sudden, impatient exclamation. Then there was silence again.

After a while he spoke slowly, and weighing his words.

'It's very strange,' he said to me, 'but tonight I have felt again what I have not felt for nearly six months. You know for a week after she died—I am speaking of my wife—I used constantly to think that she was somewhere close to me. Now, tonight, all through that game of whist, I felt it strongly. I suppose it is only the associations I have with this dahabeah. Oddly enough, it is the same one that we came up in for our honeymoon. I tried to get another one instead, but I couldn't.'

He was silent a moment and then went on.

'You-know I have always tried to avoid thinking of her,' he said. 'It is best to do so. It is no use keeping a wound open. Death is death, whatever you may say.'

He flicked the ash off his cigarette, which was nearly burned out, and lit another from the stump.

'I have always to root those memories out of my mind,' he went on, 'and I mean to go on trying. But tonight that feeling was so strong, the feeling, I mean, that she was there, that I had to speak of it. It is a great relief to speak of things. If one bottles them up inside one, they go bad, so to speak. And now I have told you, and I feel better.'

He touched a bell and the Arab servant came up.

'Whisky and soda,' said Brookfield. 'Have one, too, Vincent. Two sodas.'

He shifted his chair again, as if showing that the subject was to be changed.

'The moon is as big as a bandbox tonight,' he said. 'Don't you always imagine the moon to be as big as some small object? In England it varies between soup plates and half-crowns, but in the south it extends to bandboxes. It was almost a sin to sit in the cabin tonight, but the cards would have blown about here. By the way, did you notice Tom's play once or twice? He actually played intelligently.'

'Yes,' said I, 'but the funny thing was that he never played his own hand intelligently. It was always dummy's hand that he managed well.'

'That's odd. I didn't notice it. Usually, it is the other way round. Even a good player often spoils his dummy's hand for the sake of his own. At least a good player will often run a risk with his dummy's hand which he wouldn't with his own. Do you know Bertie Carpuncle? He plays a cautious game himself, but if he ever plays with dummy he makes his dummy do rash and brilliant things. It's the oddest thing to see.'

The whisky and soda arrived. We both silently blessed Mr Schweppe and were just preparing to turn in when Tom appeared in pyjamas.

'Greedy boys,' he remarked. 'Give me some, too. It's as hot as blazes below. My cabin had been shut up and it was stifling. By the way, which of you uses Cherry Blossom scent? My cabin smelt strongly of it.'

I saw Harry's eyes grow large and startled for a moment in the darkness, but he replied almost immediately:

'Cherry Blossom fiddlesticks! It's the bean fields. You can smell them here.'

Tom sniffed the hot night air.

'I can't. Well, here's my whisky. One long drink and then I go to bed.'

We all went down again in a few moments, but as I passed Harry's cabin he called me in.

'You never use Cherry Blossom, do you?' he asked.

'No, nor any other. I thought you said it was the bean fields.'

'Of course it was. I forgot. Well, goodnight.'

Next evening brought us to Assiout, and we spent an hour or two in the bazaars, which seemed to be full of cheap Manchester cottons. Tom thought them very native and characteristic, and bought several yards of a flimsy sort of calico, stamped with the leaves of date palms in red. He was delighted with them till he found S No 2304 in the corner. We pointed out to him that they were just as pretty whether they had S No 2304 on them or not, but he was dissatisfied.

That night, and on every night during the next week, we played whist after dinner. Each time, as I have said, Tom played with dummy, and his own play remained consistently bad, while his dummy play consistently improved. Often he would take up a bad card to lead, drop it again, and substitute a good one. It almost seemed as if one particular part of his brain played dummy and another, his normal brain, played his own cards; or as if another will was superimposed on his when playing for dummy. Harry and I laughed at it, and got accustomed to it, but Tom was always curiously unlike himself while he was playing. He was preoccupied and rather irritable. On one occasion, when it was dummy's lead, he sat looking at the cards so long that I was just going to remind him that he had to lead, when he suddenly looked up across the table, then at me, and said:

'Her lead, isn't it?'

A moment afterwards, even before Harry had time to burst out laughing, he looked at us confusedly and said:

'I beg your pardon. I don't know what I have been thinking about. Dummy to play. Small heart.'

Harry put down his cards.

'Our Thomas is asleep,' he said, 'and has been dreaming about Her. What's her name, Tommy, and when is it going to come off?'

But Tom had turned suddenly pale.

'It's stifling in here,' he said, 'and I wish to goodness one of you two wouldn't use Cherry Blossom. Scents are not meant for men.'

'It's She,' said I. 'Who is she, Tommy?'

Once again Harry's eyes grew large and startled.

'Come on,' he said, 'it's your turn, Vincent.'

That night, for the first time, I began to feel vaguely uncomfortable. At the moment when Tom said, 'Her lead, isn't it?' I found myself looking towards dummy's place quite seriously and quite instinctively. No doubt his very matter-of-fact tone had led me to do it. Of course I saw nothing there. The cards were arranged in suits on the table, and a chair, which happened to be put in such a position that if we have been playing four Tom's partner would have been sitting in it, was, of course, empty. Then Harry's laugh broke in, and I wondered what I had looked up for.

Once again Harry and I stopped up on deck for a few minutes, and he said to me:

'Do you remember me telling you a few nights ago that I had determined not to think of her? I made a great effort, and I have not failed. Ah!' he sniffed the air—'bean fields again. That accounts for Tom's Cherry Blossom.'

That night I did not get to sleep for a long time. Every now and then I dozed a little, but was recalled to my senses by a sudden whiff of some faint smell passing by me. My cabin was separated from Tom's only by a curtain, and I thought I could hear him stirring. At length I got up, and he, too, as far as I could judge by faint, rustling sounds that came from his cabin, was moving about, and I drew the curtain aside and looked in. The moonlight streamed in through the window, and by its light I could see that he was lying on his back, fast asleep.

Of course, there were a hundred explanations. He was restless in his sleep; or it was the curtain over his door that had been rustling, for a strong wind was blowing up the passage that led from the saloon to the cabins; and I went back to bed again.

Cherry Blossom! Cherry Blossom! What dim chord of memory twanged in my mind at the thought of it? Where had I smelt it? I could not remember what Cherry Blossom smelt like. Rather sickly, I should think. I dozed off again, thinking about it vaguely and dreamily, and suddenly awoke with a start. That was the smell, the smell that I could perceive in my cabin now, the smell which Harry had said was bean fields. And then, in a moment, I remembered where I had smelt it before. A crowded ball-room—a band playing a Strauss waltz—Harry's voice saying. 'Hallo! I never expected to see you here! We are just back from Egypt. Come and see my wife.' Then, finding myself on the balcony overlooking the square, where a tall, pale woman was sitting talking to half a dozen men. She saw me and smiled to me, putting out her hand, and I advanced towards her. Then a little breeze shook the awning and wafted towards me the delicate scent—not sickly—of the smell I had perceived in my cabin when I awoke. Once again that evening, when I was dancing with her, she dropped her handkerchief and I picked it up for her. Her handkerchief smelt of Cherry Blossom.

I was frightened, and fright is tiring. Soon I fell asleep.

The dragoman we had with us on the boat had taken the Brookfields up on their honeymoon, and next morning, as I was on deck, he came up to me and asked if we wanted to stop at Grigeh. There was nothing to see there, he said, and when he had been up with Mr and Mrs Brookfield before they had gone straight on. A sudden idea struck me, and I asked him which cabin Mrs Brookfield had had.

He thought for a moment and then said:

'No 3. I am sure it was No 3, and Mr Brookfield the one opposite.'

No 3 was Tom's cabin.

In the next few nights, I can only remember one thing that struck me as curious, excepting, of course, the constant improvement in Tom's dummy play, and the slight deterioration, if anything, in his own. It was this:

One night, dummy held a long hand of trumps, and it was Tom's lead. He opened with the king and ace of a common suit. Dummy only had two, the eight and the four, and Tom played out the eight first and then four. He then led another of the same suit for dummy to rough. Harry burst out laughing.

'It is pathetic,' he said. 'You make dummy call for trumps and then don't lead them to him! Poor, ill-used dummy!'

Tom looked puzzled.

'I wanted him to trump,' he said.

'Then why didn't you make him call for trumps?'

'Call for trumps? Oh, that's when you play a high one and then a low one, isn't it? He never called for trumps.'

But both Harry and I had noticed it.

Though nothing else strange happened for two or three days, an odd change had begun to come over Tom. During the day he was himself, but after dinner he always became curiously nervous and agitated. One night after I had gone to bed he came into my cabin half-undressed, and sat for an hour there. He said his cabin was so close and stuffy; though it was the coolest cabin on the boat, and for the last day or two the heat had decreased considerably. And while we were playing whist he would constantly glance up quickly and nervously, and more than once I saw him focus his eyes at the empty air in front of him, just in that same disconcerting way which dogs sometimes have towards dusk, as if they saw something which we could not see. Meanwhile, we had gone steadily on. We had passed Grigeh, and if the wind held we expected to be at Luxor, where we were to stop for a time, before the end of the week.

One night after dinner Tom and I were sitting on deck. The moon had not yet risen, but by the keen, clear starlight we could see the broad river stretched out in front of us like a plate of burnished metal. To the left rose high, orange-coloured rocks, which gave out the heat they had been baked in during the day, and on the right lay the brown expanse of desert. An Arab below was chanting some monotonous native song, and the echo was returned from the rocks in a curious plaintive whine. Suddenly the wind dropped altogether, and the great sail flapped against the mast. The current took us slowly back, and as we neared the shore the anchor was thrown out, and we stopped for the night.

Suddenly Tom caught my arm.

'There, did you not see it?' he said.

I looked quickly round in the direction of his finger, but there was only the pale, glimmering deck, and behind the circle of the sky.

'It came last night to fetch us to play whist,' he said. 'I am frightened. Let us go quick, or it will come again.'

'My dear Tom, what do you mean?' I asked.

'Never mind, it is nothing,' he said. 'Come quickly. It will be all right then.'

And he literally dragged me downstairs.

'Harry, where are you?' he called. 'Come and play whist, it's getting late.'

'Well, I've been waiting for you,' shouted a voice from the saloon. Again we cut for dummy, and again it fell to Tom. For the last week he had won steadily. That night, whether it was that Tom's strange terror had affected my nerves, I do not know, for though I had at present neither seen nor heard anything peculiar, from the moment I began to play I felt that there was something living in the room besides ourselves, and when on one occasion I looked round and found the soft-footed dragoman, who had entered the room to get orders for next day without my hearing him, standing at my elbow, I could have shrieked aloud.

It must have been about nine when we began. Harry, as usual, was absolutely absorbed in the game, but Tom's eyes went peering nervously about the cabin, and, as for me, I confess to having been absolutely upset. But the game went on quietly, and by degrees I recovered myself. Tom was playing even worse than usual, and the dummy had not much opportunity to distinguish itself. But at length there came a hand—I cannot remember all the details of it—in which, towards the end, dummy held three suits, his trumps being exhausted, in two of which, diamonds and spades, Harry and I were both over him. Tom had already run out of spades, and held only one small diamond. He led the ace of hearts, in which suit dummy held the king and knave. Tom took up the knave to put on third hand, hesitated, and played the king instead. He then led the queen, which drew the knave, and after that the ten. He was four up already, and this secured him the odd trick. Then said Tom:

'What a fool I was to play the king. I can't think what made me do it.'

Harry gasped.

'Why, man, if you'd played any other card, you'd have lost the odd. Don't you see, if dummy had not played the king, the lead would have been placed in his hand next round, and he would have had to play a diamond with a spade. You had to unblock.'

Tom said frankly that he did not understand, and the game went on. The next round dummy played the grand coup, the opportunity for which seldom occurs, and is still seldom recognised. But Tom saw it at once.

Two rounds afterwards I had just picked up my cards and was sorting them, when—it takes longer to describe than it did to take place—I was suddenly conscious of something seen out of the corner of my eye on my left. Also, I could no longer see the white flash of cards where dummy's hand was laid on the table. I saw a glimmer as of a white dress, a faintly outlined profile, and at that moment a little breeze blowing in through the open window wafted across me a faint smell of Cherry Blossom. The whole thing was instantaneous, and I looked up from the hand I was sorting. There was nothing there—dummy's cards were laid on the table, the chair was empty, and the little puff of wind had passed. Then looking at Tom, I saw that he was looking fixedly at the opposite side of the table. Moist beads of perspiration stood on his forehead, and one hand was clutching the tablecloth. Then he gave a long-drawn breath of horror, and his head fell forwards on the table.

We raised him, and soon brought him round. He had complained all day of headache, and he said he thought he had had a touch of the sun. He was sorry to break up the game, but he thought he had better go to bed. No doubt he would be all right in the morning, and—and would Harry mind his moving into the other empty cabin?

Next morning he seemed better, but nervously anxious not to be left alone. Harry spent the morning in writing letters, and Tom and I sat on the deck. I expected he would speak of something—I did not know what—and before long he did.

There had been a silence, and Tom broke it.

'Did you see nothing?' he said.

It would have been mere affectation to pretend not to know what he meant.

'I hardly know if I did nor not,' I said.

'But her face—her face,' he went on almost in a whisper. 'There was a horrible scar across it, a bar of raw, burned flesh. What happened then? I fainted, did I not?'

'Something rather like it.'

He threw himself back in his chair despairingly.

'I can't tell Harry about it,' he said. 'Besides, I don't think he knows she is there. She does not come to see him, but only to play whist. It is horrible. Even if I don't see her, I know she is there. Wait a minute.'

He got up out of his chair and ran downstairs.

Five minutes later he returned.

'Stand up,' he said, 'and look at the water behind us.'

I looked closely at the broken wake of the boat.

Thirty yards behind us in the water was covered with a quantity of little white specks.

'Why, have you thrown the cards overboard?' I asked.

'Yes, it is worth trying.'

That evening, for the first time for twenty-six nights, we did not play whist. The boat was ransacked for the cards, but they had vanished. Harry was furious, but we never told him what we had done. And with the cards vanished the Thing which had taken dummy's place.

A WINTER MORNING

FOR FOUR LONG WEEKS WE HAVE BEEN LIVING IN A WORLD of whiteness. Late in December the first snows fell, and morning after morning I have seen the fine tracery of frost thick on my windows, bringing back to me one of the earliest and most mysterious of my childish memories. It was always a matter of dim wonder, and sometimes of serious speculation to me, how in the cover of the still barren nights those aerial sheets of white vegetation grew and filled the nursery panes. I still remember the scorn poured on me by an elder brother, when I asked him what it was, though his answer that it was the frost, rendered it hardly more intelligible. These things do not get less wonderful as one gets older; the knowledge that those white forests are the effect of a condensation of the moist particles in the air, and their subsequent crystallisation, seems to me only the substitution for a simple and unknown expression, one equally unknown and more complicated.

But yesterday afternoon a message of change was whispered among the bushes, and the armies of the frost dropped their spears and swords. The soft plunge of spongy snow was busy in the shrubbery, and on the leaves the little icicles seemed to have grown less hard in outline. At nightfall a little bitter wind rose and sobbed round the house, and from time to time a cold patter of rain shivered against the windows, and with it there swept over me a memory which is ever new, but which the first relenting of the grip of frost brings back with a distinctness which does not grow less with years.

I went up to bed last night with the old pain creeping and stirring again at the heart, till at last I dropped into the vague, shadow-haunted twilight of those grey slopes that lie between the shores of living consciousness and the deeper gulfs of sleep. Whenever our souls would pass into that dark sea beyond, they have always to wade through these ill-defined shallows, where the restless little waves beat upon the land, where we feel the chill of the deeps of unconsciousness, but not their quiet, as we stumble dizzily from the shore, only wanting to rest, yet not able to lose ourselves in the still depths beyond.

All night I wandered as it seemed for long half-conscious years, on that grey borderland, not sleeping and not waking, moving painfully forward under a sunless sky, hearing strange moans and cries from the land which I could not leave, and the shrill pipe of a wind that seemed to blow all round me, and yet touched me not. Now and then that long monotony of sea and sky would resolve itself into the dim square of my window, and the blast that blew over those grey wastes was only the soughing of the breeze outside, and the flapping of the dying flame. But at last there came along the shore a little figure moving quickly towards me, and as it came nearer I saw it was no dull contortion which my tired brain drew from some object in the room, for against the greyness it glowed with a lucid outline, and when it got close to me, I seemed to mingle with it, and the weary twilight deepened into the blackness of dreamless sleep.

Today a faint sun looks on the trees that are muffled no longer, and the snow that still lies somewhat thick on the grass seems less impenetrably white; the oozy droppings from shrubs, and the last dead leaves that fell when the snow was yet thin, have stained it with an ugly brown.

To me this first false hint of spring is laden with a memory which seems to grow more vivid with each slow turning year; perhaps the dream that I had last night has made its presence more insistent, for this morning it is with me like those strange throbs of double consciousness, which most of us know, the sense that something we have just said or seen is only the repetition of a real event which is intensely vivid to us, yet which we cannot grasp or localise.

What I am going to tell you happened many years ago, twenty years ago this winter. I will try to say it in simple straightforward words, for it is a very simple story, and a very common one.

It is twenty-six years ago since my wife died, since I was left alone with a year-old baby; and it is twenty years ago since the baby died.

We had twenty years ago a month of weather very like these last four weeks. The snow had fallen thickly for a day or two, and after that, the earth had lain still and white under the grip of a windless frost. One evening I was playing billiards here in the hall with my brother. The boy, Jack, was sitting on the hearthrug teasing his dog. The dog had enough of it before Jack ceased to find it amusing, and he walked with dignity to the door. Jack was left with nothing to do, and he came to give a wide-eyed inspection to us.

After a while it became clear that the little boxes under the table that held the chalk, and the square blocks of chalk, with their green paper coverings, were quite the most fascinating things on earth. It was necessary to screw these boxes round on their pivots as fast as possible, and if the chalk flew out, it was simply charming. I have got one of these pieces of chalk still: I am going to tell you why I keep it.

Jack was in the way, and when he was told so, it hurt his feelings rather: at any-rate he did not understand it. But he retired to the hearthrug with his bit of chalk, and drew on the baize carpet a picture of a somewhat irregular horse.

In the course of a few minutes, my brother was about to make a stroke from over the box which had held Jack's piece of chalk. It was a stroke involving a certain amount of screw back, and he wished to chalk his cue. Jack's feelings were hurt again, when it was found that his chalk was wanted, and he was told not to touch it any more. Soon afterwards he went to bed.

That night the snow, which had lain thick across the fields, was breathed on by the south wind; and when we let Jack's dog out for a run, we stood in the porch for a moment and listened to the thud of the soft stuff as it slid off the labouring trees, which rustled and stirred as their burden dropped off them, and all round the bitter rain fell coldly through the dark night.

As we passed into the hall again, I happened to notice Jack's picture on the carpet. It was not quite finished, for it had only three legs, and the entire absence of any eye gave it a blind idiotic appearance.

To Jack this thaw was delightful; his pony passed from being a beautiful dream into a dear reality. After breakfast he cantered off with a groom in attendance, scattering gleefully behind him the lumps of slushy snow.

Two hours after, I was kneeling by his side in the hall. His pony had slipped on the hard treacherous ground beneath, and Jack was dying. He was quite unconscious, and it was doubtful whether he would regain consciousness again. His back—ah, God!—was broken, and he had only an hour or so to live.

He lay on a pile of rugs, close to the hearth. Near his head, on the carpet, I could see the faint outline of the unfinished horse, which the housemaids had not quite succeeded in obliterating. He lay quite still, and there was no disfigurement. His breath came evenly, and his eyes were shut. He looked like a child tired with play; but Jack never used to be tired.

Just before the end he stirred and opened his eyes, and saw me kneeling by him. The shadow of death was on his face.

'I want to tell you,' he whispered, 'I took—'

So he went out alone into the dark valley.

They took him up to his room, and laid him on the bed. Death had been very merciful; he had come swiftly and silently; there had been no struggle and no fear. But what was it he wanted to tell me?

Later in the day I went up again. His clothes were lying on a chair by the bed, and a sheet covered the still body of a child.

More than half unconsciously I took them up, and laid them in a drawer. As I carried them across the room, something fell out of his coat pocket.

It was a piece of chalk from the billiard table.

But why does that little thing stand out so clearly to me from the heavy background of my sorrow? Why is the pathos of that one moment, when Jack wished to tell me of that tiny act of disobedience before the great silence closed about him, so piercingly sharp? The thought of it must have been present to him all the morning; for, when he woke for a moment from that dim hour which preceded death, the threads of interrupted consciousness reasserted themselves, though he went out into the dark valley with his secret untold. I cannot help feeling, quite irrationally, that if I had only remembered his childish desire for that bit of chalk in the morning, and given it to him, if only he had finished drawing his horse, that the bitterness which now fills me would be measurably less. Yet there are those who in an ignorance which seems to be almost insolent, talk of little things not mattering, who would rob life of half its deepest emotions of joy and sorrow. Yet it is not that we need these little things to keep sorrow and joy alive, the strength of memory does not depend on them. Perhaps it is because those we loved and still love are human, because they were full of little wants and little failings, because the idea of a cold disembodied perfection is not so dear to us as the memory of one who was human, who was imperfect, full of little cares and trivial wants, who felt small disappointments and small homely joys, and whom, because we are human too, we loved for these little things.

The cold unkind morning creeps on to noon: the trees look drowsy and tired, as if they had been awakened in the middle of the night by some bad news that banished sleep, though not the weary craving for it. A few birds peck aimlessly among the brown leaves that are beginning to appear again through the pitted snow. They seem half to realise that this promise of warmth and spring is delusive.

Ah, my little Jack, I am very lonely and very tired.

BETWEEN THE LIGHTS

THE DAY HAD BEEN ONE UNCEASING FALL OF SNOW FROM sunrise until the gradual withdrawal of the vague white light outside indicated that the sun had set again. But as usual at this hospitable and delightful house of Everard Chandler where I often spent Christmas, and was spending it now, there had been no lack of entertainment, and the hours had passed with a rapidity that had surprised us. A short billiard tournament had filled up the time between breakfast and lunch, with Badminton and the morning papers for those who were temporarily not engaged, while afterwards, the interval till tea-time had been occupied by the majority of the party in a huge game of hide-and-seek all over the house, barring the billiard-room, which was sanctuary for any who desired peace. But few had done that; the enchantment of Christmas, I must suppose, had, like some spell, made children of us again, and it was with palsied terror and trembling misgivings that we had tip-toed up and down the dim passages, from any corner of which some wild screaming form might dart out on us. Then, wearied with exercise and emotion, we had assembled again for tea in the hall, a room of shadows and panels on which the light from the wide open fireplace, where there burned a divine mixture of peat and logs, flickered and grew bright again on the walls. Then, as was proper, ghost-stories, for the narration of which the electric light was put out, so that the listeners might conjecture anything they pleased to be lurking in the corners, succeeded, and we vied with each other in blood, bones, skeletons, armour and shrieks. I had just given my contribution, and was reflecting with some complacency that probably the worst was now known, when Everard, who had not yet administered to the horror of his guests, spoke. He was sitting opposite me in the full blaze of the fire, looking, after the illness he had gone through during the autumn, still rather pale and delicate. All the same he had been among the boldest and best in the exploration of dark places that afternoon, and the look on his face now rather startled me.

'No, I don't mind that sort of thing,' he said. 'The paraphernalia of ghosts has become somehow rather hackneyed, and when I hear of screams and skeletons I feel I am on familiar ground, and can at least hide my head under the bed-clothes.'

'Ah, but the bed-clothes were twitched away by my skeleton,' said I, in self-defence.

'I know, but I don't even mind that. Why, there are seven, eight skeletons in this room now, covered with blood and skin and other horrors. No, the nightmares of one's childhood were the really frightening things, because they were vague. There was the true atmosphere of horror about them because one didn't know what one feared. Now if one could recapture that—'

Mrs Chandler got quickly out of her seat.

'Oh, Everard,' she said, 'surely you don't wish to recapture it again. I should have thought once was enough.'

This was enchanting. A chorus of invitation asked him to proceed: the real true ghost-story first-hand, which was what seemed to be indicated, was too precious a thing to lose.

Everard laughed. 'No, dear, I don't want to recapture it again at all,' he said to his wife. Then to us: 'But really the—well, the nightmare perhaps, to which I was referring, is of the vaguest and most unsatisfactory kind. It has no apparatus about it at all. You will probably all say that it was nothing, and wonder why I was frightened. But I was; it frightened me out of my wits. And I only just saw something, without being able to swear what it was, and heard something which might have been a falling stone.'

'Anyhow tell us about the falling stone,' said I.

There was a stir of movement about the circle round the fire, and the movement was not of purely physical order. It was as if—this is only what I personally felt—it was as if the childish gaiety of the hours we had passed that day was suddenly withdrawn; we had jested on certain subjects, we had played hide-and-seek with all the power of earnestness that was in us. But now—so it seemed to me—there was going to be real hide-and-seek, real terrors were going to lurk in dark corners, or if not real terrors, terrors so convincing as to assume the garb of reality, were going to pounce on us. And Mrs Chandler's exclamation as she sat down again, 'Oh, Everard, won't it excite you?' tended in any case to excite us. The room still remained in dubious darkness except for the sudden lights disclosed on the walls by the leaping flames on the hearth, and there was wide field for conjecture as to what might lurk in the dim corners. Everard, moreover, who had been sitting in bright light before, was banished by the extinction of some flaming log into the shadows. A voice alone spoke to us, as he sat back in his low chair, a voice rather slow but very distinct.

'Last year,' he said, 'on the twenty-fourth of December, we were down here, as usual, Amy and I, for Christmas. Several of you who are here now were here then. Three or four of you at least.'

I was one of these, but like the others kept silence, for the identification, so it seemed to me, was not asked for. And he went on again without a pause.

'Those of you who were here then,' he said, 'and are here now, will remember how very warm it was this day year. You will remember, too, that we played croquet that day on the lawn. It was perhaps a little cold for croquet, and we played it rather in order to be able to say—with sound evidence to back the statement—that we had done so.'

Then he turned and addressed the whole little circle.

'We played ties of half-games,' he said, 'just as we have played billiards today, and it was certainly as warm on the lawn then as it was in the billiard-room this morning directly after breakfast, while today I should not wonder if there was three feet of snow outside. More, probably; listen.'

A sudden draught fluted in the chimney, and the fire flared up as the current of air caught it. The wind also drove the snow against the windows, and as he said 'Listen,' we heard a soft scurry of the falling flakes against the panes, like the soft tread of many little people who stepped lightly, but with the persistence of multitudes who were flocking to some rendezvous. Hundreds of little feet seemed to be gathering outside; only the glass kept them out. And of the eight skeletons present four or five anyhow turned and looked at the windows. These were small-paned, with leaden bars. On the leaden bars little heaps of snow had accumulated, but there was nothing else to be seen.

'Yes, last Christmas Eve was very warm and sunny,' went on Everard. 'We had had no frost that autumn, and a temerarious dahlia was still in flower. I have always thought that it must have been mad.'

He paused a moment.

'And I wonder if I were not mad too,' he added.

No one interrupted him; there was something arresting, I must suppose, in what he was saying; it chimed in anyhow with the hide-and-seek, with the suggestions of the lonely snow. Mrs Chandler had sat down again, but I heard her stir in her chair. But never was there a gay party so reduced as we had been in the last five minutes. Instead of laughing at ourselves for playing silly games, we were all taking a serious game seriously.

'Anyhow I was sitting out,' he said to me, 'while you and my wife played your half-game of croquet. Then it struck me that it was not so warm as I had supposed, because quite suddenly I shivered. And shivering I looked up. But I did not see you and her playing croquet at all. I saw something which had no relation to you and her—at least I hope not.'

Now the angler lands his fish, the stalker kills his stag, and the speaker holds his audience. And as the fish is gaffed, and as the stag is shot, so were we held. There was no getting away till he had finished with us.

'You all know the croquet lawn,' he said, 'and how it is bounded all round by a flower border with a brick wall behind it, through which, you will remember, there is only one gate. Well, I looked up and saw that the lawn—I could for one moment see it was still a lawn—was shrinking, and the walls closing in upon it. As they closed in too, they grew higher, and simultaneously the light began to fade and be sucked from the sky, till it grew quite dark overhead and only a glimmer of light came in through the gate.

'There was, as I told you, a dahlia in flower that day, and as this dreadful darkness and bewilderment came over me, I remember that my eyes sought it in a kind of despair, holding on, as it were, to any familiar object. But it was no longer a dahlia, and for the red of its petals I saw only the red of some feeble firelight. And at that moment the hallucination was complete. I was no longer sitting on the lawn watching croquet, but I was in a low-roofed room, something like a cattle-shed, but round. Close above my head, though I was sitting down, ran rafters from wall to wall. It was nearly dark, but a little light came in from the door opposite to me, which seemed to lead into a passage that communicated with the exterior of the place. Little, however, of the wholesome air came into this dreadful den; the atmosphere was oppressive and foul beyond all telling, it was as if for years it had been the place of some human menagerie, and for those years had been uncleaned and unsweetened by the winds of heaven. Yet that oppressiveness was nothing to the awful horror of the place from the view of the spirit. Some dreadful atmosphere of crime and abomination dwelt heavy in it, its denizens, whoever they were, were scarce human, so it seemed to me, and though men and women, were akin more to the beasts of the field. And in addition there was present to me some sense of the weight of years; I had been taken and thrust down into some epoch of dim antiquity.'

He paused a moment, and the fire on the hearth leaped up for a second and then died down again. But in that gleam I saw that all faces were turned to Everard, and that all wore some look of dreadful expectancy. Certainly I felt it myself, and waited in a sort of shrinking horror for what was coming.

'As I told you,' he continued, 'where there had been that unseasonable dahlia, there now burned a dim firelight, and my eyes were drawn there. Shapes were gathered round it; what they were I could not at first see. Then perhaps my eyes got more accustomed to the dusk, or the fire burned better, for I perceived that they were of human form, but very small, for when one rose, with a horrible chattering, to his feet, his head was still some inches off the low roof. He was dressed in a sort of shirt that came to his knees, but his arms were bare and covered with hair. Then the gesticulation and chattering increased, and I knew that they were talking about me, for they kept pointing in my direction. At that my horror suddenly deepened, for I became aware that I was powerless and could not move hand or foot; a helpless, nightmare impotence had possession of me. I could not lift a finger or turn my head. And in the paralysis of that fear I tried to scream, but not a sound could I utter.

'All this I suppose took place with the instantaneousness of a dream, for at once, and without transition, the whole thing had vanished, and I was back on the lawn again, while the stroke for which my wife was aiming was still unplayed. But my face was dripping with perspiration, and I was trembling all over.

'Now you may all say that I had fallen asleep, and had a sudden nightmare. That may be so; but I was conscious of no sense of sleepiness before, and I was conscious of none afterwards. It was as if someone had held a book before me, whisked the pages open for a second and closed them again.'

Somebody, I don't know who, got up from his chair with a sudden movement that made me start, and turned on the electric light. I do not mind confessing that I was rather glad of this.

Everard laughed.

'Really I feel like Hamlet in the play-scene,' he said, 'and as if there was a guilty uncle present. Shall I go on?'

I don't think anyone replied, and he went on:

'Well, let us say for the moment that it was not a dream exactly, but a hallucination. Whichever it was, in any case it haunted me; for months, I think, it was never quite out of my mind, but lingered somewhere in the dusk of consciousness, sometimes sleeping quietly, so to speak, but sometimes stirring in its sleep. It was no good my telling myself that I was disquieting myself in vain, for it was as if something had actually entered into my very soul, as if some seed of horror had been planted there. And as the weeks went on the seed began to sprout, so that I could no longer even tell myself that that vision had been a moment's disorderment only. I can't say that it actually affected my health. I did not, as far as I know, sleep or eat insufficiently, but morning after morning I used to wake, not gradually and through pleasant dozings into full consciousness, but with absolute suddenness, and find myself plunged in an abyss of despair. Often too, eating or drinking, I used to pause and wonder if it was worth while.

'Eventually I told two people about my trouble, hoping that perhaps the mere communication would help matters, hoping also, but very distantly, that though I could not believe at present that digestion or the obscurities of the nervous system were at fault, a doctor by some simple dose might convince me of it. In other words I told my wife, who laughed at me, and my doctor who laughed also, and assured me that my health was quite unnecessarily robust. At the same time he suggested that change of air and scene does wonders for the delusions that exist merely in the imagination. He also told me, in answer to a direct question, that he would stake his reputation on the certainty that I was not going mad.

'Well, we went up to London as usual for the season, and though nothing whatever occurred to remind me in any way of that single moment on Christmas Eve, the reminding was seen to all right, the moment itself took care of that, for instead of fading as is the way of sleeping or waking dreams, it grew every day more vivid, and ate, so to speak, like some corrosive acid into my mind, etching itself there. And to London succeeded Scotland.

'I took last year for the first time a small forest up in Sutherland, called Glen Callan, very remote and wild, but affording excellent stalking. It was not far from the sea, and the gillies used always to warn me to carry a compass on the hill, because sea-mists were liable to come up with frightful rapidity, and there was always a danger of being caught by one, and of having perhaps to wait hours till it cleared again. This at first I always used to do, but, as every one knows, any precaution that one takes which continues to be unjustified gets gradually relaxed, and at the end of a few weeks, since the weather had been uniformly clear, it was natural that, as often as not, my compass remained at home.

'One day the stalk took me on to a part of my ground that I had seldom been on before, a very high tableland on the limit of my forest, which went down very steeply on one side to a loch that lay below it, and on the other, by gentler gradations, to the river that came from the loch, six miles below which stood the lodge. The wind had necessitated our climbing up—or so my stalker had insisted—not by the easier way, but up the crags from the loch. I had argued the point with him, for it seemed to me that it was impossible that the deer could get our scent if we went by the more natural path, but he still held to his opinion, and therefore, since after all this was his part of the job, I yielded. A dreadful climb we had of it, over big boulders with deep holes in between, masked by clumps of heather, so that a wary eye and a prodding stick were necessary for each step if one wished to avoid broken bones. Adders also literally swarmed in the heather; we must have seen a dozen at least on our way up, and adders are a beast for which I have no manner of use. But a couple of hours saw us to the top, only to find that the stalker had been utterly at fault, and that the deer must quite infallibly have got wind of us, if they had remained in the place where we last saw them. That, when we could spy the ground again, we saw had happened; in any case they had gone. The man insisted the wind had changed, a palpably stupid excuse, and I wondered at that moment what other reason he had—for reason I felt sure there must be—for not wishing to take what would clearly now have been a better route. But this piece of bad management did not spoil our luck, for within an hour we had spied more deer, and about two o'clock I got a shot, killing a heavy stag. Then sitting on the heather I ate lunch, and enjoyed a well-earned bask and smoke in the sun. The pony meantime had been saddled with the stag, and was plodding homewards.

'The morning had been extraordinarily warm, with a little wind blowing off the sea, which lay a few miles off sparkling beneath a blue haze, and all morning in spite of our abominable climb I had had an extreme sense of peace, so much so that several times I had probed my mind, so to speak, to find if the horror still lingered there. But I could scarcely get any response from it. Never since Christmas had I been so free of fear, and it was with a great sense of repose, both physical and spiritual, that I lay looking up into the blue sky, watching my smoke-whorls curl slowly away into nothingness. But I was not allowed to take my ease long, for Sandy came and begged that I would move. The weather had changed, he said, the wind had shifted again, and he wanted me to be off this high ground and on the path again as soon as possible, because it looked to him as if a sea-mist would presently come up.

'"And yon's a bad place to get down in the mist," he added, nodding towards the crags we had come up.

'I looked at the man in amazement, for to our right lay a gentle slope down on to the river, and there was now no possible reason for again tackling those hideous rocks up which we had climbed this morning. More than ever I was sure he had some secret reason for not wishing to go the obvious way. But about one thing he was certainly right, the mist was coming up from the sea, and I felt in my pocket for the compass, and found I had forgotten to bring it.

'Then there followed a curious scene which lost us time that we could really ill afford to waste, I insisting on going down by the way that commonsense directed, he imploring me to take his word for it that the crags were the better way. Eventually, I marched off to the easier descent, and told him not to argue any more but follow. What annoyed me about him was that he would only give the most senseless reasons for preferring the crags. There were mossy places, he said, on the way I wished to go, a thing patently false, since the summer had been one spell of unbroken weather; or it was longer, also obviously untrue; or there were so many vipers about. But seeing that none of these arguments produced any effect, at last he desisted, and came after me in silence.

'We were not yet half down when the mist was upon us, shooting up from the valley like the broken water of a wave, and in three minutes we were enveloped in a cloud of fog so thick that we could barely see a dozen yards in front of us. It was therefore another cause for self-congratulation that we were not now, as we should otherwise have been, precariously clambering on the face of those crags up which we had come with such difficulty in the morning, and as I rather prided myself on my powers of generalship in the matter of direction, I continued leading, feeling sure that before long we should strike the track by the river. More than all, the absolute freedom from fear elated me; since Christmas I had not known the instinctive joy of that; I felt like a schoolboy home for the holidays. But the mist grew thicker and thicker, and whether it was that real rain-clouds had formed above it, or that it was of an extraordinary density itself, I got wetter in the next hour than I have ever been before or since. The wet seemed to penetrate the skin, and chill the very bones. And still there was no sign of the track for which I was making. Behind me, muttering to himself, followed the stalker, but his arguments and protestations were dumb, and it seemed as if he kept close to me, as if afraid.

'Now there are many unpleasant companions in this world; I would not for instance care to be on the hill with a drunkard or a maniac, but worse than either, I think, is a frightened man, because his trouble is infectious, and, insensibly, I began to be afraid of being frightened too. From that it is but a short step to fear. Other perplexities too beset us. At one time we seemed to be walking on flat ground, at another I felt sure we were climbing again, whereas all the time we ought to have been descending, unless we had missed the way very badly indeed. Also, for the month was October, it was beginning to get dark, and it was with a sense of relief that I remembered that the full moon would rise soon after sunset. But it had grown very much colder, and soon, instead of rain, we found we were walking through a steady fall of snow.

'Things were pretty bad, but then for the moment they seemed to mend, for, far away to the left, I suddenly heard the brawling of the river. It should, it is true, have been straight in front of me and we were perhaps a mile out of our way, but this was better than the blind wandering of the last hour, and turning to the left, I walked towards it. But before I had gone a hundred yards, I heard a sudden choked cry behind me, and just saw Sandy's form flying as if in terror of pursuit, into the mists. I called to him but got no reply, and heard only the spurned stones of his running. What had frightened him I had no idea, but certainly with his disappearance, the infection of his fear disappeared also, and I went on, I may almost say, with gaiety. On the moment, however, I saw a sudden well-defined blackness in front of me, and before I knew what I was doing I was half stumbling, half walking up a very steep grass slope.

'During the last few minutes the wind had got up, and the driving snow was peculiarly uncomfortable, but there had been a certain consolation in thinking that the wind would soon disperse these mists, and I had nothing more than a moonlight walk home. But as I paused on this slope, I became aware of two things, one, that the blackness in front of me was very close, the other that, whatever it was, it sheltered me from the snow. So I climbed on a dozen yards into its friendly shelter, for it seemed to me to be friendly.

'A wall some twelve feet high crowned the slope, and exactly where I struck it there was a hole in it, or door rather, through which a little light appeared. Wondering at this I pushed on, bending down, for the passage was very low, and in a dozen yards came out on the other side. Just as I did this the sky suddenly grew lighter, the wind, I suppose, having dispersed the mists, and the moon, though not yet visible through the flying skirts of cloud, made sufficient illumination.

'I was in a circular enclosure, and above me there projected from the walls some four feet from the ground, broken stones which must have been intended to support a floor. Then simultaneously two things occurred.

'The whole of my nine months' terror came back to me, for I saw that the vision in the garden was fulfilled, and at the same moment I saw stealing towards me a little figure as of a man, but only about three foot six in height. That my eyes told me; my ears told me that he stumbled on a stone; my nostrils told me that the air I breathed was of an overpowering foulness, and my soul told me that it was sick unto death. I think I tried to scream, but could not, I know I tried to move and could not. And it crept closer.

'Then I suppose the terror which held me spellbound so spurred me that I must move, for next moment I heard a cry break from my lips, and was stumbling through the passage. I made one leap of it down the grass slope, and ran as I hope never to have to run again. What direction I took I did not pause to consider, so long as I put distance between me and that place. Luck, however, favoured me, and before long I struck the track by the river, and an hour afterwards reached the lodge.

'Next day I developed a chill, and as you know pneumonia laid me on my back for six weeks.

'Well, that is my story, and there are many explanations. You may say that I fell asleep on the lawn, and was reminded of that by finding myself, under discouraging circumstances, in an old Picts' castle, where a sheep or a goat that, like myself, had taken shelter from the storm, was moving about. Yes, there are hundreds of ways in which you may explain it. But the coincidence was an odd one, and those who believe in second sight might find an instance of their hobby in it.'

'And that is all?' I asked.

'Yes, it was nearly too much for me. I think the dressing-bell has sounded.'

THE THING IN THE HALL

THE FOLLOWING PAGES ARE THE ACCOUNT GIVEN ME BY DR Assheton of the Thing in the Hall. I took notes, as copious as my quickness of hand allowed me, from his dictation, and subsequently read to him this narrative in its transcribed and connected form. This was on the day before his death, which indeed probably occurred within an hour after I had left him, and, as readers of inquests and such atrocious literature may remember, I had to give evidence before the coroner's jury. Only a week before Dr Assheton had to give similar evidence, but as a medical expert, with regard to the death of his friend, Louis Fielder, which occurred in a manner identical with his own. As a specialist, he said he believed that his friend had committed suicide while of unsound mind, and the verdict was brought in accordingly. But in the inquest held over Dr Assheton's body, though the verdict eventually returned was the same, there was more room for doubt.

For I was bound to state that only shortly before his death, I read what follows to him; that he corrected me with extreme precision on a few points of detail, that he seemed perfectly himself, and that at the end he used these words:

'I am quite certain as a brain specialist that I am completely sane, and that these things happened not merely in my imagination, but in the external world. If I had to give evidence again about poor Louis, I should be compelled to take a different line.

Please put that down at the end of your account, or at the beginning, if it arranges itself better so.'

There will be a few words I must add at the end of this story, and a few words of explanation must precede it. Briefly, they are these.

Francis Assheton and Louis Fielder were up at Cambridge together, and there formed the friendship that lasted nearly till their death. In general attributes no two men could have been less alike, for while Dr Assheton had become at the age of thirty-five the first and final authority on his subject, which was the functions and diseases of the brain, Louis Fielder at the same age was still on the threshold of achievement. Assheton, apparently without any brilliance at all, had by careful and incessant work arrived at the top of his profession, while Fielder, brilliant at school, brilliant at college and brilliant ever afterwards, had never done anything. He was too eager, so it seemed to his friends, to set about the dreary work of patient investigation and logical deductions; he was for ever guessing and prying, and striking out luminous ideas, which he left burning, so to speak, to illumine the work of others. But at bottom, the two men had this compelling interest in common, namely, an insatiable curiosity after the unknown, perhaps the most potent bond yet devised between the solitary units that make up the race of man. Both—till the end—were absolutely fearless, and Dr Assheton would sit by the bedside of the man stricken with bubonic plague to note the gradual surge of the tide of disease to the reasoning faculty with the same absorption as Fielder would study X-rays one week, flying machines the next, and spiritualism the third. The rest of the story, I think, explains itself—or does not quite do so. This, anyhow, is what I read to Dr Assheton, being the connected narrative of what he had himself told me. It is he, of course, who speaks.

* * *

After I returned from Paris, where I had studied under Charcot, I set up practice at home. The general doctrine of hypnotism, suggestion, and cure by such means had been accepted even in London by this time, and, owing to a few papers I had written on the subject, together with my foreign diplomas, I found that I was a busy man almost as soon as I had arrived in town. Louis Fielder had his ideas about how I should make my début (for he had ideas on every subject, and all of them original), and entreated me to come and live not in the stronghold of doctors, 'Chloroform Square,' as he called it, but down in Chelsea, where there was a house vacant next his own.

'Who cares where a doctor lives,' he said, 'so long as he cures people? Besides you don't believe in old methods; why believe in old localities? Oh, there is an atmosphere of painless death in Chloroform Square! Come and make people live instead! And on most evenings I shall have so much to tell you; I can't "drop in" across half London.'

Now if you have been abroad for five years, it is a great deal to know that you have any intimate friend at all still left in the metropolis, and, as Louis said, to have that intimate friend next door, is an excellent reason for going next door. Above all, I remembered from Cambridge days, what Louis' 'dropping in' meant. Towards bed-time, when work was over, there would come a rapid step on the landing, and for an hour, or two hours, he would gush with ideas. He simply diffused life, which is ideas, wherever he went. He fed one's brain, which is the one thing which matters. Most people who are ill, are ill because their brain is starving, and the body rebels, and gets lumbago or cancer. That is the chief doctrine of my work such as it has been. All bodily disease springs from the brain. It is merely the brain that has to be fed and rested and exercised properly to make the body absolutely healthy, and immune from all disease. But when the brain is affected, it is as useful to pour medicines down the sink, as make your patient swallow them, unless—and this is a paramount limitation—unless he believes in them.

I said something of the kind to Louis one night, when, at the end of a busy day, I had dined with him. We were sitting over coffee in the hall, or so it is called, where he takes his meals. Outside, his house is just like mine, and ten thousand other small houses in London, but on entering, instead of finding a narrow passage with a door on one side, leading into the dining-room, which again communicates with a small back room called 'the study,' he has had the sense to eliminate all unnecessary walls, and consequently the whole ground floor of his house is one room, with stairs leading up to the first floor. Study, dining-room and passage have been knocked into one; you enter a big room from the front door. The only drawback is that the postman makes loud noises close to you, as you dine, and just as I made these commonplace observations to him about the effect of the brain on the body and the senses, there came a loud rap, somewhere close to me, that was startling.

'You ought to muffle your knocker,' I said, 'anyhow during the time of meals.'

Louis leaned back and laughed.

'There isn't a knocker,' he said. 'You were startled a week ago, and said the same thing. So I took the knocker off. The letters slide in now. But you heard a knock, did you?'

'Didn't you?' said I.

'Why, certainly. But it wasn't the postman. It was the Thing. I don't know what it is. That makes it so interesting.'

Now if there is one thing that the hypnotist, the believer in unexplained influences, detests and despises, it is the whole root-notion of spiritualism. Drugs are not more opposed to his belief than the exploded, discredited idea of the influence of spirits on our lives. And both are discredited for the same reason; it is easy to understand how brain can act on brain, just as it is easy to understand how body can act on body, so that there is no more difficulty in the reception of the idea that the strong mind can direct the weak one, than there is in the fact of a wrestler of greater strength overcoming one of less. But that spirits should rap at furniture and divert the course of events is as absurd as administering phosphorus to strengthen the brain. That was what I thought then.

However, I felt sure it was the postman, and instantly rose and went to the door. There were no letters in the box, and I opened the door. The postman was just ascending the steps. He gave the letters into my hand.

Louis was sipping his coffee when I came back to the table.

'Have you ever tried table-turning?' he asked. 'It's rather odd.'

'No, and I have not tried violet-leaves as a cure for cancer,' I said.

'Oh, try everything,' he said. 'I know that that is your plan, just as it is mine. All these years that you have been away, you have tried all sorts of things, first with no faith, then with just a little faith, and finally with mountain-moving faith. Why, you didn't believe in hypnotism at all when you went to Paris.'

He rang the bell as he spoke, and his servant came up and cleared the table. While this was being done we strolled about the room, looking at prints, with applause for a Bartolozzi that Louis had bought in the New Cut, and dead silence over a 'Perdita' which he had acquired at considerable cost. Then he sat down again at the table on which we had dined. It was round, and mahogany-heavy, with a central foot divided into claws.

'Try its weight,' he said; 'see if you can push it about.'

So I held the edge of it in my hands, and found that I could just move it. But that was all; it required the exercise of a good deal of strength to stir it.

'Now put your hands on the top of it,' he said, 'and see what you can do.'

I could not do anything, my fingers merely slipped about on it. But I protested at the idea of spending the evening thus.

'I would much sooner play chess or noughts and crosses with you,' I said, 'or even talk about politics, than turn tables. You won't mean to push, nor shall I, but we shall push without meaning to.'

Louis nodded.

'Just a minute,' he said, 'let us both put our fingers only on the top of the table and push for all we are worth, from right to left.'

We pushed. At least I pushed, and I observed his finger-nails. From pink they grew to white, because of the pressure he exercised. So I must assume that he pushed too. Once, as we tried this, the table creaked. But it did not move.

Then there came a quick peremptory rap, not I thought on the front door, but somewhere in the room.

'It's the Thing,' said he.

Today, as I speak to you, I suppose it was. But on that evening it seemed only like a challenge. I wanted to demonstrate its absurdity.

'For five years, on and off, I've been studying rank spiritualism,' he said. 'I haven't told you before, because I wanted to lay before you certain phenomena, which I can't explain, but which now seem to me to be at my command. You shall see and hear, and then decide if you will help me.'

'And in order to let me see better, you are proposing to put out the lights,' I said.

'Yes; you will see why.'

'I am here as a sceptic,' said I.

'Scep away,' said he.

Next moment the room was in darkness, except for a very faint glow of firelight. The window-curtains were thick, and no street-illumination penetrated them, and the familiar, cheerful sounds of pedestrians and wheeled traffic came in muffled. I was at the side of the table towards the door; Louis was opposite me, for I could see his figure dimly silhouetted against the glow from the smouldering fire.

'Put your hands on the table,' he said, 'quite lightly, and—how shall I say it—expect.'

Still protesting in spirit, I expected. I could hear his breathing rather quickened, and it seemed to me odd that anybody could find excitement in standing in the dark over a large mahogany table, expecting. Then—through my finger-tips, laid lightly on the table, there began to come a faint vibration, like nothing so much as the vibration through the handle of a kettle when water is beginning to boil inside it. This got gradually more pronounced and violent till it was like the throbbing of a motor-car. It seemed to give off a low humming note. Then quite suddenly the table seemed to slip from under my fingers and began very slowly to revolve.

'Keep your hands on it and move with it,' said Louis, and as he spoke I saw his silhouette pass away from in front of the fire, moving as the table moved.

For some moments there was silence, and we continued, rather absurdly, to circle round keeping step, so to speak, with the table. Then Louis spoke again, and his voice was trembling with excitement.

'Are you there?' he said.

There was no reply, of course, and he asked it again. This time there came a rap like that which I had thought during dinner to be the postman. But whether it was that the room was dark, or that despite myself I felt rather excited too, it seemed to me now to be far louder than before. Also it appeared to come neither from here nor there, but to be diffused through the room.

Then the curious revolving of the table ceased, but the intense, violent throbbing continued. My eyes were fixed on it, though owing to the darkness I could see nothing, when quite suddenly a little speck of light moved across it, so that for an instant I saw my own hands. Then came another and another, like the spark of matches struck in the dark, or like fire-flies crossing the dusk in southern gardens. Then came another knock of shattering loudness, and the throbbing of the table ceased, and the lights vanished.

Such were the phenomena at the first séance at which I was present, but Fielder, it must be remembered, had been studying, 'expecting,' he called it, for some years. To adopt spiritualistic language (which at that time I was very far from doing), he was the medium, I merely the observer, and all the phenomena I had seen that night were habitually produced or witnessed by him. I make this limitation since he told me that certain of them now appeared to be outside his own control altogether. The knockings would come when his mind, as far as he knew, was entirely occupied in other matters, and sometimes he had even been awakened out of sleep by them. The lights were also independent of his volition.

Now my theory at the time was that all these things were purely subjective in him, and that what he expressed by saying that they were out of his control, meant that they had become fixed and rooted in the unconscious self, of which we know so little, but which, more and more, we see to play so enormous a part in the life of a man. In fact, it is not too much to say that the vast majority of our deeds spring, apparently without volition, from this unconscious self. All hearing is the unconscious exercise of the aural nerve, all seeing of the optic, all walking, all ordinary movement seem to be done without the exercise of will on our part. Nay more, should we take to some new form of progression, skating, for instance, the beginner will learn with falls and difficulty the outside edge, but within a few hours of his having learned his balance on it, he will give no more thought to what he learned so short a time ago as an acrobatic feat, than he gives to the placing of one foot before the other.

But to the brain specialist all this was intensely interesting, and to the student of hypnotism, as I was, even more so, for (such was the conclusion I came to after this first séance), the fact that I saw and heard just what Louis saw and heard was an exhibition of thought-transference which in all my experience in the Charcot-schools I had never seen surpassed, if indeed rivalled. I knew that I was myself extremely sensitive to suggestion, and my part in it this evening I believed to be purely that of the receiver of suggestions so vivid that I visualised and heard these phenomena which existed only in the brain of my friend.

We talked over what had occurred upstairs. His view was that the Thing was trying to communicate with us. According to him it was the Thing that moved the table and tapped, and made us see streaks of light.

'Yes, but the Thing,' I interrupted, 'what do you mean? Is it a great-uncle—oh, I have seen so many relatives appear at séances, and heard so many of their dreadful platitudes—or what is it? A spirit? Whose spirit?'

Louis was sitting opposite to me, and on the little table before us there was an electric light. Looking at him I saw the pupil of his eye suddenly dilate. To the medical man—provided that some violent change in the light is not the cause of the dilation—that meant only one thing, terror. But it quickly resumed its normal proportion again.

Then he got up, and stood in front of the fire.

'No, I don't think it is great-uncle anybody,' he said, 'I don't know, as I told you, what the Thing is. But if you ask me what my conjecture is, it is that the Thing is an Elemental.'

'And pray explain further. What is an Elemental?'

Once again his eye dilated.

'It will take two minutes,' he said. 'But, listen. There are good things in this world, are there not, and bad things? Cancer, I take it is bad, and—and fresh air is good; honesty is good, lying is bad. Impulses of some sort direct both sides, and some power suggests the impulses. Well, I went into this spiritualistic business impartially. I learned to "expect," to throw open the door into the soul, and I said, "Anyone may come in." And I think Something has applied for admission, the Thing that tapped and turned the table and struck matches, as you saw, across it. Now the control of the evil principle in the world is in the hands of a power which entrusts its errands to the things which I call Elementals. Oh, they have been seen; I doubt not that they will be seen again. I did not, and do not ask good spirits to come in. I don't want "The Church's one foundation" played on a musical box. Nor do I *want* an Elemental. I only threw open the door. I believe the Thing has come into my house, and is establishing communication with me. Oh, I want to go the whole hog. What is it? In the name of Satan, if necessary, what is it? I just want to know.'

What followed I thought then might easily be an invention of the imagination, but what I believed to have happened was this. A piano with music on it was standing at the far end of the room by the door, and a sudden draught entered the room, so strong that the leaves turned. Next the draught troubled a vase of daffodils, and the yellow heads nodded. Then it reached the candles that stood close to us, and they fluttered, burning blue and low. Then it reached me, and the draught was cold, and stirred my hair. Then it eddied, so to speak, and went across to Louis, and his hair also moved, as I could see. Then it went downwards towards the fire, and flames suddenly started up in its path, blown upwards. The rug by the fireplace flapped also.

'Funny, wasn't it?' he asked.

'And has the Elementa gone up the chimney?' said I.

'Oh, no,' said he, 'the Thing only passed us.'

Then suddenly he pointed at the wall just behind my chair, and his voice cracked as he spoke.

'Look, what's that?' he said. 'There on the wall.'

Considerably startled I turned in the direction of his shaking finger. The wall was pale grey in tone, and sharp-cut against it was a shadow that, as I looked, moved. It was like the shadow of some enormous slug, legless and fat, some two feet high by about four feet long. Only at one end of it was a head shaped like the head of a seal, with open mouth and panting tongue.

Then even as I looked it faded, and from somewhere close at hand there sounded another of those shattering knocks.

For a moment after there was silence between us, and horror was thick as snow in the air. But, somehow neither Louis nor I were frightened for more than one moment. The whole thing was so absorbingly interesting.

'That's what I mean by its being outside my control,' he said. 'I said I was ready for any—any visitor to come in, and by God, we've got a beauty.'

Now I was still, even in spite of the appearance of this shadow, quite convinced that I was only taking observations of a most curious case of disordered brain accompanied by the most vivid and remarkable thought-transference. I believed that I had not seen a slug-like shadow at all, but that Louis had visualised this dreadful creature so intensely that I saw what he saw. I found also that his spiritualistic trash-books which I thought a truer nomenclature than text-books, mentioned this as a common form for Elementals to take. He on the other hand was more firmly convinced than ever that we were dealing not with a subjective but an objective phenomenon.

For the next six months or so we sat constantly, but made no further progress, nor did the Thing or its shadow appear again, and I began to feel that we were really wasting time. Then it occurred to me, to get in a so-called medium, induce hypnotic sleep, and see if we could learn anything further. This we did, sitting as before round the dining-room table. The room was not quite dark, and I could see sufficiently clearly what happened.

The medium, a young man, sat between Louis and myself, and without the slightest difficulty I put him into a light hypnotic sleep. Instantly there came a series of the most terrific raps, and across the table there slid something more palpable than a shadow, with a faint luminance about it, as if the surface of it was smouldering. At the moment the medium's face became contorted to a mask of hellish terror; mouth and eyes were both open, and the eyes were focussed on something close to him. The Thing waving its head came closer and closer to him, and reached out towards his throat. Then with a yell of panic, and warding off this horror with his hands, the medium sprang up, but It had already caught hold, and for the moment he could not get free. Then simultaneously Louis and I went to his aid, and my hands touched something cold and slimy. But pull as we could we could not get it away. There was no firm hand-hold to be taken; it was as if one tried to grasp slimy fur, and the touch of it was horrible, unclean, like a leper. Then, in a sort of despair, though I still could not believe that the horror was real, for it must be a vision of diseased imagination, I remembered that the switch of the four electric lights was close to my hand. I turned them all on. There on the floor lay the medium, Louis was kneeling by him with a face of wet paper, but there was nothing else there. Only the collar of the medium was crumpled and torn, and on his throat were two scratches that bled.

The medium was still in hypnotic sleep, and I woke him. He felt at his collar, put his hand to his throat and found it bleeding, but, as I expected, knew nothing whatever of what had passed. We told him that there had been an unusual manifestation, and he had, while in sleep, wrestled with something. We had got the result we wished for, and were much obliged to him.

I never saw him again. A week after that he died of blood-poisoning.

From that evening dates the second stage of this adventure. The Thing had materialised (I use again spiritualistic language which I still did not use at the time). The huge slug, the Elemental, manifested itself no longer by knocks and waltzing tables, nor yet by shadows. It was there in a form that could be seen and felt. But it still—this was my strong point—was only a thing of twilight; the sudden kindling of the electric light had shown us that there was nothing there. In this struggle perhaps the medium had clutched his own throat, perhaps I had grasped Louis' sleeve, he mine. But though I said these things to myself, I am not sure that I believed them in the same way that I believe the sun will rise tomorrow.

Now as a student of brain-functions and a student in hypnotic affairs, I ought perhaps to have steadily and unremittingly pursued this extraordinary series of phenomena. But I had my practice to attend to, and I found that with the best will in the world, I could think of nothing else except the occurrence in the hall next door. So I refused to take part in any further séance with Louis. I had another reason also. For the last four or five months he was becoming depraved. I have been no prude or Puritan in my own life, and I hope I have not turned a Pharisaical shoulder on sinners. But in all branches of life and morals, Louis had become infamous. He was turned out of a club for cheating at cards, and narrated the event to me with gusto. He had become cruel; he tortured his cat to death; he had become bestial. I used to shudder as I passed his house, expecting I knew not what fiendish thing to be looking at me from the window.

Then came a night only a week ago, when I was awakened by an awful cry, swelling and falling and rising again. It came from next door. I ran downstairs in my pyjamas, and out into the street. The policeman on the beat had heard it too, and it came from the hall of Louis' house, the window of which was open. Together we burst the door in. You know what we found. The screaming had ceased but a moment before, but he was dead already. Both jugulars were severed, torn open.

It was dawn, early and dusky when I got back to my house next door. Even as I went in something seemed to push by me, something soft and slimy. It could not be Louis' imagination this time. Since then I have seen glimpses of it every evening. I am awakened at night by tappings, and in the shadows in the corner of my room there sits something more substantial than a shadow.

* * *

Within an hour of my leaving Dr Assheton, the quiet street was once more aroused by cries of terror and agony. He was already dead, and, in no other manner than his friend, when they got into the house.

THE PASSENGER

On a certain Tuesday night during last October I was going home down war-darkened Piccadilly on the top of a westering bus. It still wanted a few minutes to eleven o'clock, the theatres had not yet disgorged their audiences, and I was quite alone up aloft, though inside the vehicle was full to repletion. But the chilliness of the evening and a certain bitter quality in the south-east wind accounted for this, and also led me to sit on the hindmost of the seats, close to the stairs, where my back was defended from the bite of the draught by the protective knife-board.

I had barely taken my seat when an incident that for the moment just a little startled me occurred, for I thought I felt something (or somebody) push by me, brushing lightly against my right arm and leg. This impression was vivid enough to make me look round, expecting a fellow-passenger or perhaps the conductor. We were just passing underneath a shaded lamp in the middle of the street when this happened, and I perceived, without any doubt whatever, that my nerves or a sudden draught must have deceived my senses into imagining this, for there was nobody there. But, though I did not give two further thoughts to this impression, I knew that at that moment my pleasurable anticipations from this dark and keen-aired progression had vanished, and, with rather bewildering suddenness, a mood uneasy and ominous had taken possession of me.

I did not, as far as I am aware, make in the smallest degree any mental connection between this sense of being brushed against by something unseen and the vanishing of the contented mood. I put the one down to imagination, the other to the desolate twilight of the streets and the inclemency of the night. A falling barometer portended storm, there had been disquieting news from the Western battleline that afternoon, and those causes seemed sufficient (or nearly sufficient) to account for the sudden dejection that had taken hold of me. And yet, even as I told myself that these were causes enough, I knew that there was another symptom in my disquietude for which they did not account.

This was the sense that I had suddenly been brought into touch with something that lay outside the existing world as I had known it two minutes before. There was something more in my surroundings than could be accounted for by eye and ear. I heard the boom and rattle of the bus as we roared down the decline of Piccadilly, I saw the shaded lamps, the infrequent pedestrians, the tall houses with blinds drawn down according to regulations, for fear of enemy aircraft, and soon across the sky were visible the long luminous pencils cast on to the mottled floor of clouds overhead by the searchlights at Hyde Park Corner; but I knew that none of these, these wars and rumours of wars, entirely accounted for my sudden and fearful alacrity of soul. There was something else; it was as if in a darkened room I had been awakened by the tingling noise of a telephone bell, had been torn from sleep by it, as if some message was even now coming through from unseen and discarnate realms. And on the moment I saw that I was not alone on the top of the bus.

There was someone with his back to me on the seat right in front. For a second or two he was sharply silhouetted against the lamps of a motor coming down the hill towards us, and I could see that he sat with head bent forward and coat-collar turned up. And at that instant I knew that it was this figure unaccountably appearing there that caused the telephone-tingle in my brain. It was not merely that it had appeared there when I was certain that I was the sole passenger up on the top; had the roof been crowded in every seat I should have known that one of those heads, that belonging to the man who sat leaning forward, was not of this world as represented by the tall houses, the searchlight beams, the other passengers. Then, mixed up with this horror of the spirit, there came to me also a feeling of intense and invincible curiosity. I had penetrated again into the psychical world, into the realm of the unseen and real existences that surround us.

Precisely then, while those impressions took form and coherence in my mind, the conductor came up the stairs. Simultaneously the bell sounded, and as the bus slackened speed and stopped, he leant over the side by me, so that I saw his face very clearly. In another moment he stamped, signalling the driver to go on again, and turned to me with hand out for my fare. He punched a twopenny ticket for me, and then walked forward along the gangway towards the front seat where the unexplained passenger sat. But halfway there he stopped and turned back again.

'Funny thing, sir,' he said. 'I thought I saw another fare sitting there.'

He turned to go down the stairs, and, watching him, I saw, just before his head vanished, that he looked forward again along the roof, shading his eyes with his hand. Then he came back a couple of steps, still looking forward, then finally turned and left me alone on the top there—or not quite alone...

After leaving Hyde Park Corner a somewhat grosser darkness pervaded the streets, but still I believed that I could see faintly the outline of the bowed head of the man who sat on the front seat of the bus. But in that dim, uncertain light, flecked with odd shadows, I felt that my certainty that it was still there faded, as I strained my eyes to pierce the ambient dimness.

Looking forward eagerly and intently then, I was suddenly startled again by the feeling that somebody (or something) brushed by me. Instantly I started to my feet, and with one step got to the head of the stairs leading down. Certainly there was no one on them, and equally certainly there was no one now on the front seat, or on any other seat.

A fine rain had begun to fall, blown stingingly by the wind that was increasing every moment, and having completely satisfied myself that there was no one there, I descended from the top of the bus to go inside if there was a seat to be had.

I was delayed, still standing on the stairs, by the stream of passengers leaving the bus, and when I got down to the ground floor I found that as I had had the top to myself on the first part of my journey, I was to enjoy an untenanted interior now. I sat close to the door, and presently beckoned to the conductor.

'Did anyone leave the top of the bus,' I asked, 'just before we stopped here?'

He looked at me sideways a little curiously.

'Not as I know of, sir,' he said.

We drew up, and a number of cheerful soldiers invaded the place.

*

For some reason I could not get the thought of this dim, inconclusive experience out of my head. It was not at all impossible that all I had seen—namely, the head and shoulders of a man seated on the front bench of the bus—was accounted for by the tricky shadows and veiled light of the streets; or, again, it was within the bounds of possibility that in the darkness a real living man might have come up there, and in the same confusion of shade and local illumination have left again.

It was conceivable also that the same queer lights and shadows deceived the conductor even as they had deceived me; while, as for the brushing against my arm and leg, which I thought I had twice experienced, that might possibly have been the stir and eddy of some draught on this windy night buffeting round the corner by the stairs. And yet with every desire to think reasonably about it, I could not make myself believe that this was all. Deep down in me I knew I was convinced that what I had seen and felt was not on the ordinary planes of perceptible things. Furthermore, I knew that there was more connected with that figure on the front seat that should sometime be revealed to me. What it was I had no idea, but the sense that more was coming, some development which I felt sure would be tragic and terrible, while it filled me with some befogged and nightmarish horror, yet inspired me with an invincible curiosity.

Accordingly, next evening I stationed myself at the place where I had boarded this particular bus some quarter of an hour before the time that it passed there the previous night. It appeared probable that the phantom, whatever it was, was local; that it might appear again (as in a haunted house) on the bus on which I had seen it before. I guessed, furthermore, that, its habitat being a particular bus, the locality of its appearance otherwise was between the Ritz Hotel and the top of Sloane Street.

My knowledge of the organisation of the traffic service was *nil*, it was but guesswork that led me to suppose that the conductor would be on the same bus tonight as that on which he had been the evening before. And, after waiting ten minutes or so, I saw him.

Tonight the bus was moderately full both inside and on the top, and it was with a certain sense of comfort that I found myself gregariously placed. The front seat where it had sat before, however, was empty, and I placed myself on the seat immediately behind.

Just on my right were a man in khaki and a girl, uproariously cheerful. The sound of human talk and laughter made an encouraging music, but in spite of that, I felt some undefined and chilly fear creeping over me as we bounced down the dip of Piccadilly, while I kept my eyes steadily on the vacant couple of seats in front of me. And then I felt something brush by me, and, turning my head to look, saw nothing that could account for it. But when I looked in front of me again, I saw that on the vacant seat there was sitting a man with coat collar turned up and head bent forward. He was not in the act of sitting down—he was there.

We stopped at that moment at Hyde Park Corner; the rain had begun to fall more heavily, and I saw that all the occupants of the top of the bus had risen to take shelter inside or in the Tube station; one alone, sitting just in front of me, did not move.

At the thought of being alone again with him, a sudden panic seized me, and I rose also to follow the others down. But even as I stood at the top of the stairs, something of courage, or at least of curiosity, prevailed, and instead I sat down again on the back seat (nearer than that I felt I could not go) and watched for what should be. In a moment or two we started off again.

Tonight, in spite of the falling rain, there was more light; behind the clouds, probably the moon had risen, and I could see with considerable distinctness the figure that shared the top with me. I longed to be gone, so cold was the fear that gripped my heart, but still insatiable curiosity held me where I was.

Inwardly I felt convinced that something was going to happen, and, though the sweat of terror stood on my face at the thought of what it might be, I knew that the one thing even more unfaceable was to turn tail and never know what it was.

On the right the leafless plane-trees in the Park stretched angled fingers against the muffled sky, and below, the pavements and roadway gleamed with moisture. Traffic was infrequent, infrequent also were the figures of pedestrians; never in my life had I felt so cut off from human intercourse.

Close round me were secure, normal rooms, tenanted by living men and women, where cheerful fires burnt and steady lights illuminated the solid walls. But here companionless, except for the motionless form crouched in front of me, I sped between earth and sky, among dim shadows and fugitive lights. And all the time I knew, though not knowing how I knew, some dreadful drama was immediately to be unrolled in front of me. Whether that would prove to be some re-enactment of what in the world of time and space had already occurred, or whether, by the stranger miracle of second-sight, I was to behold something which had not happened yet, I had no idea. All I was certain of was that I sat in the presence of things not normally seen; in the world which, for the sake of sanity, is but rarely made manifest.

I kept my eye fixed on the figure in front of me, and saw that its bowed head was supported by its hands, which seemed to hold it up. Then came a step on the stairs, and the conductor was by me demanding my fare. Having given it, a sudden idea struck me as he was about to leave the top again.

'You haven't collected the fare from that man in front there,' I said.

The conductor looked forward, then at me again.

'Sure enough, there is someone there,' he said, 'and can you see him, too?'

'Certainly,' said I.

This appeared to me at the moment to reassure him; it occurred to me also that perhaps I was utterly wrong, and that the figure was nothing but a real passenger.

What followed happened in a dozen seconds.

The conductor advanced up the bus, and, having spoken without attracting the passenger's attention, touched him on the shoulder, and I saw his hand go into it, as it plunged in water. Simultaneously the figure turned round in its seat, and I saw its face. It was that of a young man, absolutely white and colourless. I saw, too, why it held its head up in its hands, for its throat was cut from ear to ear.

The eyes were closed, but as it raised its head in its hands, looking at the conductor, it opened them, and from within them there came a light as from the eye of a cat.

Then, in an awful voice, half squeal, half groan, I heard the conductor cry out:

'O my God! O my God!' he said.

The figure rose, and cowering as from a blow, he turned and fled before it. Whether he jumped into the roadway from the top of the stairs, or in his flight fell down them, I do not know, but I heard the thud of his body as it fell, and was alone once more on the top of the bus.

I rang the bell violently, and in a few yards we drew up. Already there was a crowd round the man on the road, and presently he was carried in an ambulance, alive, but not much more than alive, to St George's Hospital.

He died from his injuries a few days later, and the discovery of a certain pearl necklace concealed in the clothes of his room, about which he gave information, makes it probable that the confession he made just before he died was true.

The conductor, William Larkins, had been in gaol on a charge of stealing six months before, and on his release, by means of a false name and forged references, he had got this post, with every intention of keeping straight. But he had lost money racing, and ten days before his death was in serious want of cash.

That night an old acquaintance of his, who had been associated with him in burglaries, boarded the bus, heard his story, and tried to persuade him to come back into his old way of life. By way of recommendation, he opened a small dressing-bag he had with him, and showed him, wrapped away in a corner, the pearl necklace which subsequently was discovered in Larkins' room. The two were alone on the top of the bus, and, yielding to the ungovernable greed, Larkins next moment had his arm over the passenger's face, and with a razor out of his dressing-bag had cut his throat.

He kept his wits about him, pocketed the pearls, left the bag open and the razor on the floor, and descended to the footboard again.

Immediately afterwards, having ascertained that there were no blood stains on him, he ascended again and instantly stopped the bus, having discovered the body of a passenger there with his throat cut and the razor on the floor. The body was identified as that of a well-known burglar, and the coroner's jury had brought in a verdict of suicide.

THE LIGHT IN THE GARDEN

THE HOUSE AND THE DOZEN ACRES OF GARDEN AND PASture-land surrounding it, which had been left me by my uncle, lay at the top end of one of those remote Yorkshire valleys carved out among the hills of the West Riding. Above it rose the long moors of bracken and heather, from which flowed the stream that ran through the garden, and, joining another tributary, brawled down the valley into the Nidd, and at the foot of its steep fields lay the hamlet—a dozen of houses and a small grey church. I had often spent half my holidays there when a boy, but for the last twenty years my uncle had become a confirmed recluse, and lived alone, seeing neither kith nor kin nor friends from January to December.

It was, therefore, with a sense of clearing old memories from the dust and dimness with which the lapse of years had covered them that I saw the dale again on a hot July afternoon in this year of drought and rainlessness. The house, as his agent had told me, was sorely in need of renovation and repair, and my notion was to spend a fortnight here in personal supervision. I had arranged that the foreman of a firm of decorators in Harrogate should meet me here next day and discuss what had to be done. I was still undecided whether to live in the house myself or let or sell it. As it would be impossible to stay there while painting and cleaning and repairing were going on, the agent had recommended me to inhabit for the next fortnight the lodge which stood at the gate on to the high road. My friend, Hugh Grainger, who was to have come up with me, had been delayed by business in London, but he would join me tomorrow.

It is strange how the revisiting of places which one has known in youth revives all sorts of memories which one had supposed must have utterly faded from the mind. Such recollections crowded fast in upon me, jostling each other for recognition and welcome, as I came near to the place. The sight of the church recalled a Sunday of disgrace, when I had laughed at some humorous happening during the progress of the prayers; the sight of the coffee-coloured stream recalled memories of trout fishing; and, most of all, the sight of the lodge, built of brown stone, with the high wall enclosing the garden, reawoke the most vivid and precise recollections. My uncle's butler, of the name of Wedge—how it all came back!—lived there, coming up to the house of a morning, and going back there with his lantern at night, if it was dark and moonless, to sleep; Mrs Wedge, his wife, had the care of the locked gate, and opened it to visiting or outgoing vehicles. She had been rather a formidable figure to a small boy, a dark, truculent woman, with a foot curiously malformed, so twisted that it pointed outwards and at right angles to the other. She scowled at you when you knocked at the door and asked her to open the gate, and came hobbling out with a dreadful rocking movement. It was, in fact, worth the trouble of going round by a path through the plantation in order to avoid an encounter with Mrs Wedge, especially after one occasion, when, not being able to get any response to my knockings, I opened the door of the lodge and found her lying on the floor, flushed and tipsily snoring… Then the last year that I ever came here Mrs Wedge went off to Whitby or Scarborough on a fortnight's holiday. Wedge had not waited at breakfast that morning, for he was said to have driven the dogcart to take Mrs Wedge to the station at Harrogate, ten miles away. There was something a little odd about this, for I had been early abroad that morning, and thought I had seen the dogcart bowling along the road with Wedge, indeed, driving it, but no wife beside him. How odd, I thought now, that I should recollect that, and even while I wondered that I should have retained so insignificant a memory, the sequel, which made it significant, flashed into my mind, for a few days afterwards Wedge was absent again, having been sent for to go to his wife, who was dying. He came back a widower. A woman from the village was installed as lodge-keeper, a pleasant body, who seemed to enjoy opening the gate to a young gentleman with a fishing-rod... Just at that moment my rummaging among old memories ceased, for here was the agent, warned by the motor-horn, coming out of the brown stone lodge.

There was time before sunset to stroll up to the house and form a general idea of what must be done in the way of decoration and repair, and not till we had got back to the lodge again did the thought of Wedge re-occur to me.

'My uncle's butler used to live here,' I said. 'Is he alive still? Is he here now?'

'Mr Wedge died a fortnight ago,' said the agent. 'It was of the suddenest; he was looking forward to your coming and to attending to you, for he remembered you quite well.'

Though I had so vivid a mental picture of Mrs Wedge, I could not recall in the least what Wedge looked like.

'I, too, can remember all about him,' I said. 'But I can't remember him. What was he like?'

Mr Harkness described him to me, of course, as he knew him, an old man of middle height, grey-haired, and much wrinkled, with the habit of looking round quickly when he spoke to you; but his description roused no response whatever in my memory. Naturally, the grey hair and the wrinkles, and, for that matter, perhaps the habit of 'looking round quickly,' delineated an older man than he was when I knew him, and anyhow, among so much that was vivid in recollection, the appearance of Wedge was to me not even dim, but had no existence at all.

I found that Mr Harkness had made thoughtful arrangements for my comfort in the lodge. A woman from the village and her daughter were to come in early every morning for cooking and housework, and leave again at night after I had had my dinner. I was served with an excellent plain meal, and presently, as I sat watching the fading of the long twilight, there came past my open window, the figures of the woman and the girl going home to the village. I heard the gate clang as they passed out, and knew that I was alone in the house. To cheerful folk of solitude, such as myself, that is a rare but pleasant sensation; there is the feeling that by no possibility can one be interrupted, and I prepared to spend a leisurely evening over a book that had beguiled my journey and a pack of Patience cards. It was fast growing dark, and before settling down I turned to the chimney-piece to light a pair of candles. Perhaps the kindling of the match cast some momentary shadow, for I found myself looking quickly across to the window, under the impression that some black figure had gone past it along the garden path outside. The illusion was quite momentary, but I knew that I was thinking about Wedge again. And still I could not remember in the least what Wedge was like.

My book that had begun so well in the train proved disappointing in its development, and my thoughts began to wander from the printed page, and presently I rose to pull down the blinds which till now had remained unfurled. The room was at an angle of the cottage; one window looked up to the little high-walled garden, the other up the road towards my uncle's house. As I drew down the blind here I saw up the road the light as of some lantern, which bobbed and oscillated as if to the steps of someone who carried it, and the thought of Wedge coming home at night when his work at the house was done re-occurred to my memory. Then, even as I watched, the light, whatever it was, ceased to oscillate, but burned steadily. At a guess, I should have said it was about a hundred yards distant. It remained like that a few seconds and then went out, as if the bearer had extinguished it. As I pulled down the blind I found that my breath came quick and shallow, as if I had been running.

It was with something of an effort that I sat myself down to play patience, and with an effort that I congratulated myself on being alone and secure from interruptions. I did not feel quite so secure now, and I did not know what the interruption might be… There was no sense of any presence but my own being in the house with me, but there was a sense, deny it though I might, of there being some presence outside. A shadow had seemed to cross the window looking on to the garden; on the road a light had appeared, as if carried by some nocturnal passenger, and somehow the two seemed to have a common source, as if some presence that hovered about the place was striving to manifest itself…

At that moment there came on the door of the house, just outside the room where I sat, a sharp knock, followed by silence, and then once more a knock. And instantaneous, as a blink of lightning, there flashed unbidden into my mind the image of the lantern-bearer who, seeing me at the window, had extinguished his light, and in the darkness had crept up to the house and was now demanding admittance. I knew that I was frightened now, but I knew also that I was hugely interested, and, taking one of the candles in my hand, I went quietly to the door.

Just then the knocking was renewed outside, three raps in quick succession, and I had to wait until mere curiosity was ascendant again over some terror that came welling up to my forehead in beads of moisture. It might be that I should find outside some tenant or dependent of my uncle, who, unaware of my advent, wondered who might have business in this house lately vacated, and in that case my terror would vanish; or I should find outside either nothing or some figure as yet unconjecturable, and my curiosity and interest would flame up again. And then, holding the candle above my head so that I could look out undazzled, I pulled back the latch of the door and opened it wide.

Though but a few seconds ago the door had sounded with the knockings, there was no one there, neither in front of it nor to the right or left of it. But though to my physical eye no one was visible, I must believe that to the inward eye of soul or spirit there was apparent that which my grosser bodily vision could not perceive. For as I scrutinised the empty darkness it was as if I was gazing on the image of the man whom I had so utterly forgotten, and I knew what Wedge was like when I had seen him last. 'In his habit as he lived' he sprang into my mind, his thick brown hair not yet tinged with grey, his hawk-like nose, his thin, compressed mouth, his eyes set close together, which shifted if you gave him a straight gaze. No less did I know his low, broad shoulders and the mole on the back of his left hand, his heavy watch-chain, his dark striped trousers. Externally and materially my questing eyes saw but the empty circle of illumination cast by my candle, but my soul's vision beheld Wedge standing on the doorstep. It was his shadow that had passed the window as I lit my lights after dinner, his lantern that I had seen on the road, his knocking that I had heard.

Then I spoke to him who stood there so minutely seen and yet so invisible.

'What do you want with me, Wedge?' I asked. 'Why are you not at rest?'

A draught of wind came round the corner, extinguishing my light. At that a gust of fear shook me, and I slammed to the door and bolted it. I could not be there in the darkness with that which indubitably stood on the threshold.

The mind is not capable of experiencing more than a certain degree of any emotion. A climax arrives, and an assuagement, a diminution follows. That was certainly the case with me now, for though I had to spend the night alone here, with God knew what possible visitations before day, the terror had reached its culminating point and ebbed away again. Moreover, that haunting presence, which I now believed I had identified, was without and not within the house. It had not, to the psychical sense, entered through the open door, and I faced my solitary night with far less misgiving than would have been mine if I had been obliged now to fare forth into the darkness. I slept and woke again, and again slept, but never with panic of nightmare, or with the sense, already once or twice familiar to me, that there was any presence in the room beside my own, and when finally I dropped into a dreamless slumber I woke to find the cheerful day already bright, and the dawn-chorus of the birds in full harmony.

My time was much occupied with affairs of restorations and repairs that day, but I did a little private thinking about Wedge, and made up my mind that I would not tell Hugh Grainger any of my experiences on the previous evening. Indeed, they seemed now of no great evidential value: the shape that had passed my window might so easily have been some queer shadow cast by the kindling of my match; the lantern-light I had seen up the road—if, indeed, it was a lantern at all—might easily have been a real lantern, and who knew whether those knocks at the door might not have been vastly exaggerated by my excitement and loneliness, and be found only to have been the tapping of some spray of ivy or errant creeper? As for the sudden recollection of Wedge, which had eluded me before, it was but natural that I should sooner or later have recaptured the memory of him. Besides, supposing there was anything supernormal about these things, and supposing that they or similar phenomena appeared to Hugh also, his evidence would be far more weighty, if it was come at independently, without the prompting of suggestions from me.

He arrived, as I had done the day before, a little before sunset, big and jovial, and rather disposed to reproach me for holding out trout-fishing as an attraction, when the stream was so dwindled by the drought.

'But there's rain coming,' said he. 'Can't you smell it?'

The sky certainly was thickly overcast and sultry with storm, and before dinner was over the shrubs outside began to whisper underneath the first drops. But the shower soon passed, and while I was busy with some estimate which I had promised the contractor to look at before he came again next morning, Hugh strolled out along the road up to the house for a breath of air. I had finished before he came back, and we sat down to picquet. As he cut, he said:

'I thought you told me the house above was unoccupied. But I passed a man apparently coming down from there, carrying a lantern.'

'I don't know who that could be,' said I. 'Did you see him at all clearly?'

'No, he put out his lantern as I approached; I turned immediately afterwards, and caught him up, and passed him again.'

There came a knock at the front door, then silence, and then a repetition.

'Shall I see who it is while you are dealing?' he said.

He took a candle from the table, but, leaving the deal incomplete, I followed him, and saw him open the door. The candlelight shone out into the darkness, and under Hugh's uplifted arm I beheld, vaguely and indistinctly, the shape of a man. Then the light fell full on to his face, and I recognised him.

'Yes, what do you want?' said Hugh, and just as had happened last night a puff of wind blew the flame off the candle-wick and left us in the dark.

Then Hugh's voice, suddenly raised, came again.

'Here, get out,' he said. 'What do you want?'

I threw open the door into the sitting-room close at hand, and the light within illuminated the narrow passage of the entry. There was no one there but Hugh and myself.

'But where's the beggar gone?' said Hugh. 'He pushed in by me. Did he go into the sitting-room? And where on earth is he?'

'Did you see him?' I asked.

'Of course I saw him. A little man, hook-nosed, with eyes close together. I never liked a man less... Look here, we must search through the house. He did come in.'

Together, not singly, we went through the few rooms which the cottage contained, the two living rooms and the kitchen below, and the three bedrooms upstairs. All was empty and quiet.

'It's a ghost,' said Hugh; and then I told him my experience on the previous evening. I told him also that I knew of Wedge, and of his wife, and of her sudden death when on her holiday. Once or twice as I spoke I saw that Hugh put up his hand as if to shade the flame of the candle from shining out into the garden, and as I finished he suddenly blew it out and came close to me.

'I thought it was the reflection of the candlelight on the panes,' he said, 'but it isn't. Look out there.'

There was a light burning at the far end of the garden, visible in glimpses through a row of tall peas, and there was something moving beside it. A piece of an arm appeared there, as of a man digging, a shoulder and head...

'Come out,' whispered Hugh. 'That's our man. And what is he doing?'

Next moment we were gazing into blackness; the light had vanished.

We each took a candle and went out through the kitchen door. The flames burned steady in the windless air as in a room, and in five minutes we had peered behind every bush, and looked into every cranny. Then suddenly Hugh stopped.

'Did you leave a light in the kitchen?' he asked.

'No.'

'There's one there now,' he said, and my eye followed his pointing finger.

There was a communicating door between our bedrooms, both of which looked out on to the garden, and before getting into bed I made myself some trivial excuse of wanting to speak to Hugh, and left it open. He was already in bed.

'You'd like to fish tomorrow?' I asked.

Before he could answer the room leaped into light, and simultaneously the thunder burst overhead. The fountains of the clouds were unsealed, and the deluge of the rain descended. I took a step across to the window with the idea of shutting it, and across the dark streaming cave of the night outside, again, and now unobscured from the height of the upper floor, I saw the lantern light at the far end of the garden, and the figure of a man bending and rising again as he plied his secret task... The downpour continued; sometimes I dozed for a little, but through dozing and waking alike, my mind was delving and digging as to why out there in the hurly-burly of the storm, the light burned and the busy figure rose and fell. There was haste and bitter urgency in that hellish gardening, which recked nothing of the rain.

I awoke suddenly from an uneasy doze, and felt the skin of my scalp grow tight with some nameless terror. Hugh apparently had lit his candle again, for light came in through the open door between our rooms. Then came the click of a turned handle, and the other door into the passage slowly opened. I was sitting up in bed now with my eyes fixed on it, and round it came the figure of Wedge. He carried a lantern, and his hands were black with mould. And at that sight the whole of my self-control was shattered.

'Hugh!' I yelled. 'Hugh! He is here.'

Hugh came hurrying in, and for one second I turned my eyes to him.

'There by the door!' I cried.

When I looked back the apparition was no longer there. But the door was open, and on the floor by it fragments of mud and soaked soil...

The sequel is soon told. Where we had seen the figure digging in the garden was a row of lavender bushes. These we pulled up, and three feet below came on the huddled remains of a woman's body. The skull had been beaten in by some crashing blow; fragments of clothing and the malformation of one of the feet were sufficient to establish identification. The bones lie now in the churchyard close by the grave of her husband and murderer.

THE OUTCAST

WHEN MRS ACRES BOUGHT THE GATE-HOUSE AT TARLETON, which had stood so long without a tenant, and appeared in that very agreeable and lively little town as a resident, sufficient was already known about her past history to entitle her to friendliness and sympathy. Hers had been a tragic story, and the account of the inquest held on her husband's body, when, within a month of their marriage, he had shot himself before her eyes, was recent enough, and of as full a report in the papers as to enable our little community of Tarleton to remember and run over the salient grimness of the case without the need of inventing any further details—which, otherwise, it would have been quite capable of doing.

Briefly, then, the facts had been as follows. Horace Acres appeared to have been a heartless fortune-hunter—a handsome, plausible wretch, ten years younger than his wife. He had made no secret to his friends of not being in love with her but of having a considerable regard for her more than considerable fortune. But hardly had he married her than his indifference developed into violent dislike, accompanied by some mysterious, inexplicable dread of her. He hated and feared her, and on the morning of the very day when he had put an end to himself he had begged her to divorce him; the case he promised would be undefended, and he would make it indefensible. She, poor soul, had refused to grant this; for, as corroborated by the evidence of friends and servants, she was utterly devoted to him, and stated with that quiet dignity which distinguished her throughout this ordeal, that she hoped that he was the victim of some miserable but temporary derangement, and would come to his right mind again. He had dined that night at his club, leaving his month-old bride to pass the evening alone, and had returned between eleven and twelve that night in a state of vile intoxication. He had gone up to her bedroom, pistol in hand, had locked the door, and his voice was heard screaming and yelling at her. Then followed the sound of one shot. On the table in his dressing-room was found a half-sheet of paper, dated that day, and this was read out in court. 'The horror of my position,' he had written, 'is beyond description and endurance. I can bear it no longer: my soul sickens…' The jury, without leaving the court, returned the verdict that he had committed suicide while temporarily insane, and the coroner, at their request, expressed their sympathy and his own with the poor lady, who, as testified on all hands, had treated her husband with the utmost tenderness and affection.

For six months Bertha Acres had travelled abroad, and then in the autumn she had bought Gate-house at Tarleton, and settled down to the absorbing trifles which make life in a small country town so busy and strenuous.

Our modest little dwelling is within a stone's throw of the Gate-house; and when, on the return of my wife and myself from two months in Scotland, we found that Mrs Acres was installed as a neighbour, Madge lost no time in going to call on her. She returned with a series of pleasant impressions. Mrs Acres, still on the sunny slope that leads up to the tableland of life which begins at forty years, was extremely handsome, cordial, and charming in manner, witty and agreeable, and wonderfully well dressed. Before the conclusion of her call Madge, in country fashion, had begged her to dispose with formalities, and, instead of a frigid return of the call, to dine with us quietly next day. Did she play bridge? That being so, we would just be a party of four; for her brother, Charles Alington, had proposed himself for a visit…

I listened to this with sufficient attention to grasp what Madge was saying, but what I was really thinking about was a chess-problem which I was attempting to solve. But at this point I became acutely aware that her stream of pleasant impressions dried up suddenly, and she became stonily silent. She shut speech off as by the turn of a tap, and glowered at the fire, rubbing the back of one hand with the fingers of another, as is her habit in perplexity.

'Go on,' I said.

She got up, suddenly restless.

'All I have been telling you is literally and soberly true,' she said. 'I thought Mrs Acres charming and witty and good-looking and friendly. What more could you ask from a new acquaintance? And then, after I had asked her to dinner, I suddenly found for no earthly reason that I very much disliked her; I couldn't bear her.'

'You said she was wonderfully well dressed,' I permitted myself to remark… If the Queen took the Knight—

'Don't be silly!' said Madge. 'I am wonderfully well dressed too. But behind all her agreeableness and charm and good looks I suddenly felt there was something else which I detested and dreaded. It's no use asking me what it was, because I haven't the slightest idea. If I knew what it was, the thing would explain itself. But I felt a horror—nothing vivid, nothing close, you understand, but somewhere in the background. Can the mind have a "turn," do you think, just as the body can, when for a second or two you suddenly feel giddy? I think it must have been that—oh! I'm sure it was that. But I'm glad I asked her to dine. I mean to like her. I shan't have a "turn" again, shall I?'

'No, certainly not,' I said... If the Queen refrained from taking the tempting Knight—

'Oh, do stop your silly chess-problem!' said Madge. 'Bite him, Fungus!'

Fungus, so called because he is the son of Humour and Gustavus Adolphus, rose from his place on the hearthrug, and with a horse laugh nuzzled against my leg, which is his way of biting those he loves. Then the most amiable of bull-dogs, who has a passion for the human race, lay down on my foot and sighed heavily. But Madge evidently wanted to talk, and I pushed the chessboard away.

'Tell me more about the horror,' I said.

'It was just horror,' she said—'a sort of sickness of the soul.'

I found my brain puzzling over some vague reminiscence, surely connected with Mrs Acres, which those words mistily evoked. But next moment that train of thought was cut short, for the old and sinister legend about the Gate-house came into my mind as accounting for the horror of which Madge spoke. In the days of Elizabethan religious persecutions it had, then newly built, been inhabited by two brothers, of whom the elder, to whom it belonged, had Mass said there every Sunday. Betrayed by the younger, he was arrested and racked to death. Subsequently the younger, in a fit of remorse, hanged himself in the panelled parlour. Certainly there was a story that the house was haunted by his strangled apparition dangling from the beams, and the late tenants of the house (which now had stood vacant for over three years) had quitted it after a month's occupation, in consequence, so it was commonly said, of unaccountable and horrible sights. What was more likely, then, than that Madge, who from childhood has been intensely sensitive to occult and psychic phenomena, should have caught, on that strange wireless receiver which is characteristic of 'sensitives,' some whispered message?

'But you know the story of the house,' I said. 'Isn't it quite possible that something of that may have reached you? Where did you sit, for instance? In the panelled parlour?'

She brightened at that.

'Ah, you wise man!' she said. 'I never thought of that. That may account for it all. I hope it does. You shall be left in peace with your chess for being so brilliant.'

I had occasion half an hour later to go to the post-office, a hundred yards up the High Street, on the matter of a registered letter which I wanted to despatch that evening. Dusk was gathering, but the red glow of sunset still smouldered in the west, sufficient to enable me to recognise familiar forms and features of passers-by. Just as I came opposite the post-office there approached from the other direction a tall, finely built woman, whom, I felt sure, I had never seen before. Her destination was the same as mine, and I hung on my step a moment to let her pass in first. Simultaneously I felt that I knew, in some vague, faint manner, what Madge had meant when she talked about a 'sickness of the soul.' It was no nearer realisation to me than is the running of a tune in the head to the audible external hearing of it, and I attributed my sudden recognition of her feeling to the fact that in all probability my mind had subconsciously been dwelling on what she had said, and not for a moment did I connect it with any external cause. And then it occurred to me who, possibly, this woman was...

She finished the transaction of her errand a few seconds before me, and when I got out into the street again she was a dozen yards down the pavement, walking in the direction of my house and of the Gate-house. Opposite my own door I deliberately lingered, and saw her pass down the steps that led from the road to the entrance of the Gate-house. Even as I turned into my own door the unbidden reminiscence which had eluded me before came out into the open, and I cast my net over it. It was her husband, who, in the inexplicable communication he had left on his dressing-room table, just before he shot himself, had written 'my soul sickens.' It was odd, though scarcely more than that, for Madge to have used those identical words.

Charles Alington, my wife's brother, who arrived next afternoon, is quite the happiest man whom I have ever come across. The material world, that perennial spring of thwarted ambition, physical desire, and perpetual disappointment, is practically unknown to him. Envy, malice, and all uncharitableness are equally alien, because he does not want to obtain what anybody else has got, and has no sense of possession, which is queer, since he is enormously rich. He fears nothing, he hopes for nothing, he has no abhorrences or affections, for all physical and nervous functions are in him in the service of an intense inquisitiveness. He never passed a moral judgment in his life, he only wants to explore and to know. Knowledge, in fact, is his entire preoccupation, and since chemists and medical scientists probe and mine in the world of tinctures and microbes far more efficiently than he could do, as he has so little care for anything that can be weighed or propagated, he devotes himself, absorbedly and ecstatically, to that world that lies about the confines of conscious existence. Anything not yet certainly determined appeals to him with the call of a trumpet: he ceases to take an interest in a subject as soon as it shows signs of assuming a practical and definite status. He was intensely concerned, for instance, in wireless transmission until Signor Marconi proved that it came within the scope of practical science, and then Charles abandoned it as dull. I had seen him last two months before, when he was in a great perturbation, since he was speaking at a meeting of Anglo-Israelites in the morning, to show that the Scone Stone, which is now in the Coronation Chair at Westminster, was for certain the pillow on which Jacob's head had rested when he saw the vision at Bethel; was addressing the Psychical Research Society in the afternoon on the subject of messages received from the dead through automatic script, and in the evening was, by way of a holiday, only listening to a lecture on reincarnation. None of these things could, as yet, be definitely proved, and that was why he loved them. During the intervals when the occult and the fantastic do not occupy him, he is, in spite of his fifty years and wizened mien, exactly like a schoolboy of eighteen back on his holidays and brimming with superfluous energy.

I found Charles already arrived when I got home next afternoon, after a round of golf. He was betwixt and between the serious and the holiday mood, for he had evidently been reading to Madge from a journal concerning reincarnation, and was rather severe to me...

'Golf!' he said, with insulting scorn. 'What is there to know about golf? You hit a ball into the air—'

I was a little sore over the events of the afternoon.

'That's just what I don't do,' I said. 'I hit it along the ground!'

'Well, it doesn't matter where you hit it,' said he. 'It's all subject to known laws. But the guess, the conjecture: there's the thrill and the excitement of life. The charlatan with his new cure for cancer, the automatic writer with his messages from the dead, the reincarnationist with his positive assertions that he was Napoleon or a Christian slave—they are the people who advance knowledge. You have to guess before you know. Even Darwin saw that when he said you could not investigate without a hypothesis!'

'So what's your hypothesis this minute?' I asked.

'Why, that we've all lived before, and that we're going to live again here on this same old earth. Any other conception of a future life is impossible. Are all the people who have been born and have died since the world emerged from chaos going to become inhabitants of some future world? What a squash, you know, my dear Madge! Now, I know what you're going to ask me. If we've all lived before, why can't we remember it? But that's so simple! If you remembered being Cleopatra, you would go on behaving like Cleopatra; and what would Tarleton say? Judas Iscariot, too! Fancy knowing you had been Judas Iscariot! You couldn't get over it! you would commit suicide, or cause everybody who was connected with you to commit suicide from their horror of you. Or imagine being a grocer's boy who knew he had been Julius Cæsar... Of course, sex doesn't matter: souls, as far as I understand, are sexless—just sparks of life, which are put into physical envelopes, some male, some female. You might have been King David, Madge and poor Tony here one of his wives.'

'That would be wonderfully neat,' said I.

Charles broke out into a shout of laughter.

'It would indeed,' he said. 'But I won't talk sense any more to you scoffers. I'm absolutely tired out, I will confess, with thinking. I want to have a pretty lady to come to dinner, and talk to her as if she was just herself and I myself, and nobody else. I want to win two-and-sixpence at bridge with the expenditure of enormous thought. I want to have a large breakfast tomorrow and read *The Times* afterwards, and go to Tony's club and talk about crops and golf and Irish affairs and Peace Conferences, and all the things that don't matter one straw!'

'You're going to begin your programme tonight, dear,' said Madge. 'A very pretty lady is coming to dinner, and we're going to play bridge afterwards.'

Madge and I were ready for Mrs Acres when she arrived, but Charles was not yet down. Fungus, who has a wild adoration for Charles, quite unaccountable, since Charles has no feelings for dogs, was helping him to dress, and Madge, Mrs Acres, and I waited for his appearance. It was certainly Mrs Acres whom I had met last night at the door of the post-office, but the dim light of sunset had not enabled me to see how wonderfully handsome she was. There was something slightly Jewish about her profile: the high forehead, the very full-lipped mouth, the bridged nose, the prominent chin, all suggested rather than exemplified an Eastern origin. And when she spoke she had that rich softness of utterance, not quite hoarseness, but not quite of the clear-cut distinctness of tone which characterises northern nations. Something southern, something Eastern...

'I am bound to ask one thing,' she said, when, after the usual greetings, we stood round the fireplace, waiting for Charles—'but have you got a dog?'

Madge moved towards the bell.

'Yes, but he shan't come down if you dislike dogs,' she said. 'He's wonderfully kind, but I know—'

'Ah, it's not that,' said Mrs Acres. 'I adore dogs. But I only wished to spare your dog's feelings. Though I adore them, they hate me, and they're terribly frightened of me. There's something anti-canine about me.'

It was too late to say more. Charles's steps clattered in the little hall outside, and Fungus was hoarse and amused. Next moment the door opened, and the two came in.

Fungus came in first. He lolloped in a festive manner into the middle of the room, sniffed and snored in greeting, and then turned tail. He slipped and skidded on the parquet outside, and we heard him bundling down the kitchen stairs.

'Rude dog,' said Madge. 'Charles, let me introduce you to Mrs Acres. My brother, Mrs Acres: Sir Charles Alington.'

Our little dinner-table of four would not permit of separate conversations, and general topics, springing up like mushrooms, wilted and died at their very inception. What mood possessed the others I did not at that time know, but for myself I was only conscious of some fundamental distaste of the handsome, clever woman who sat on my right, and seemed quite unaffected by the withering atmosphere. She was charming to the eye, she was witty to the ear, she had grace and gracefulness, and all the time she was something terrible. But by degrees, as I found my own distaste increasing, I saw that my brother-in-law's interest was growing correspondingly keen. The 'pretty lady' whose presence at dinner he had desired and obtained was enchaining him—not, so I began to guess, for her charm and her prettiness, but for some purpose of study, and I wondered whether it was her beautiful Jewish profile that was confirming to his mind some Anglo-Israelitish theory, whether he saw in her fine brown eyes the glance of the seer and the clairvoyante, or whether he divined in her some reincarnation of one of the famous or the infamous dead. Certainly she had for him some fascination beyond that of the legitimate charm of a very handsome woman; he was studying her with intense curiosity.

'And you are comfortable in the Gate-house?' he suddenly rapped out at her, as if asking some question of which the answer was crucial.

'Ah! but so comfortable,' she said—'such a delightful atmosphere. I have never known a house that "felt" so peaceful and homelike. Or is it merely fanciful to imagine that some houses have a sense of tranquillity about them and others are uneasy and even terrible?'

Charles stared at her a moment in silence before he recollected his manners.

'No, there may easily be something in it, I should say,' he answered. 'One can imagine long centuries of tranquillity actually investing a home with some sort of psychical aura perceptible to those who are sensitive.'

She turned to Madge.

'And yet I have heard a ridiculous story that the house is supposed to be haunted,' she said. 'If it is, it is surely haunted by delightful, contented spirits.'

Dinner was over. Madge rose.

'Come in very soon, Tony,' she said to me, 'and let's get to our bridge.'

But her eyes said, 'Don't leave me long alone with her.'

Charles turned briskly round when the door had shut.

'An extremely interesting woman,' he said.

'Very handsome,' said I.

'Is she? I didn't notice. Her mind, her spirit—that's what intrigued me. What is she? What's behind? Why did Fungus turn tail like that? Queer, too, about her finding the atmosphere of the Gate-house so tranquil. The late tenants, I remember, didn't find that soothing touch about it!'

'How do you account for that?' I asked.

'There might be several explanations. You might say that the late tenants were fanciful, imaginative people, and that the present tenant is a sensible, matter-of-fact woman. Certainly she seemed to be.'

'Or—' I suggested.

He laughed.

'Well, you might say—mind, I don't say so—but you might say that the—the spiritual tenants of the house find Mrs Acres a congenial companion, and want to retain her. So they keep quiet, and don't upset the cook's nerves!'

Somehow this answer exasperated and jarred on me.

'What do you mean?' I said. 'The spiritual tenant of the house, I suppose, is the man who betrayed his brother and hanged himself. Why should he find a charming woman like Mrs Acres a congenial companion?'

Charles got up briskly. Usually he is more than ready to discuss such topics, but tonight it seemed that he had no such inclination.

'Didn't Madge tell us not to be long?' he asked. 'You know how I run on if I once get on that subject, Tony, so don't give me the opportunity.'

'But why did you say that?' I persisted.

'Because I was talking nonsense. You know me well enough to be aware that I am an habitual criminal in that respect.'

It was indeed strange to find how completely both the first impression that Madge had formed of Mrs Acres and the feeling that followed so quickly on its heels were endorsed by those who, during the next week or two, did a neighbour's duty to the newcomer. All were loud in praise of her charm, her pleasant, kindly wit, her good looks, her beautiful clothes, but even while this *Lob-gesang* was in full chorus it would suddenly die away, and an uneasy silence descended, which somehow was more eloquent than all the appreciative speech. Odd, unaccountable little incidents had occurred, which were whispered from mouth to mouth till they became common property. The same fear that Fungus had shown of her was exhibited by another dog. A parallel case occurred when she returned the call of our parson's wife. Mrs Dowlett had a cage of canaries in the window of her drawing-room. These birds had manifested symptoms of extreme terror when Mrs Acres entered the room, beating themselves against the wires of their cage, and uttering the alarm-note... She inspired some sort of inexplicable fear, over which we, as trained and civilised human beings, had control, so that we behaved ourselves. But animals, without that check, gave way altogether to it, even as Fungus had done.

Mrs Acres entertained; she gave charming little dinner-parties of eight, with a couple of tables at bridge to follow, but over these evenings there hung a blight and a blackness. No doubt the sinister story of the panelled parlour contributed to this.

This curious secret dread of her, of which as on that first evening at my house, she appeared to be completely unconscious differed very widely in degree. Most people, like myself, were conscious of it, but only very remotely so, and we found ourselves at the Gate-house behaving quite as usual, though with this unease in the background. But with a few, and most of all with Madge, it grew into a sort of obsession. She made every effort to combat it; her Will was entirely set against it, but her struggle seemed only to establish its power over her. The pathetic and pitiful part was that Mrs Acres from the first had taken a tremendous liking to her, and used to drop in continually, calling first to Madge at the window, in that pleasant, serene voice of hers, to tell Fungus that the hated one was imminent.

Then came a day when Madge and I were bidden to a party at the Gate-house on Christmas evening. This was to be the last of Mrs Acres's hospitalities for the present, since she was leaving immediately afterwards for a couple of months in Egypt. So, with this remission ahead, Madge almost gleefully accepted the bidding. But when the evening came she was seized with so violent an attack of sickness and shivering that she was utterly unable to fulfil her engagement. Her doctor could find no physical trouble to account for this: it seemed that the anticipation of her evening alone caused it, and here was the culmination of her shrinking from our kindly and pleasant neighbour. She could only tell me that her sensations, as she began to dress for the party, were like those of that moment in sleep when somewhere in the drowsy brain nightmare is ripening. Something independent of her will revolted at what lay before her...

Spring had begun to stretch herself in the lap of winter when next the curtain rose on this veiled drama of forces but dimly comprehended and shudderingly conjectured; but then, indeed, nightmare ripened swiftly in broad noon. And this was the way of it.

Charles Alington had again come to stay with us five days before Easter, and expressed himself as humorously disappointed to find that the subject of his curiosity was still absent from the Gate-house. On the Saturday morning before Easter he appeared very late for breakfast, and Madge had already gone her ways. I rang for a fresh teapot, and while this was on its way he took up *The Times*.

'I only read the outside page of it,' he said. 'The rest is too full of mere materialistic dullnesses—politics, sports, money-market—'

He stopped, and passed the paper over to me.

'There, where I'm pointing,' he said—'among the deaths. The first one.'

What I read was this:

> ACRES, BERTHA. Died at sea, Thursday night, 30th March, and by her own request buried at sea. (Received by wireless from P. & O. steamer *Peshawar*.)

He held out his hand for the paper again, and turned over the leaves.

'Lloyd's,' he said. 'The *Peshawar* arrived at Tilbury yesterday afternoon. The burial must have taken place somewhere in the English Channel.'

On the afternoon of Easter Sunday Madge and I motored out to the golf links three miles away. She proposed to walk along the beach just outside the dunes while I had my round, and return to the club-house for tea in two hours' time. The day was one of most lucid spring: a warm south-west wind bowled white clouds along the sky, and their shadows jovially scudded over the sandhills. We had told her of Mrs Acres's death, and from that moment something dark and vague which had been lying over her mind since the autumn seemed to join this fleet of the shadows of clouds and leave her in sunlight. We parted at the door of the club-house, and she set out on her walk.

Half an hour later, as my opponent and I were waiting on the fifth tee, where the road crosses the links, for the couple in front of us to move on, a servant from the club-house, scudding along the road, caught sight of us, and, jumping from his bicycle, came to where we stood.

'You're wanted at the club-house, sir,' he said to me. 'Mrs Carford was walking along the shore, and she found something left by the tide. A body, sir. 'Twas in a sack, but the sack was torn, and she saw—It's upset her very much, sir. We thought it best to come for you.'

I took the boy's bicycle and went back to the club-house as fast as I could turn the wheel. I felt sure I knew what Madge had found, and, knowing that, realised the shock... Five minutes later she was telling me her story in gasps and whispers.

'The tide was going down,' she said, 'and I walked along the high-water mark... There were pretty shells; I was picking them up... And then I saw it in front of me—just shapeless, just a sack... and then, as I came nearer, it took shape; there were knees and elbows. It moved, it rolled over, and where the head was the sack was torn, and I saw her face. Her eyes were open, Tony, and I fled... All the time I felt it was rolling along after me. Oh, Tony! she's dead, isn't she? She won't come back to the Gate-house? Do you promise me?... There's something awful! I wonder if I guess. The sea gives her up. The sea won't suffer her to rest in it.'...

The news of the finding had already been telephoned to Tarleton, and soon a party of four men with a stretcher arrived. There was no doubt as to the identity of the body, for though it had been in the water for three days no corruption had come to it. The weights with which at burial it had been laden must by some strange chance have been detached from it, and by a chance stranger yet it had drifted to the shore closest to her home. That night it lay in the mortuary, and the inquest was held on it next day, though that was a bank-holiday. From there it was taken to the Gate-house and coffined, and it lay in the panelled parlour for the funeral on the morrow.

Madge, after that one hysterical outburst, had completely recovered herself, and on the Monday evening she made a little wreath of the spring-flowers which the early warmth had called into blossom in the garden, and I went across with it to the Gate-house. Though the news of Mrs Acres's death and the subsequent finding of the body had been widely advertised, there had been no response from relations or friends, and as I laid the solitary wreath on the coffin a sense of the utter loneliness of what lay within seized and encompassed me. And then a portent, no less, took place before my eyes. Hardly had the freshly gathered flowers been laid on the coffin than they drooped and wilted. The stalks of the daffodils bent, and their bright chalices closed; the odour of the wallflowers died, and they withered as I watched... What did it mean, that even the petals of spring shrank and were moribund?

I told Madge nothing of this; and she, as if through some pang of remorse, was determined to be present next day at the funeral. No arrival of friends or relations had taken place, and from the Gate-house there came none of the servants. They stood in the porch as the coffin was brought out of the house, and even before it was put into the hearse had gone back again and closed the door. So, at the cemetery on the hill above Tarleton, Madge and her brother and I were the only mourners.

The afternoon was densely overcast, though we got no rainfall, and it was with thick clouds above and a sea-mist drifting between the gravestones that we came, after the service in the cemetery-chapel, to the place of interment. And then—I can hardly write of it now—when it came for the coffin to be lowered into the grave, it was found that by some faulty measurement it could not descend, for the excavation was not long enough to hold it.

Madge was standing close to us, and at this moment I heard her sob.

'And the kindly earth will not receive her,' she whispered.

There was awful delay: the diggers must be sent for again, and meantime the rain had begun to fall thick and tepid. For some reason—perhaps some outlying feeler of Madge's obsession had wound a tentacle round me—I felt that I must know that earth had gone to earth, but I could not suffer Madge to wait. So, in this miserable pause, I got Charles to take her home, and then returned.

Pick and shovel were busy, and soon the resting-place was ready. The interrupted service continued, the handful of wet earth splashed on the coffin-lid, and when all was over I left the cemetery, still feeling, I knew not why, that all was *not* over. Some restlessness and want of certainty possessed me, and instead of going home I fared forth into the rolling wooded country inland, with the intention of walking off these bat-like terrors that flapped around me. The rain had ceased, and a blurred sunlight penetrated the sea-mist which still blanketed the fields and woods, and for half an hour, moving briskly, I endeavoured to fight down some fantastic conviction that had gripped my mind in its claws. I refused to look straight at that conviction, telling myself how fantastic, how unreasonable it was; but as often as I put out a hand to throttle it there came the echo of Madge's words: 'The sea will not suffer her; the kindly earth will not receive her.' And if I could shut my eyes to that there came some remembrance of the day she died, and of half-forgotten fragments of Charles's superstitious belief in reincarnation. The whole thing, incredible though its component parts were, hung together with a terrible tenacity.

Before long the rain began again, and I turned, meaning to go by the main-road into Tarleton, which passes in a wide-flung curve some half-mile outside the cemetery. But as I approached the path through the fields, which, leaving the less direct route, passes close to the cemetery and brings you by a steeper and shorter descent into the town, I felt myself irresistibly impelled to take it. I told myself, of course, that I wished to make my wet walk as short as possible; but at the back of my mind was the half-conscious, but none the less imperative need to know by ocular evidence that the grave by which I had stood that afternoon had been filled in, and that the body of Mrs Acres now lay tranquil beneath the soil. My path would be even shorter if I passed through the graveyard, and so presently I was fumbling in the gloom for the latch of the gate, and closed it again behind me. Rain was falling now thick and sullenly, and in the bleared twilight I picked my way among the mounds and slipped on the dripping grass, and there in front of me was the newly turned earth. All was finished: the gravediggers had done their work and departed, and earth had gone back again into the keeping of the earth.

It brought me some great lightening of the spirit to know that, and I was on the point of turning away when a sound of stir from the heaped soil caught my ear, and I saw a little stream of pebbles mixed with clay trickle down the side of the mound above the grave: the heavy rain, no doubt, had loosened the earth. And then came another and yet another, and with terror gripping at my heart I perceived that this was no loosening from without, but from within, for to right and left the piled soil was falling away with the press of something from below. Faster and faster it poured off the grave, and ever higher at the head of it rose a mound of earth pushed upwards from beneath. Somewhere out of sight there came the sound as of creaking and breaking wood, and then through that mound of earth there protruded the end of the coffin. The lid was shattered: loose pieces of the boards fell off it, and from within the cavity there faced me white features and wide eyes. All this I saw, while sheer terror held me motionless; then, I suppose, came the breaking-point, and with such panic as surely man never felt before I was stumbling away among the graves and racing towards the kindly human lights of the town below.

I went to the parson who had conducted the service that afternoon with my incredible tale, and an hour later he, Charles Alington, and two or three men from the undertaker's were on the spot. They found the coffin, completely disinterred, lying on the ground by the grave, which was now three-quarters full of the earth which had fallen back into it. After what had happened it was decided to make no further attempt to bury it; and next day the body was cremated.

Now, it is open to anyone who may read this tale to reject the incident of this emergence of the coffin altogether, and account for the other strange happenings by the comfortable theory of coincidence. He can certainly satisfy himself that one Bertha Acres did die at sea on this particular Thursday before Easter, and was buried at sea: there is nothing extraordinary about that. Nor is it the least impossible that the weights should have slipped from the canvas shroud, and that the body should have been washed ashore on the coast by Tarleton (why not Tarleton, as well as any other little town near the coast?); nor is there anything inherently significant in the fact that the grave, as originally dug, was not of sufficient dimensions to receive the coffin. That all these incidents should have happened to the body of a single individual is odd, but then the nature of coincidence is to be odd. They form a startling series, but unless coincidences are startling they escape observation altogether. So, if you reject the last incident here recorded, or account for it by some local disturbance, an earthquake, or the breaking of a spring just below the grave, you can comfortably recline on the cushion of coincidence...

For myself, I give no explanation of these events, though my brother-in-law brought forward one with which he himself is perfectly satisfied. Only the other day he sent me, with considerable jubilation, a copy of some extracts from a mediæval treatise on the subject of reincarnation which sufficiently indicates his theory. The original work was in Latin, which, mistrusting my scholarship, he kindly translated for me. I transcribe his quotations exactly as he sent them to me.

'We have these certain instances of his reincarnation. In one his spirit was incarnated in the body of a man; in the other, in that of a woman, fair of outward aspect, and of a pleasant conversation, but held in dread and in horror by those who came into more than casual intercourse with her... She, it is said, died on the anniversary of the day on which he hanged himself, after the betrayal, but of this I have no certain information. What is sure is that, when the time came for her burial, the kindly earth would receive her not, but though the grave was dug deep and well it spewed her forth again... Of the man in whom his cursed spirit was reincarnated it is said that, being on a voyage when he died, he was cast overboard with weights to sink him; but the sea would not suffer him to rest in her bosom, but slipped the weights from him, and cast him forth again on to the coast... Howbeit, when the full time of his expiation shall have come and his deadly sin forgiven, the corporal body which is the cursed receptacle of his spirit shall at length be purged with fire, and so he shall, in the infinite mercy of the Almighty, have rest, and shall wander no more.'

THE TOP LANDING

I HAD BOUGHT THAT AFTERNOON FROM A TWOPENNY BOOK-stall a shabby little volume entitled *Commerce with the Dead*, and I was glancing through it with growing derision when Geoffrey Halton looked in. As I considered him to be a dabbler in the superstitious, I read out to him with contempt the sentence I had got to when he came in. It was as follows:

> The possibility of communication with departed spirits is no longer open to doubt, but the enquirer will certainly expose himself to grave dangers. When once he has opened the door, as he may easily do, between the dead and the living, he cannot be sure what evil and potent intelligences may not be let loose. They are of terrible power: they may drive the communicator to madness or suicide—

'Oh, what rot!' said I, closing the book.

Geoffrey was silent a moment.

'It isn't rot,' he said quietly. 'It's deadly and awful truth. I have seen it happen.'

In answer to my incredulous enquiry he told me the following story:

'My cousin, Phil Halton, and I,' said he, 'found ourselves a couple of years ago reluctantly facing the conclusion that, after two idle and expensive months in London, we must devote August and September to industry and economy. He had to compose the incidental music to Shakespeare's *Tempest*, which was to be produced in November, and I to write a novel for serial publication, of which at present I had only conceived the outline, though in detail. But just as we were settling down for August in London Phil, during a week-end in the country, came across a small Queen Anne house in the little town of Adelsham, which was to be let furnished for the ridiculous sum of five guineas a week, including the ministrations of the cook-housekeeper who was in charge. Naturally, he suspected imperfect drains or leaking roofs, but the agent assured him, as proved to be the case, that all was in perfect repair. So within three days we were established there; I had brought down from London my manservant and a housemaid, and our first dinner in the house convinced us of the abilities of Mrs Ayton. She was a shrivelled little old woman, quick and nimble and silent, and as for the house, if Providence had specially planned an ideal retreat for Phil and me he could not have bettered it. It stood on the top of the hill above the Romney Marsh in a cobbled, sequestered street. There was a sitting-room for each of us, two good bedrooms on the first floor, and above four smaller rooms for servants. One of these was locked, and contained, so Mrs Ayton told us, the more private possessions of the owner, who was spending the summer abroad. To the garden, framed in tall walls of mellow brick, there was the access of French windows from the dining-room and the downstairs sitting-room, in which was a piano at Phil's disposal. All was exactly perfect.

'We plunged at once into our belated labours, and for the first week or so I can tell you of no unusual or sinister happening except that both of us, and that increasingly, had the sense that we were being watched. It seemed a fantastic idea, and we used to laugh at each other and ourselves, but a dozen times a day one or other of us would find ourselves suddenly looking round with the notion that there was some presence other than our own in the room. All the time, too, I was cudgelling my memory to recollect what story I had once read about some dreadful occurrence at Adelsham, but at present it was stored in some sealed cell in my brain, and I could not get access to it.

'We were sitting one sultry evening after dinner out in the garden, and dusk was deepening into the night. We had been talking about this odd fancy that something was watching us, when Phil pointed to the house.

'"Look at the light in that window," he said. "Isn't that the closed room?"

'There, sure enough, on the top storey, the windows of which appeared above the low brick balustrade, was a light coming from the locked room. There was also someone in the room for across the illuminated square appeared the black silhouette of a head and shoulders.

'"Probably Mrs Ayton," said I, getting up. "Come in and play picquet."

'When I looked again the figure was gone. But my heart missed a beat, for I clearly saw that it was not a figure of a woman, but of a man. I felt, too, that it was from there that we were being watched.

'Next morning a domestic bombshell exploded. My servant Manders, who had been with me for ten years, came to me after breakfast and asked if he and my housemaid might go back to London. It was reasonable to ask for an explanation.

'"We can neither of us stand it any longer," he said. "I'm very sorry, sir, but I can't stop here, and it's the same with Edith."

'"And if I refuse?" I asked.

'Manders wiped his forehead with the back of his hand, and I saw that his face was white and his hand trembled.

'"Then we shall both ask to give you notice, sir," he said, "and forfeit a month's wages."

'"What's the matter, Manders?" I asked. "You're frightened. Can't you tell me what it is?"

'He looked round with a scared eye.

'"There's something on the top landing, sir," he said in a whisper. "I don't know what it is, but I can't bear it."

'"Have you seen anything, or heard anything?" I asked.

'"No, sir. But it's there, and it's getting worse."

'He took a step towards me.

'"I wish I could persuade you and Mr Phil to come too," he said. "Don't stop here, sir!"

'It was evident that they were determined not to stop here, and unless I was prepared to lose these admirable people altogether I must let them go. But I tried one more appeal.

'"And what's to happen to us if you and Edith go?" I asked.

'"Mrs Ayton says she can manage everything," he said.

'"You can go this afternoon," I said.

'Manders lingered a moment.

'"I'm very sorry, sir," he said.

'A few days after their departure the sudden spate of work which had descended over Phil and me dried up, and, finding that there was a golf links in the neighbourhood, Phil went out to sample and report on it, leaving me with some overdue letters to write. He returned at lunch-time, rather silent and preoccupied.

'"And the links?" I asked.

'"Oh, they're quite good," he said. "I had half a round with the secretary. He—he told me some strange things."

'"Such as?"

'"Well, he began talking about this house, not knowing we were in it. During this last year it has been let three times, but the tenants never stopped more than a fortnight. And the owner isn't abroad. She's in the house now, and the late owner is in the churchyard. I also found out what you had forgotten about Adelsham. There was a certain Dr Hoart who lived here—actually here, I mean—who conducted curious experiments in raising spirits."

'Then I remembered the rest.

'"And hanged himself," I said.

'"Yes."

'"About the present owner?" I said. "I suppose you mean Mrs Ayton. Did Dr Hoart leave the house to her?"

'"Yes, on the condition that she went on with the experiments they had conducted together."

'That afternoon I sat in the garden, reading over what I had written since I came to Adelsham. So deep was I in it that I leaped from my chair when I heard a voice addressing me, for I had seen no one approach.

'"I came to ask if I might have my evening out after I have served your dinner, sir?" said Mrs Ayton. "I have a bit of business."

'"Certainly," I said. "But are you sure you don't want help? You've got a lot to do, Mrs Ayton."

'She looked at me with a secret sort of smile on her withered old face.

'"No, I can manage," she said. "Two such quiet gentlemen, one with his pretty music and one with his pretty story."

'I made up my mind to spring a surprise on her.

'"You managed for Dr Hoart?" I asked.

'Not a tremor betrayed her.

'"And who might Dr Hoart be?" she asked.

'The evening became dark and overcast, and when we had finished our dinner we went upstairs to the little sitting-room where I worked. The staircase was very dark, for Mrs Ayton had drawn the curtains in the hall, and the only illumination came from the skylight above the top landing where was the locked room. As I fumbled for the electric light I looked up and saw dimly, but distinctly, the figure of a man leaning over the banisters at the top. Next moment the light shone out, and there was no one there... I cannot describe the awful shock this gave me, and it required every ounce of my courage to run upstairs and look into the rooms there. Two, lately vacated by my servants, were empty; the other two, the closed room and Mrs Ayton's room, were locked. But again, more vividly than on that first evening, I had the sense of being watched. I said nothing of this to Phil, and presently we were engaged over picquet. We went to bed early that night, each confessing to a weariness and oppression, and for my part I fell asleep instantly. I woke to find my room lit and Phil standing by me.

'"Something is happening," he said. "Listen!"

'From the landing overhead there was the sound of muffled footsteps and a drone of voices, two of them. Then there came a sudden loud creak from the banisters above and a noise as of rustling leaves... We hurried out on to the lit landing, and there, convulsed and quivering, was suspended a woman's figure. It turned as it oscillated to and fro, and we saw who it was—who, with eyes and tongue protruding, dangled there.

'Before we could get to her came the crowning horror. The rope was pulled up again from above by some agency there, and once more the body descended and jumped on the cord that was round the neck. And then the quivering and convulsions ceased.

'We ran up to untie the rope, but it was too late. The two rooms that had been locked up were open, and there was no one within. In the one there was just the furniture of an ordinary bedroom; the other was absolutely empty.'

THE FACE

HESTER WARD, SITTING BY THE OPEN WINDOW ON THIS hot afternoon in June, began seriously to argue with herself about the cloud of foreboding and depression which had encompassed her all day, and, very sensibly, she enumerated to herself the manifold causes for happiness in the fortunate circumstances of her life. She was young, she was extremely good-looking, she was well-off, she enjoyed excellent health, and above all, she had an adorable husband and two small, adorable children. There was no break, indeed, anywhere in the circle of prosperity which surrounded her, and had the wishing-cap been handed to her that moment by some beneficent fairy, she would have hesitated to put it on her head, for there was positively nothing that she could think of which would have been worthy of such solemnity. Moreover, she could not accuse herself of a want of appreciation of her blessings; she appreciated enormously, she enjoyed enormously, and she thoroughly wanted all those who so munificently contributed to her happiness to share in it.

She made a very deliberate review of these things, for she was really anxious, more anxious, indeed, than she admitted to herself, to find anything tangible which could possibly warrant this ominous feeling of approaching disaster. Then there was the weather to consider; for the last week London had been stiflingly hot, but if that was the cause, why had she not felt it before? Perhaps the effect of these broiling, airless days had been cumulative. That was an idea, but, frankly, it did not seem a very good one, for, as a matter of fact, she loved the heat; Dick, who hated it, said that it was odd he should have fallen in love with a salamander.

She shifted her position, sitting up straight in this low window-seat, for she was intending to make a call on her courage. She had known from the moment she awoke this morning what it was that lay so heavy on her, and now, having done her best to shift the reason of her depression on to anything else, and having completely failed, she meant to look the thing in the face. She was ashamed of doing so, for the cause of this leaden mood of fear which held her in its grip, was so trivial, so fantastic, so excessively silly.

'Yes, there never was anything so silly,' she said to herself. 'I must look at it straight, and convince myself how silly it is.' She paused a moment, clenching her hands.

'Now for it,' she said.

She had had a dream the previous night, which, years ago, used to be familiar to her, for again and again when she was a child she had dreamed it. In itself the dream was nothing, but in those childish days, whenever she had this dream which had visited her last night, it was followed on the next night by another which contained the source and the core of the horror, and she would awake screaming and struggling in the grip of overwhelming nightmare. For some ten years now she had not experienced it, and would have said that, though she remembered it, it had become dim and distant to her. But last night she had had that warning dream, which used to herald the visitation of the nightmare, and now that whole store-house of memory crammed as it was with bright things and beautiful contained nothing so vivid.

The warning dream, the curtain that was drawn up on the succeeding night, and disclosed the vision she dreaded, was simple and harmless enough in itself. She seemed to be walking on a high sandy cliff covered with short down-grass; twenty yards to the left came the edge of this cliff, which sloped steeply down to the sea that lay at its foot. The path she followed led through fields bounded by low hedges, and mounted gradually upwards. She went through some half-dozen of these, climbing over the wooden stiles that gave communication; sheep grazed there, but she never saw another human being, and always it was dusk, as if evening was falling, and she had to hurry on, because someone (she knew not whom) was waiting for her, and had been waiting not a few minutes only, but for many years. Presently, as she mounted this slope, she saw in front of her a copse of stunted trees, growing crookedly under the continual pressure of the wind that blew from the sea, and when she saw those she knew her journey was nearly done, and that the nameless one, who had been waiting for her so long was somewhere close at hand. The path she followed was cut through this wood, and the slanting boughs of the trees on the seaward side almost roofed it in; it was like walking through a tunnel. Soon the trees in front began to grow thin, and she saw through them the grey tower of a lonely church. It stood in a graveyard, apparently long disused, and the body of the church, which lay between the tower and the edge of the cliff, was in ruins, roofless, and with gaping windows, round which ivy grew thickly.

At that point this prefatory dream always stopped. It was a troubled, uneasy dream, for there was over it the sense of dusk and of the man who had been waiting for her so long, but it was not of the order of nightmare. Many times in childhood had she experienced it, and perhaps it was the subconscious knowledge of the night that so surely followed it, which gave it its disquiet. And now last night it had come again, identical in every particular but one. For last night it seemed to her that in the course of these ten years which had intervened since last it had visited her, the glimpse of the church and churchyard was changed. The edge of the cliff had come nearer to the tower, so that it now was within a yard or two of it, and the ruined body of the church, but for one broken arch that remained, had vanished. The sea had encroached, and for ten years had been busily eating at the cliff.

Hester knew well that it was this dream and this alone which had darkened the day for her, by reason of the nightmares that used to follow it, and, like a sensible woman, having looked it once in the face, she refused to admit into her mind any conscious calling-up of the sequel. If she let herself contemplate that, as likely or not the very thinking about it would be sufficient to ensure its return, and of one thing she was very certain, namely, that she didn't at all want it to do so. It was not like the confused jumble and jangle of ordinary nightmare, it was very simple, and she felt it concerned the nameless one who waited for her... But she must not think of it; her whole will and intention was set on not thinking of it, and to aid her resolution, there was the rattle of Dick's latchkey in the front-door, and his voice calling her.

She went out into the little square front hall; there he was, strong and large, and wonderfully undreamlike.

'This heat's a scandal, it's an outrage, it's an abomination of desolation,' he cried, vigorously mopping. 'What have we done that Providence should place us in this frying-pan? Let us thwart him, Hester! Let us drive out of this inferno and have our dinner at—I'll whisper it so that he shan't overhear—at Hampton Court!'

She laughed: this plan suited her excellently. They would return late, after the distraction of a fresh scene; and dining out at night was both delicious and stupefying.

'The very thing,' she said, 'and I'm sure Providence didn't hear. Let's start now!'

'Rather. Any letters for me?'

He walked to the table where there were a few rather uninteresting-looking envelopes with half penny stamps.

'Ah, receipted bill,' he said. 'Just a reminder of one's folly in paying it. Circular... unasked advice to invest in German marks... Circular begging letter, beginning "Dear Sir or Madam." Such impertinence to ask one to subscribe to something without ascertaining one's sex... Private view, portraits at the Walton Gallery.... Can't go: business meetings all day. You might like to have a look in, Hester. Some one told me there were some fine Vandycks. That's all: let's be off.'

Hester spent a thoroughly reassuring evening, and though she thought of telling Dick about the dream that had so deeply imprinted itself on her consciousness all day, in order to hear the great laugh he would have given her for being such a goose, she refrained from doing so, since nothing that he could say would be so tonic to these fantastic fears as his general robustness. Besides, she would have to account for its disturbing effect, tell him that it was once familiar to her, and recount the sequel of the nightmares that followed. She would neither think of them, nor mention them: it was wiser by far just to soak herself in his extraordinary sanity, and wrap herself in his affection... They dined out-of-doors at a riverside restaurant and strolled about afterwards, and it was very nearly midnight when, soothed with coolness and fresh air, and the vigour of his strong companionship, she let herself into the house, while he took the car back to the garage. And now she marvelled at the mood which had beset her all day, so distant and unreal had it become. She felt as if she had dreamed of shipwreck, and had awoke to find herself in some secure and sheltered garden where no tempest raged nor waves beat. But was there, ever so remotely, ever so dimly, the noise of far-off breakers somewhere?

He slept in the dressing-room which communicated with her bedroom, the door of which was left open for the sake of air and coolness, and she fell asleep almost as soon as her light was out, and while his was still burning. And immediately she began to dream.

She was standing on the sea-shore; the tide was out, for level sands strewn with stranded jetsam glimmered in a dusk that was deepening into night. Though she had never seen the place it was awfully familiar to her. At the head of the beach there was a steep cliff of sand, and perched on the edge of it was a grey church tower. The sea must have encroached and undermined the body of the church, for tumbled blocks of masonry lay close to her at the bottom of the cliff, and there were gravestones there, while others still in place were silhouetted whitely against the sky. To the right of the church tower there was a wood of stunted trees, combed sideways by the prevalent sea-wind, and she knew that along the top of the cliff a few yards inland there lay a path through fields, with wooden stiles to climb, which led through a tunnel of trees and so out into the churchyard. All this she saw in a glance, and waited, looking at the sand-cliff crowned by the church tower, for the terror that was going to reveal itself. Already she knew what it was, and, as so many times before, she tried to run away. But the catalepsy of nightmare was already on her; frantically she strove to move, but her utmost endeavour could not raise a foot from the sand. Frantically she tried to look away from the sand-cliffs close in front of her, where in a moment now the horror would be manifested...

It came. There formed a pale oval light, the size of a man's face, dimly luminous in front of her and a few inches above the level of her eyes. It outlined itself, short reddish hair grew low on the forehead, below were two grey eyes, set very close together, which steadily and fixedly regarded her. On each side the ears stood noticeably away from the head, and the lines of the jaw met in a short pointed chin. The nose was straight and rather long, below it came a hairless lip, and last of all the mouth took shape and colour, and there lay the crowning terror. One side of it, soft-curved and beautiful, trembled into a smile, the other side, thick and gathered together as by some physical deformity, sneered and lusted.

The whole face, dim at first, gradually focused itself into clear outline: it was pale and rather lean, the face of a young man. And then the lower lip dropped a little, showing the glint of teeth, and there was the sound of speech. 'I shall soon come for you now,' it said, and on the words it drew a little nearer to her, and the smile broadened. At that the full hot blast of nightmare poured in upon her. Again she tried to run, again she tried to scream, and now she could feel the breath of that terrible mouth upon her. Then with a crash and a rending like the tearing asunder of soul and body she broke the spell, and heard her own voice yelling, and felt with her fingers for the switch of her light. And then she saw that the room was not dark, for Dick's door was open, and the next moment, not yet undressed, he was with her.

'My darling, what is it?' he said. 'What's the matter?'

She clung desperately to him, still distraught with terror.

'Ah, he has been here again,' she cried. 'He says he will soon come to me. Keep him away, Dick.'

For one moment her fear infected him, and he found himself glancing round the room.

'But what do you mean?' he said. 'No one has been here.'

She raised her head from his shoulder.

'No, is was just a dream,' she said. 'But it was the old dream, and I was terrified. Why, you've not undressed yet. What time is it?'

'You haven't been in bed ten minutes, dear,' he said. 'You had hardly put out your light when I heard you screaming.'

She shuddered.

'Ah, it's awful,' she said. 'And he will come again...'

He sat down by her.

'Now tell me all about it,' he said.

She shook her head.

'No, it will never do to talk about it,' she said, 'it will only make it more real. I suppose the children are all right, are they?'

'Of course they are. I looked in on my way upstairs.'

'That's good. But I'm better now, Dick. A dream hasn't anything real about it, has it? It doesn't mean anything?'

He was quite reassuring on this point, and soon she quieted down. Before he went to bed he looked in again on her, and she was asleep.

Hester had a stern interview with herself when Dick had gone down to his office next morning. She told herself that what she was afraid of was nothing more than her own fear. How many times had that ill-omened face come to her in dreams, and what significance had it ever proved to possess? Absolutely none at all, except to make her afraid. She was afraid where no fear was: she was guarded, sheltered, prosperous, and what if a nightmare of childhood returned? It had no more meaning now than it had then, and all those visitations of her childhood had passed away without trace… And then, despite herself, she began thinking over that vision again. It was grimly identical with all its previous occurrences, except… And then, with a sudden shrinking of the heart, she remembered that in earlier years those terrible lips had said: 'I shall come for you when you are older,' and last night they had said: 'I shall soon come for you now.' She remembered, too, that in the warning dream the sea had encroached, and it had now demolished the body of the church. There was an awful consistency about these two changes in the otherwise identical visions. The years had brought their change to them, for in the one the encroaching sea had brought down the body of the church, in the other the time was now near…

It was no use to scold or reprimand herself, for to bring her mind to the contemplation of the vision meant merely that the grip of terror closed on her again; it was far wiser to occupy herself, and starve her fear out by refusing to bring it the sustenance of thought. So she went about her household duties, she took the children out for their airing in the park, and then, determined to leave no moment unoccupied, set off with the card of invitation to see the pictures in the private view at the Walton Gallery. After that her day was full enough, she was lunching out, and going on to a matinée, and by the time she got home Dick would have returned, and they would drive down to his little house at Rye for the week-end. All Saturday and Sunday she would be playing golf, and she felt that fresh air and physical fatigue would exorcise the dread of these dreaming fantasies.

The gallery was crowded when she got there; there were friends among the sightseers, and the inspection of the pictures was diversified by cheerful conversation. There were two or three fine Raeburns, a couple of Sir Joshuas, but the gems, so she gathered, were three Vandycks that hung in a small room by themselves. Presently she strolled in there, looking at her catalogue. The first of them, she saw, was a portrait of Sir Roger Wyburn. Still chatting to her friend she raised her eye and saw it...

Her heart hammered in her throat, and then seemed to stand still altogether. A qualm, as of some mental sickness of the soul overcame her, for there in front of her was he who would soon come for her. There was the reddish hair, the projecting ears, the greedy eyes set close together, and the mouth smiling on one side, and on the other gathered up into the sneering menace that she knew so well. It might have been her own nightmare rather than a living model which had sat to the painter for that face.

'Ah, what a portrait, and what a brute!' said her companion. 'Look, Hester, isn't that marvellous?'

She recovered herself with an effort. To give way to this ever-mastering dread would have been to allow nightmare to invade her waking life, and there, for sure, madness lay. She forced herself to look at it again, but there were the steady and eager eyes regarding her; she could almost fancy the mouth began to move. All round her the crowd bustled and chattered, but to her own sense she was alone there with Roger Wyburn.

And yet, so she reasoned with herself, this picture of him—for it was he and no other—should have reassured her. Roger Wyburn, to have been painted by Vandyck, must have been dead near on two hundred years; how could he be a menace to her? Had she seen that portrait by some chance as a child; had it made some dreadful impression on her, since overscored by other memories, but still alive in the mysterious subconsciousness, which flows eternally, like some dark underground river, beneath the surface of human life? Psychologists taught that these early impressions fester or poison the mind like some hidden abscess. That might account for this dread of one, nameless no longer, who waited for her.

That night down at Rye there came again to her the prefatory dream, followed by the nightmare, and clinging to her husband as the terror began to subside, she told him what she had resolved to keep to herself. Just to tell it brought a measure of comfort, for it was so outrageously fantastic, and his robust common sense upheld her. But when on their return to London there was a recurrence of these visions, he made short work of her demur and took her straight to her doctor.

'Tell him all, darling,' he said. 'Unless you promise to do that, I will. I can't have you worried like this. It's all nonsense, you know, and doctors are wonderful people for curing nonsense.'

She turned to him.

'Dick, you're frightened,' she said quietly.

He laughed.

'I'm nothing of the kind,' he said, 'but I don't like being awakened by your screaming. Not my idea of a peaceful night. Here we are.'

The medical report was decisive and peremptory. There was nothing whatever to be alarmed about; in brain and body she was perfectly healthy, but she was run down. These disturbing dreams were, as likely as not, an effect, a symptom of her condition, rather than the cause of it, and Dr Baring unhesitatingly recommended a complete change to some bracing place. The wise thing would be to send her out of this stuffy furnace to some quiet place to where she had never been. Complete change; quite so. For the same reason her husband had better not go with her; he must pack her off to, let us say, the East coast. Sea-air and coolness and complete idleness. No long walks; no long bathings; a dip, and a deck-chair on the sands. A lazy, soporific life. How about Rushton? He had no doubt that Rushton would set her up again. After a week or so, perhaps, her husband might go down and see her. Plenty of sleep—never mind the nightmares—plenty of fresh air.

Hester, rather to her husband's surprise, fell in with this suggestion at once, and the following evening saw her installed in solitude and tranquillity. The little hotel was still almost empty, for the rush of summer tourists had not yet begun, and all day she sat out on the beach with the sense of a struggle over. She need not fight the terror any more; dimly it seemed to her that its malignancy had been relaxed. Had she in some way yielded to it and done its secret bidding? At any rate no return of its nightly visitations had occurred, and she slept long and dreamlessly, and woke to another day of quiet. Every morning there was a line for her from Dick, with good news of himself and the children, but he and they alike seemed somehow remote, like memories of a very distant time. Something had driven in between her and them, and she saw them as if through glass. But equally did the memory of the face of Roger Wyburn, as seen on the master's canvas or hanging close in front of her against the crumbling sand-cliff, become blurred and indistinct, and no return of her nightly terrors visited her. This truce from all emotion reacted not on her mind alone, lulling her with a sense of soothed security, but on her body also, and she began to weary of this day-long inactivity.

The village lay on the lip of a stretch of land reclaimed from the sea. To the north the level marsh, now beginning to glow with the pale bloom of the sea-lavender, stretched away featureless till it lost itself in distance, but to the south a spur of hill came down to the shore ending in a wooded promontory. Gradually, as her physical health increased, she began to wonder what lay beyond this ridge which cut short the view, and one afternoon she walked across the intervening level and strolled up its wooded slopes. The day was close and windless, the invigorating sea-breeze which till now had spiced the heat with freshness had died, and she looked forward to finding a current of air stirring when she had topped the hill. To the south a mass of dark cloud lay along the horizon, but there was no imminent threat of storm. The slope was easily surmounted, and presently she stood at the top and found herself on the edge of a tableland of wooded pasture, and following the path, which ran not far from the edge of the cliff, she came out into more open country. Empty fields, where a few sheep were grazing, mounted gradually upwards. Wooden stiles made a communication in the hedges that bounded them. And there, not a mile in front of her, she saw a wood, with trees growing slantingly away from the push of the prevalent sea winds, crowning the upward slope, and over the top of it peered a grey church tower.

For the moment, as the awful and familiar scene identified itself, Hester's heart stood still: the next a wave of courage and resolution poured in upon her. Here, at last was the scene of that prefatory dream, and here was she presented with the opportunity of fathoming and dispelling it. Instantly her mind was made up, and under the strange twilight of the shrouded sky, she walked swiftly on through the fields she had so often traversed in sleep, and up to the wood, beyond which he was waiting for her. She closed her ears against the clanging bell of terror, which now she could silence for ever, and unfalteringly entered that dark tunnel of wood. Soon in front of her the trees began to thin, and through them, now close at hand, she saw the church tower. In a few yards farther she came out of the belt of trees, and round her were the monuments of a graveyard long disused. The cliff was broken off close to the church tower: between it and the edge there was no more of the body of the church than a broken arch, thick hung with ivy. Round this she passed and saw below the ruin of fallen masonry, and the level sands strewn with headstones and disjected rubble, and at the edge of the cliff were graves already cracked and toppling. But there was no one here, none waited for her, and the churchyard where she had so often pictured him was as empty as the fields she had just traversed.

A huge elation filled her; her courage had been rewarded, and all the terrors of the past became to her meaningless phantoms. But there was no time to linger, for now the storm threatened, and on the horizon a blink of lightning was followed by a crackling peal. Just as she turned to go her eye fell on a tombstone that was balanced on the very edge of the cliff, and she read on it that here lay the body of Roger Wyburn.

Fear, the catalepsy of nightmare, rooted her for the moment to the spot; she stared in stricken amazement at the moss-grown letters; almost she expected to see that fell terror of a face rise and hover over his resting-place. Then the fear which had frozen her lent her wings, and with hurrying feet she sped through the arched pathway in the wood and out into the fields. Not one backward glance did she give till she had come to the edge of the ridge above the village, and, turning. saw the pastures she had traversed empty of any living presence. None had followed; but the sheep, apprehensive of the coming storm, had ceased to feed, and were huddling under shelter of the stunted hedges.

Her first idea, in the panic of her mind, was to leave the place at once, but the last train for London had left an hour before, and besides, where was the use of flight if it was the spirit of a man long dead from which she fled? The distance from the place where his bones lay did not afford her safety; that must be sought for within. But she longed for Dick's sheltering and confident presence; he was arriving in any case tomorrow, but there were long dark hours before tomorrow, and who could say what the perils and dangers of the coming night might be? If he started this evening instead of tomorrow morning, he could motor down here in four hours, and would be with her by ten o'clock or eleven. She wrote an urgent telegram: 'Come at once,' she said. 'Don't delay.'

The storm which had flickered on the south now came quickly up, and soon after it burst in appalling violence. For preface there were but a few large drops that splashed and dried on the roadway as she came back from the post-office, and just as she reached the hotel again the roar of the approaching rain sounded, and the sluices of heaven were opened. Through the deluge flared the fire of the lightning, the thunder crashed and echoed overhead, and presently the street of the village was a torrent of sandy turbulent water, and sitting there in the dark one picture leapt floating before her eyes, that of the tombstone of Roger Wyburn, already tottering to its fall at the edge of the cliff of the church tower. In such rains as these, acres of the cliffs were loosened; she seemed to hear the whisper of the sliding sand that would precipitate those perished sepulchres and what lay within to the beach below.

By eight o'clock the storm was subsiding, and as she dined she was handed a telegram from Dick, saying that he had already started and sent this off *en route*. By half-past ten, therefore, if all was well, he would be here. and somehow he would stand between her and her fear, Strange how a few days ago both it and the thought of him had become distant and dim to her; now the one was as vivid as the other, and she counted the minutes to his arrival. Soon the rain ceased altogether, and looking out of the curtained window of her sitting-room where she sat watching the slow circle of the hands of the clock, she saw a tawny moon rising over the sea. Before it had climbed to the zenith, before her clock had twice told the hour again, Dick would be with her.

It had just struck ten when there came a knock at her door, and the page-boy entered with the message that a gentleman had come for her. Her heart leaped at the news; she had not expected Dick for half an hour yet, and now the lonely vigil was over. She ran downstairs, and there was the figure standing on the step outside. His face was turned away from her; no doubt he was giving some order to his chauffeur. He was outlined against the white moonlight, and in contrast with that, the gas-jet in the entrance just above his head gave his hair a warm, reddish tinge.

She ran across the hall to him.

'Ah, my darling, you've come,' she said. 'It was good of you. How quick you've been!' Just as she laid her hand on his shoulder he turned. His arm was thrown out round her, and she looked into a face with eyes close set, and a mouth smiling on one side, the other, thick and gathered together as by some physical deformity, sneered and lusted.

The nightmare was on her; she could neither run nor scream, and supporting her dragging steps, he went forth with her into the night.

Half an hour later Dick arrived. To his amazement he heard that a man had called for his wife not long before, and that she had gone out with him. He seemed to be a stranger here, for the boy who had taken his message to her had never seen him before, and presently surprise began to deepen into alarm; enquiries were made outside the hotel, and it appeared that a witness or two had seen the lady whom they knew to be staying there walking, hatless, along the top of the beach with a man whose arm was linked in hers. Neither of them knew him, but one had seen his face and could describe it.

The direction of the search thus became narrowed down, and though with a lantern to supplement the moonlight they came upon footprints which might have been hers, there were no marks of any who walked beside her. But they followed these until they came to an end, a mile away, in a great landslide of sand, which had fallen from the old churchyard on the cliff, and had brought down with it half the tower and a gravestone, with the body that had lain below.

The gravestone was that of Roger Wyburn, and his body lay by it, untouched by corruption or decay, though two hundred years had elapsed since it was interred there. For a week afterwards the work of searching the landslide went on, assisted by the high tides that gradually washed it away. But no further discovery was made.

THE CORNER HOUSE

FIRHAM-BY-SEA HAD LONG BEEN KNOWN TO JIM PURLEY AND myself, though we had been careful not to talk about it, and for years we had been accustomed to skulk quietly away from London, either alone or together, for a day or two of holiday at that delightful and unheard-of little village. It was not, I may safely say, any secretive or dog-in-the-manger instinct of keeping a good thing to ourselves that was the cause of this reticence, but it was because if Firham had become known at all the whole charm of it would have vanished. A popular Firham, in fact, would cease to be Firham, and while we should lose it nobody else would gain it. Its remoteness, its isolation, its emptiness were its most essential qualities; it would have been impossible, so we both of us felt, to have gone to Firham with a party of friends, and the idea of its little inn being peopled with strangers, or its odd little nine-hole golf-course with the small corrugated-iron shed for its club-house becoming full of serious golfers would certainly have been sufficient to make us desire never to play there again. Nor, indeed, were we guilty of any selfishness in keeping the knowledge of that golf-course to ourselves, for the holes were short and dull and the fairway badly kept. It was only because we were at Firham that we so often strolled round it, losing balls in furse bushes and marshy ground, and considering it quite decent putting if we took no more than three putts on a green. It was bad golf in fact, and no one in his senses would think of going to Firham to play bad golf, when good golf was so vastly more accessible. Indeed, the only reason why I have spoken of the golf-links is because in an indirect and distant manner they were connected with the early incidents of the story which strung itself together there, and which, to me at any rate, has destroyed the secure tranquillity of our remote little hermitage.

To get to Firham at all from London, except by a motor drive of some hundred and twenty miles, is a slow progress, and after two changes the leisurely railway eventually lands you no nearer than five miles from your destination. After that a switch-back road terminating in a long decline brings you off the inland Norfolk hills, and into the broad expanse of lowland, once reclaimed from the sea, and now protected from marine invasion by big banks and dykes. From the top of the last hill you get your first sight of the village, its brick-built houses with their tiled roofs smouldering redly in the sunset, like some small, glowing island anchored in that huge expanse of green, and, a mile beyond it, the dim blue of the sea. There are but few trees to be seen on that wide landscape, and those stunted and slanted in their growth by the prevailing wind off the coast, and the great sweep of the country is composed of featureless fields intersected with drainage dykes, and dotted with sparse cattle. A sluggish stream, fringed with reed-beds and loose-strife, where moor-hens chuckle, passes just outside the village, and a few hundred yards below it is spanned by a bridge and a sluice-gate. From there it broadens out into an estuary, full of shining water at high tide, and of grey mud-banks at the ebb, and passes between rows of tussocked sand-dunes out to sea.

The road, descending from the higher inlands, strikes across these reclaimed marshes, and after a mile of solitary travel enters the village of Firham. To right and left stand a few outlying cottages, whitewashed and thatched, each with a strip of gay garden in front and perhaps a fisherman's net spread out to dry on the wall, but before they form anything that could be called a street the road takes a sudden sharp-angled turn, and at once you are in the square which, indeed, forms the entire village. On each side of the broad cobbled space is a line of houses, on one side a post office and police-station with a dozen small shops where may be bought the more rudimentary needs of existence, a baker's, a butcher's, a tobacconists'. Opposite is a row of little residences midway between villa and cottage, while at the far end stands the dumpy grey church with the vicarage, behind green and rather dilapidated palings, beside it. At the near end is the 'Fisherman's Arms,' the modest hostelry at which we always put up, flanked by two or three more small red-brick houses, of which the farthest, where the road leaves the square again, is the Corner House of which this story treats.

The Corner House was an object of mild curiosity to Jim and me, for while the rest of the houses in the square, shops and residences alike, had a tidy and well-cared-for appearance, with an air of prosperity on a small contented scale, the Corner House presented a marked and curious contrast. The faded paint on the door was blistered and patchy, the step of the threshold always unwhitened and partly overgrown with an encroachment of moss, as if there was little traffic across it. Over the windows inside were stretched dingy casement curtains, and the Virginia creeper which straggled untended up the discoloured front of the house drooped over the dull panes like the hair over a terrier's eyes. Sometimes in one or other of these windows, between the curtains and the glass, there sat a mournful grey cat, but all day long no further sign of life within gave evidence of occupation. Behind the house was a spacious square of garden enclosed by a low brick wall, and from the upper windows of 'The Fisherman's Arms' it was was possible to look into it. There was a gravel path running round it, entirely overgrown, and a flower-bed underneath the wall was a jungle of rank weeds among which, in summer, two or three neglected rose trees put out a few meagre flowers. A broken water-butt stood at the end of it, and in the middle a rusty iron seat, but never at morning or at noon or at evening did I see any human figure in it; it seemed entirely derelict and unvisited.

At dusk shabby curtains were drawn across the windows that looked into the square, and then between chinks you could see that one room was lit within. The house, it was evident, had once been a very dignified little residence; it was built of red brick and was early Georgian in date, square and comfortable with its enclosed plot behind; one wondered, as I have said, with mild curiosity what blight had fallen on it, what manner of folk moved silent and unseen behind the dingy casement curtains all day and sat in that front room when night had fallen.

It was not only to us but also to the Firhamites generally that the inhabitants of the Corner House were veiled in some sort of mystery. The landlord of our inn, for instance, in answer to casual questions, could tell us very little of their life nowadays, but what he knew of them indicated that something rather grim lurked behind the drawn curtains. It was a married couple who lived there, and he could remember the arrival of Mr and Mrs Labson some ten years before.

'She was a big, handsome woman,' he said, 'and her age might have been thirty. He was a good deal younger; at that time he looked hardly out of his teens, a slim little slip of a fellow, half a head shorter than his wife. I daresay you've seen him on the golf-links, knocking a ball about by himself, for he goes out there every afternoon.'

I had more than once noticed a man playing alone, and carrying a couple of clubs. If he was on a green, and saw us coming up, he always went hurriedly on or stood aside at a little distance, with back turned, and waited for us to pass. But neither of us had paid any particular attention to him.

'She doesn't go out with him?' I asked.

'She never leaves the house at all to my knowledge,' said the landlord, 'though to be sure it wasn't always like that. When first they came here they were always out together, playing golf or boating or fishing, and in the evening there would be the sound of singing or piano-playing from that front room of theirs. They didn't live here entirely, but came down from London, where they had a house, for two or three months in the summer and perhaps a month at Christmas and another month at Easter. There would be friends staying with them much of the time, and merriment and games always going on, and dancing, too, with a gramophone to play their tunes for them till midnight and later. And then, all of a sudden, five years ago now or perhaps a little more, something happened and everything was changed. Yes, that was a queer thing, and sudden, as I say, like a clap of thunder.'

'Interesting,' said Jim. 'What was it that happened?'

'Well, as we saw it, it was like this,' said he, 'Mr and Mrs Labson were down here together in the summer, and one morning as I passed their door I heard her voice inside scolding and swearing at him or at some one. Him it must have been, as we knew later. All that day she went on at him; it was a wonder to think that a woman had so much breath in her body or so much rage in her mind. Next day all their servants, five or six they kept then, butler and lady's maid and valet and housemaid and cook, were all dismissed and off they went. The gardener got his month's wages, too, and was told he'd be wanted no more, and so there were Mr and Mrs Labson alone in the house. But half that day, too, she went on shouting and yelling, so it must have been him she was scolding and swearing at. Like a mad woman she was, and never a word from him. Then there would be silence a bit, and she'd break out again, and day after day it was like that, silence and then that screaming voice of hers. As the weeks went on, silence shut down on them; now and then she'd break out again, even as she does to this day, but a month and more will pass now, and you'll never hear a sound from within the house.'

'And what had been the cause of it all?' I asked.

'That came out in the papers,' said he, 'when Mr Labson was made a bankrupt. He had been speculating on the Stock Exchange, not with his own money alone, but with hers, and had lost nigh every penny. His house in London was sold, and all they had left was this house which belonged to her, and a bit of money he hadn't got at, which brings them in a pound or two a week. They keep no servants, and every morning Mr Labson goes out early with his basket on his arm and brings provisions for their dinner with the shilling or two she gives him. They say he does the cooking as well, and the housework too, though there's not too much of that, if you can judge from what you see from outside, while she sits with her hands in her lap doing nothing from morning till night. Sitting there and hating him, you may say.'

It was a weird, grim sort of story, and from that moment the house, to my mind, took on, as with a deeper dye of forbiddingness, something of its quality. Its desolate and untended aspect was fully earned, the uncleaned windows and discoloured door seemed a fit expression of the spirit that dwelt there: the house was the faithful expression of those who lived in it, of the man whose folly or knavery had brought them to a penury that was near ruin, and of the woman who was never seen, but sat behind the dirty curtained windows hating him, and making him her drudge. He was her slave; those hours when she screamed and raved at him must surely have broken his spirit utterly, or, whatever his fault had been, he must have rebelled against so servile and dismal an existence. Just that hour or two of remission she gave him in the afternoon that he might get air and exercise to keep his health, and continue his life of bondage, and then back again he went to the seclusion and the simmering hostility.

As sometimes happens when a subject has got started, the round of trivial, everyday experiences begins to bristle with allusions and hints that bear on it, so now when this matter of the Corner House had been set going, Jim and I began to be constantly aware of its ticking. It was just that: it was as if a clock had been wound up and started off, and now we were aware in a way we had not been before that it was steadily ticking on, and the hands silently moving towards some unconjecturable hour. Fancifully, and fantastically enough I wondered what the hour would be towards which the silent pointers were creeping. Would there be some sort of jarring whirr that gave warning that the hour was imminent, or should we miss that, and be suddenly startled by some reverberating shock? Such an idea was, of course, purely an invention of the imagination, but somehow it had got hold of me, and I used to pass the Corner House with an uneasy glance at its dingy windows, as if they were the dial that interpreted the progress of the sombre mechanism within.

The reader must understand that all this formed no continuous series of impressions. Jim and I were at Firham only on short visits, with intervals of weeks or even of months in between. But certainly after the subject had been started we had more frequent glimpses of Mr Labson. Day after day we saw his flitting figure on the links, keeping its distance, and retreating before us, but once we approached close up to him before he was aware of our presence. It was an afternoon that threatened rain, and in order to be nearer shelter if the storm burst suddenly we had cut two holes and walked across an intervening tract of rough ground to a hole which took us in a homeward direction. He was just addressing his ball on this teeing-ground when, looking up, he saw that we were beside him; he gave a little squeal as of terror, picked up his ball, and scuttled away, at a shuffling run, with abject terror written on his lean white face. Not a word did he give us in answer to Jim's begging him to precede us, not once did he look round.

'But the man's quaking with fear,' said I, as he disappeared. 'He could hardly pick up his ball.'

'Poor devil!' said Jim. 'There's something formidable at the Corner House.'

He had hardly spoken when the rain began in torrents, and we trotted with the best speed of middle-aged gentlemen towards the corrugated-iron shed of the club-house. But Mr Labson did not join us there for shelter; for we saw him plodding homewards through the downpour rather than face his fellow-creatures.

That close glimpse of Mr Labson had made the affair of the Corner House much more real. Behind the curtains where the light was lit in the evening there sat a man in whose soul terror was enthroned. Was it terror of his companion who sat there with him that reigned so supreme that even when he was away out on the links it still was master of him? Had it also so drained from him all dregs of manhood and of courage that he could not even run away, but must return to the grim house for fear of his fear, as a rabbit on whose track is a weasel has not the courage to gallop off and easily save itself from the sharp white teeth? Or were there ties of affection between him and the woman whom his folly had brought to penury, so that as a willing penance he cooked and drudged for her? And then I thought of the voice that had yelled at him all day; it was more likely that, as Jim had said, there was something formidable at the Corner House, before which he cowered and from which he had not the strength to fly.

There were other glimpses of him as, with his basket on his arm in the early morning, he brought home bread and milk and some cheap cut from the butcher's. Once I saw him enter his house on his return from his marketing. He must have locked the door before going out, for now he unlocked it again, slipped in, and I heard the key click in the wards again. Once, too, though only in featureless outline, I saw her who shared his solitude, for passing by the Corner House in the dusk, the lamp had been lit within, and I had a glimpse through the thin casement blinds of a carpetless room, a blackened ceiling and one big armchair drawn up to the fire. And at that moment the form of a woman silhouetted itself between me and the light. She was very tall, and immensely broad and stout, and her hands, large as a man's, grasped the curtain. Next moment, with a jingle of running rings, she had drawn it, and shut up herself and the man for the long winter evening and the night that followed.

The same evening, I remember, Jim had occasion to go to the post office and came back to our snug little sitting-room with something of horror in his eyes.

'You've seen her today,' he said, 'and I've heard her.'

'Who? Oh! at the Corner House?' I asked.

'Yes. I was just passing it, when she began. I tell you it scared me. It was scarcely like a human voice at all, or at any rate not like a sane voice. A shrill, swearing gabble all on one note, and going on without a pause. Maniac.'

The conjectured picture of the two grew more grim. It was an awful thought that behind those dingy curtains in the bare room there were the pair of them, the little terrified man, and that greater monster of a woman, yelling and bawling at him. Yet what could we do? It seemed impossible to interfere in any way. It was not the business of a couple of visitors from London to intrude on the domestic differences of total strangers. And yet the sequel showed that any interference would have been justified.

The day following was wet from morning till night. A gale of rain mingled with sleet roared in from the northeast, and neither of us stirred abroad, but kept close by the fire listening to the wind bugling in the chimney, and the gale flinging the sheets of water solidly against the window-pane. But after nightfall the wind abated and the sky cleared, and when I went up to bed, sleepy with the day indoors, I saw the shadows of the window bars black against a brightness outside, and pulling up the blind looked on to a blaze of moonlight. Below, a little to the left, was the neglected garden of the Corner House, and there, standing on the grass-grown path, was the figure of the woman I had seen in black silhouette against the lamplight in her room. Now the moonlight shone full on her face and my breath caught in my throat as I looked on that appalling countenance. It was fat and bloated beyond belief, the eyes were but slits above her cheeks, and the lines of her mouth were invisible in their shadows. But even the whiteness of the moonlight gave no pallor to her face, for it was flushed with some purplish hue that seemed nearly black. One glimpse only I had for perhaps she had heard the rattle of my blind, and she looked up and next minute had stepped back into the house again. But that moment was enough; I felt that I had looked on something hellish, something almost outside the wide range of humanity. It was not only the appalling physical ugliness of that monstrous face that was so shocking; it was the expression in the eyes and mouth, visible in that second when she raised her face to look upwards to my window. An inhuman hatred and cruelty were there that made the heart quake; the featureless outline was filled in with details more awful than I had ever conjectured.

We were out on the links again next afternoon on a day of liquid sunshine and brisk air, but some nameless oppression of the spirits held me sundered from the genial and bracing warmth. The idea of that frightened little man being imprisoned all day and night, but for his brief outing, with her who at any moment might break into that screaming torrent of speech, was like a nightmare that came between me and the sun. It would have been something to have seen him out today, and know that he was having a respite from that terrible presence; but we caught no sight of him, and when we returned and passed the Corner House the curtains were already drawn, and, as usual, there was silence within.

Jim touched me on the arm as we walked by the windows.

'But there's no light inside this evening,' he said.

This was quite true; the curtains were torn, as I knew, in half a dozen places, but neither through these holes nor from the chinks at their edges was there any light showing. Somehow this gave an added horror, which set my nerves jangling.

'Well, we can't knock and tell them they've forgotten to light the lamp,' I said.

We had halted for a moment, and even as I spoke I saw coming across the square towards us in the gathering dusk the figure of the man whom we had missed on the links that afternoon. Though I had not seen him approach, nor heard the noise of his footfall on the cobbles, he was now within a few yards of us.

'Here *he* is anyhow,' I said.

Jim turned.

'Where?' he asked.

We were standing perhaps two yards apart, and as he asked that the man stepped between us and advanced to the door of the Corner House. And then, instantaneously, I saw that Jim and I were alone. The door of the Corner House had not opened, but there was no one there.

Jim gave a startled exclamation.

'What was that?' he said. 'Something brushed by me.'

'Didn't you see anything?' I asked.

'No, but I felt something. I don't know what it was.'

'I saw him,' said I.

My jangled nerves seemed to have infected Jim.

'Nonsense!' he said. 'How could you have seen him? Where has he gone if you saw him? And I don't know what we're standing here for.'

Before I could answer I heard from within the Corner House the sound of heavy and shuffling steps; a key grated in the lock, and the door was flung open. Out of it, panting and heaving with some strange agitation, came the woman I had seen last night in her garden.

She had shut the door and locked it before she saw us. She was hatless and shod in great carpet slippers the heels of which tapped on the pavement as she moved, and on her face was the vacancy of some nameless terror. Her mouth, a cavern in that mountain of flesh, was wide, and now there came from it something between a gasp and a rattle. Then, seeing us, quick as a lizard, she whisked round again, fumbled for a moment with the key which she still held in her hand, and there once more was the shut door and the empty pavement. The whole scene passed like a blink of strong light seen in the dusk and vanishing again. She had come out, driven by some terror of her own; she had gone back in terror, it would seem, of us.

It was without a word passing between us that we went back to the inn. Just then there was nothing to be said; for myself, at least. I knew that there was, covering my brain, so to speak, some frozen surface of abject fear which must be thawed. I knew that I had seen, I knew that Jim had felt, something which had no tangible existence in the material world. He had felt what I had seen, and I had seen the form and bodily semblance of the man who lived at the Corner House. But what his wife had seen that drove her from the house, and why, seeing us, she had whisked back into it again I had no notion. Perhaps when a certain physical horror in my brain was uncongealed I should know.

Presently we were sitting in the small, cosy room, with our tea ready for us, and the fire burning bright on the hearth. We talked, odd as it may appear, of anything else but *that*. But the silences between the abandonment of our topic and the introduction of another grew longer, and at last Jim spoke.

'Something has happened,' he said. 'You saw what wasn't there, and I felt what wasn't there. What did we see or feel? And what did *she* see or feel?'

He had hardly spoken when there came a rap at the door, and our landlord entered. For the moment, during which the door was open, I heard from the bar of the inn a shrill, gabbling voice, which I had never heard before, but which I knew Jim had heard.

'There's Mrs Labson come into the bar, gentlemen,' he said, 'and she wants to know if it was you who were standing outside her house ten minutes ago. She's got a notion—'

He paused.

'It's hard to make out what she's after,' he said. 'Her husband has not been at home all day, and he's not home yet, and she thinks you may have seen him on the golf-links. And then she says she's thinking of letting her house for a month, and wonders if you would care to take it, but she runs on so—'

The door opened again, and there she stood, filling the doorway. She had on her head a great feathered hat, and over her shoulders a red satin evening cloak, now moth-eaten and ragged, while on her feet were still those carpet slippers.

'So odd it must seem to you for a lady to intrude like this,' she said, 'but you are the gentlemen, are you not, whom I saw admiring my house just now?'

Her eyes, now utterly vacant, now suddenly keen and searching, fell on the window. The curtains were not drawn and outside the last of the daylight was fading. She shuffled quickly across the floor and rattled the blind down, first peering out into the dusk.

'I'm sure I don't wonder at that,' she gabbled on, 'for my house is much admired by visitors here. I was thinking of letting it for a few weeks, though I am not sure that it would be convenient to do so just yet, and even if I did, I should have to put some of my treasures away in a little attic at the top of the house, and lock that up. Some heirlooms, you understand. But that's all by the way. I came in, a very odd intrusion I know, to ask if either of you had seen my husband, Mr Labson—I am Mrs Labson, as I should have told you—if you'd seen him on the golf-links this afternoon. He went out about two o'clock, and he's not been back. Most unusual, for there's his tea ready for him always at half-past four.'

She paused and seemed to listen intently, then went across to the window again and drew the blind aside.

'I thought I heard a step in my garden just out there,' she said, 'and I wondered if it was Mr Labson. Such a pleasant little garden, a bit overgrown maybe; I think I saw one of you gentlemen looking down into it last night, when I was taking a breath of air. Or even if you didn't care to take the whole of my house, perhaps you would like a couple of rooms there. I could make everything most comfortable for you, for Mr Labson always said I was a wonderful cook and manager, and not a word of complaint have I ever had from him all these years. Still, if he's taken it into his head to go off suddenly like this, I should be pleased to have a lodger in the house, for I'm not accustomed to be alone. Being alone in a house was a thing I never could bear.'

She turned to our landlord:

'I'll take a room here for tonight,' she said, 'if Mr Labson doesn't come back. Perhaps you would send across for a bag into which I have put what I shall want. No; that would never do; I'll go and get it myself, if you would be so good as to come with me as far as the door. One never knows who is about at this time of night. And if Mr Labson should come here to look for me, don't let him in whatever you do. Say I'm not here; say I've left home for a day or two and have given no address. You don't want Mr Labson here, for he's not got a penny of his own, and couldn't pay for his board and lodging, and I won't support him in idleness any longer. He ruined me and I'll be even with him yet. I told him—'

The stream of insane babble suddenly ceased; her eyes, fixing themselves on a dusky corner of the room behind where I stood, grew wide with terror, and her mouth gaped. Simultaneously I heard a gasp of startled amazement from Jim, and turned quickly to see what he and Mrs Labson was looking at.

There he stood, he whom I had seen half an hour ago appearing suddenly in the square, and as suddenly disappearing as he came to the Corner House. Next minute she had flung the door wide and bolted out. Jim and I followed and saw her rush down the passage outside, and through the open door of the bar into the square. Terror winged her feet, and that great misshapen bulk sped away and was lost in the darkness of the fallen night.

We went straight to the police office, and the country was scoured for the mad woman who, I felt sure, was also a murderess. The river was dragged, and about midnight two fishermen found the body below the sluice-gate at the head of the estuary. Search meantime had been made in the Corner House, and her husband's corpse was discovered, strangled with a silk handkerchief, behind the water-butt in the corner of the garden. Close by was a half-dug excavation, where no doubt she had intended to bury him.

BY THE SLUICE

MY FRIEND LOUIS CARRINGTON, WITH WHOM I WAS TO spend a liberal week-end, met me in his car at Whitford Station on Friday afternoon. There had been a long spell of damp and windless weather, and the fog which had been so thick in London was scarcely less dense down here; the whole of Surrey seemed to be blanketed in this white opacity. Even when we got free of the town we could do no more than crawl along the road with prolonged hoots at every turn and corner. Occasionally, when the air was somewhat clearer, a glimpse could be seen of a sombre copper-plate low in the west, which one supposed was the sun, for the reason that it could scarcely be anything else.

Louis was unusually silent; his attention, of course, was largely taken up by this blind progression, but I soon became aware, through that perception which long intimacy gives, that there was something on his mind. In answer to a direct question he admitted this was so, and said he would tell me about what he called 'this very painful affair' when we got home. It did not, he relieved me by saying, directly affect him or his immediate circle, but it was a very sad thing, very sad indeed, and he fell to silence and knitted brow again.

We arrived at the end of our four-mile drive without accident, and found his wife in the jolly, spacious hall which they used as a general sitting-room. It was pleasant to come out of that inhospitable dimness into the warmth and light, but over Margaret also there was this same shadow of anxiety or suspense, and even as she greeted me she said to him:

'Any news yet about him, Louis?'

'No, poor chap, not a word,' said he; 'I've communicated with the police, and search parties are going out.'

'And you've advertised?' she asked.

'Yes: county and London papers, telling him to come back without any fear. I signed it myself, and I think he trusts me. Now I'm going to tell Frank the whole story to see if there is anything else he can suggest.'

The story certainly was a painful one, though to me, personally, it concerned a man whom I had never seen in my life, and of whose existence till this moment I had never heard. Louis is the manager of the local branch of a big banking house in Whitford, and his sub-manager, Thomas Oulton, had worked his way up through thirty years of industrious and honourable service to his present position. He was respected and liked in the town, he had a good salary with an ample pension ahead, and, as far as was known, he had no money worries of any kind.

'And then without warning,' said Louis, 'only yesterday came the crash. A client of ours came to see me about some securities we held for him. Among them were a hundred shares of a certain cement company, which had lately offered new shares to its holders at a price considerably below the market quotation. They had the right to purchase at par one new share for every four they held; our client therefore could buy twenty-five of these for twenty-five pounds. We had advised him to do so, and at his orders had applied for them, and in his pass-book there duly appeared this sum in payment of them. His list of investments, which we held for him, had lately been made up, and we noticed that though he was debited with the payment of them, they did not appear in it.

'I felt sure that there was some explanation of this; probably the new certificates had not been issued yet, and sent for Oulton. My clerk came back, saying that Oulton had left the bank, saying he was going out for lunch, a few minutes before; he had left, in fact, when he saw this client of ours come in and ask to see me.

'Half an hour passed, and an hour. Oulton did not come back at all. I sent round to the restaurant where he usually had his lunch, but he had not been there. Soon after I rang up his house in the village here to know if he had been home. He had been in, and told his wife that he had to go up to our head office in London over some business, and might not get back, if the fog was bad, till next morning. Accordingly he took away with him a suitcase with the few things he would want. Now I knew there was nothing connected with the bank that could have taken him to London, but I rang up the head office. He had not appeared there. Then, still almost incredulous that there could be anything wrong in the case of so steady a man, I went into the affair myself. I found that the certificates had been issued some days before, and soon there was no longer any doubt that Oulton had debited our client's account with this paltry sum and taken the money.'

'And then I suppose you found other defalcations?' I asked.

'Not one. All other accounts with which he had anything to do were perfectly in order. I am quite positive that Oulton had never done such a thing before. He knew that our client was a very rich man, and that the chances were a hundred to one that he would never notice so small an omission. But he just happened to do so. Oulton must have known, too, that if he had come to me and told me what he had done I could have managed something. I should not have proceeded against a man who had served us so long and faithfully for a sudden madness—for it was no less—of this kind. But I suppose that the sight of the client he had defrauded coming in and asking to see me broke his nerve, for he must have guiltily guessed what his errand was. Even now, if he can only be found, or if, seeing my advertisement, he comes back, I shall somehow get him out of trouble. I daresay it is my duty to have him prosecuted, but I consider it no less my duty to save a man with a long and blameless record like his from ruin. And when duties conflict you have to choose between them.'

We assented to this and sat silent a few moments. But there seemed nothing more that could be done; Louis's advertisement was the best chance of getting hold of the unfortunate man, and the only course at present was to wait in the hope that some news of him, or, best of all, he himself, should turn up. Soon other, more cheerful, topics unfolded themselves, and we talked of agreeable schemes for the spending of the next few days, should the fog permit us to do anything at all.

Golf was one, for there was a good links near by on the stretch of sandy, heathered country outside Louis's wooded domain; another, particularly dear to him in this season of April, was observing the arrivals of migrating birds. The open heath, the woods below his house, and his fine sheet of water that lay deep within them, ringed with copses and banks of sedge, should all be alive with movements of the northerly travelling hosts.

To the best of my belief Oulton was not mentioned again that evening, but I have to record what now seems to me the first in the series of those odd occurrences which I do not profess to explain. At the time it struck me as a mere fanciful impression on my part, but in the light of what soon happened it seems more reasonable to suppose it was a manifestation—faint, and scarcely coming 'through'—of the power (whatever that was) which soon gave clearer evidence of itself.

Louis, after tea, went to his room to finish up some business, and Margaret to the nursery to play with her two small children, and thus I was left alone in the hall, thinking, as far as I am aware, of birds and golf rather than Oulton. As I mused, rather drowsily, by the fire, I thought I heard a very faint tinkle from the telephone at the far end of the hall. It certainly was not the usual peremptory summons, and I lazily waited for it to be repeated.

It came again, still faint and far-away, and I went to the instrument. There were little clicks and buzzings to be heard, and then I thought I heard a voice in a whisper saying something inaudible.

'Who is it?' I asked. 'I can't hear you.'

I had hardly spoken when a voice from the exchange said, 'Number, please?' I explained that there was some message coming through, and was told that no connection had been made through the exchange. But, though I felt sure there had been someone there, I might have been mistaken. The bell that summoned me had not sounded as it generally did. The impression, however, remained that someone wanted to communicate with this house.

The evening passed in a perfectly normal manner. We dined and played cut-throat, but all the time, still fancifully I suppose, the idea remained in my head, sometimes growing very insistent, that there was someone trying to make his presence felt. We went to bed shortly after midnight, and I instantly fell asleep.

*

I awoke out of a perfectly dreamless sleep with the impression that I had heard the bell of the church clock strike; indeed, some vibration of it still lingered in the air. It was perfectly natural that I should have done so, for the church stood only a few hundred yards away, at the bottom of the steep slope by the garden.

I was drowsy, but certainly still awake, when I heard it again; it struck one, but now I was sure it was not the chime of the clock, but one of the church bells. After an interval it came again, and yet again; the bell was tolling as if for a death. It was odd that it should be rung in the middle of the night, and I wondered what the reason for that could be.

And then, quite suddenly, there came into my mind the thought that Oulton was dead. Where, so to speak, it came from, I had no idea, but it instantly crystallised into a conviction.

My room was almost completely dark; from the windows came no ray of light at all, but there was still a red coal or two smouldering out in the fireplace. And then I was aware that over the end of my bed there was forming in the air a patch of something dimly luminous, an oval of greyish light. It seemed to hang unsupported, and as I watched it, not exactly frightened, but in some numb suspense of the mind, it defined itself a little more and took the shape of a human face. The outline grew complete and firm; I could see the form of ears jutting out rather prominently from the side of the head, but of features there was no trace at all.

Then suddenly the suspense of my mind broke, and in an access of panic terror I felt for the switch of the electric light, still keeping an eye glued to that developing face, and throttled by the horror of perhaps seeing eyes and mouth form themselves in the blankness of it. Then the room leaped into brightness, and there was nothing there but the safe-curtained emptiness of it, with the dying embers clinking in the grate.

As I recovered from the grip of the terror, my curiosity, I suppose, awoke, and it cured my cowardice. I turned out my light again and watched, but there was no sign of it now, and the tolling of the bell had ceased. Already it seemed to my normal consciousness quite unreal, and I wondered if I had dreamed it all. But if so, the night-hag had ridden me with a spur, for my forehead dripped with the dews of that moment's terror.

I slept late, and found Louis and his wife already at breakfast. Just as I entered I heard him say to her:

'But the child must have dreamt it. The bell could not have been tolling in the middle of the night... Ah, good morning, Frank; fog as bad as ever, I'm afraid. Putting on the hearthrug, and books about birds instead of the real thing.'

'But what's that about a bell tolling?' I asked. 'Did one of your children hear it? Because I did, too.'

'Both dreaming,' said Louis. 'How is it possible?'

'The only explanation I can think of is that somebody was ringing it,' I said.

He had finished breakfast and got up.

'Well, I'll make a bet with you,' he said, 'that no one was. I've got to go down to the village, and I'll enquire. Any other adventures last night?'

I decided at once not to tell him about the other adventure, for, horribly real as it had been at the time, it seemed, over eggs and bacon, to be too fantastic to recount. But still somewhere in the back of my mind there was the idea that some wave from the infinite sea which laps round the coast of material things had at that moment hissed up to me on the shore and withdrawn again.

'The adventure of a great many hours' uninterrupted sleep,' I said.

The day outside was certainly desolation; the fog pressed its grey face close to the windows, and it was scarcely possible to see across the terraced walk that ran along the house. But the prospect of a snug morning indoors was not disagreeable, and when Louis set off to the village, I encamped myself very comfortably by the fire in the hall. He was back in half-an-hour and joined me there.

'The church was locked all night,' he said, 'and opened again by the vicar at eight for morning prayers. My errand, of course, you can guess. I went to see Mrs Oulton, in case she had heard anything from her husband. But there was nothing. Surely, don't you think he must see my advertisement this morning? If we hear nothing today I shall begin to be afraid—Well, it's no use thinking about that yet.'

He had seated himself on the window-seat, and was looking out into the denseness. Suddenly he sprang up, pointing.

'Look!' he said. 'Why, that's he! The man who walked by the window just then. Didn't you see him?'

I had seen nothing, but now I followed Louis as he rushed across the hall, and ran out with him from the front door into the fog. We sped round the corner of the house on to the terrace, and along it to the end, where a flight of stone steps descended to the garden, without seeing a sign of any human being.

'But where is he, where is he?' cried Louis. 'He can't have gone more than a dozen yards since I saw him. Perhaps he has gone to the back door. I'll go round there, and you go down the steps into the garden. He must be quite close somewhere.'

I ran down the steps, and searched this way and that, and found no one but a gardener coming up with vegetables to the house. He had passed nobody on his way, and presently I came up on to the terrace again from the far end of it, and heard Louis calling me.

'I've been all round the house,' he said, 'and to the garage, but there's not a trace of him.'

'But are you sure it was he?' I asked.

'Not a doubt of it. Besides, whoever it was, what has happened to him? I must ring up the police at Whitford and tell them. And yet I wonder if that's wise. The poor chap may have seen my advertisement and be wanting to steal back quietly to see me. When we ran out together he wouldn't be able to see who we were in the fog, and may have thought that there were two men running to capture him. He may be hiding till he can get at me alone. And yet where can he have hidden?'

So Louis decided, for fear of scaring the man, to postpone his information to the police that he had seen him. Oulton, he believed, had concealed himself somewhere (and, indeed, this fog made the idea feasible) till he could slip into the house undetected, and Louis settled to remain quietly at home all day, strolling perhaps in the garden so as to give him his opportunity.

This sounded sensible, and yet even while we were discussing it, the futility of such a plan struck me. I knew in my own mind that the figure Louis had seen was not that of a living man, any more than that white sketch of a human face which had hung in the darkness of my room last night was an effect of material light and shadow, or the imagining of a dream.

Something was astir in the discarnate kingdom, some soul seeking to manifest itself.

During the afternoon the fog began to clear, and about four o'clock I went out with my binoculars for an ornithological tramp. Louis would not join me, for he was determined to stay close to the house so that Oulton might find him, and I set off across the heath with the intention of making a wide circuit there, and then walking through the woods and home by the lake. But though my occupation was congenial, and since one had to keep the eye very alert it should have claimed my close attention, I found myself barely heeding where I went or what I saw. Some invisible influence was at work; I was being detached from the myriad points of contact between myself and the material world, and there was waking within me the perception of things occult that, perhaps luckily for us, is usually dormant, and only enters the field of consciousness for rare and brief periods.

Just as the comprehension of some difficult idea slowly dawns on the mind, so now (I can express it in no other way) I felt that some inward eye was being unsealed. At present there was nothing for it to look on, its horizon was empty, but it was ready for the moment which I felt sure was coming, when there should appear to it, perhaps very horribly, in the manner of that blank face in the darkness last night, some phantom from the unseen world. A hundred times I tried to recall myself to the normal sights and sounds about me, but they were becoming more and more meaningless, and had no reality compared with the reality for which, shuddering in spirit, I waited.

I had made a long beat across the open, and was working round towards the belt of woods through which I purposed to go, when once more the fog began to gather. I had no mind to be caught by it on this huge unfeatured upland, for one might wander far and long if all landmarks were blotted out, and I hastened to get into the woods, for there, as I knew, a path would lead me down to the lake, and passing the head of it, take me back to the house.

I found the gate at the entrance to this path just before the fog grew suddenly much more dense, and I congratulated myself on having got off the open before it gathered like this, and entered the wood.

It was very dark under the trees, and the wind which earlier in the afternoon had cleared the air outside had not penetrated here, and the mist hung thick and white between the veiled forms of the tree-trunks. Darker yet it grew as the light from the sky outside was expunged by the fog, but I could just see the path ahead of me, and I went quickly, for there was closing in upon me not the fog alone, but some nameless horror of the spirit.

What exactly I feared I could not have said; but something, as yet unseen, was stirring, and in this forlorn dimness of the wood I longed for any companionship from the familiar world. Once I stopped to listen for any sound that would give evidence that there was life, even if only of birds or woodland beasts, somewhere near me, but not a note nor the patter of feet in the undergrowth came to me. The path was mossy and even my own footfalls were dumb.

Suddenly I heard the rustle of dead leaves from my feet, and I saw that I had somehow got off the path. I scouted this way and that for it, and retraced my steps, but in the deep, thick dusk I was quite unable to find it again, and the only thing to be done was to keep on going downhill, for somewhere at the bottom I knew that I must strike the lake or the stream that flowed from it, and could orientate myself again. The ground was uneven, and more than once I stumbled over some root, caught my foot in a spray of bramble, and all the time I was fighting with this rising tide of fear.

At last the darkness began to lift a little, and ahead there was no longer the same density of trees, but an open space to which I quickly drew nearer, and there in front of me lay the lake. I had greatly miscalculated my direction, for I found that instead of being at the upper end of it I had come to the lower end, where was the sluice from which the water poured down a steep bank and formed the stream that passed by the village.

A belt of thick undergrowth lay between me and the path that led along the banks of the sluice, and I was threading my way slowly through this when once again I stumbled against some unseen obstacle and fell. I picked myself up unhurt, and then looked to see what had caused me this fall. I saw that it was a small suitcase.

In a flash I remembered that Oulton had gone home from the bank and packed a few things for his pretended visit to London. I lit a match, and found his initials, 'T. O.', stamped on the side of it. I took it up, and with it in my hand struggled out on to the open path, past the sluice. I must clearly carry it home to Louis, for it might prove a valuable clue in the search for the missing man. He had certainly been in this wood, bewildered perhaps by the thick fog, and having missed his way as I had done. But I wondered how he came to be here at all, for if he had been going up to London he would have gone from his house to the station. Or—

I had come to the sluice; on my left the mist-veiled lake lay leaden and deep, and a row of young willows edged the bank. I saw forming itself in the air just above them a pale oval of light.

It oscillated slightly, as if stirred by some breath of wind, and as I watched it the outline grew firm and definite. Terror screamed to me to run from the place, but the same terror held me fast.

On each side of the face, blank as yet, there grew the form of rather prominent ears, and then above them came the semblance of grey hair hanging down over the forehead in dank straight lines, as if dripping wet. The shadowed eye-sockets appeared below thick-arched eyebrows, a nose long for the face ruled itself downwards between them, and below that a mouth, slack and open, with tongue lolling over the livid underlip. And now the eye-sockets were empty no longer; eyes with the lids half shut down on to them peered at me, though fixed and glassy, with an infinite and despairing sadness.

Then, like a screen picture coming into better focus, smaller details fixed themselves. I saw the puckered skin at the outer corner of the eyes, the darkness of the shaved jaw and upper lip, the modelling of the high cheekbones, an upright crease between the eyes. All the time the face oscillated gently sideways.

How long I watched it with cold horror clutching at my heart I do not know. A few seconds, I expect, was the duration of this unbodied vision, but such moments are immeasurable in terms of time. Then it was there no more; in front of me was the mist-swathed lake and the row of young willows just stirring in the air, and in my hand the suitcase of Thomas Oulton.

But with the vanishing of the vision, of the hallucination, whatever you may call it, the terror vanished too, and there I was, hearing the suck and splash of the sluice, master of myself, and knowing that the manifestation I had abjectly dreaded was part and parcel of all that is. The kindly woodland lay about me, the earth was drinking in, like a baby at the breast, the moisture of its nourishment, and beyond and behind, imminent and remote, was the power which had let me look through the transient veil of material limitation. What I had seen, what for the moment had filled my soul with the ultimate terror, was no more shocking than the wild whirling of the planets in space, or the sudden melody of the thrush that bubbled from the covert by the waterside, for all were subject to the same law that 'moved the sun and the other stars'.

The sequel can be told very shortly, though the reconstruction of the whole history can never be known for certain. I described the face that I had seen to Louis, and it answered so closely to the appearance of the missing man that the lake just above the sluice was dragged, and the body found there. In the breast-pocket of the coat was an envelope addressed to him; the ink had run owing to the long immersion in the water, but his name was still legible. In it were twenty-five Treasury notes of a pound each. Oulton's intention therefore seems clear, but there are several hypotheses which roughly fit to facts.

Perhaps he left his home, having told his wife that he was summoned up to London on business, with the intention of going there and of trying to evade pursuit. Against that there is the fact that he did not go to the station, but went, with his suitcase, into the woods through which a path led to Louis's house. But the two are reconcilable, for we may suppose that though he meant to disappear, he wanted first to restore the money of which he had defrauded the bank. Again, though his leaving his suitcase in that thicket where I found it, and the recovery of his body from the deep water not fifty yards away, might indicate that he deliberately committed suicide, it is yet possible that he hid his suitcase there with the intention of coming back for it after he had left the envelope at the house, and that in the dense and blinding fog he accidentally fell into the water. The path by the sluice is very narrow, and such a mishap perfectly possible. He was encumbered with a long greatcoat, and a false step on the slippery stone edging there might easily have been fatal.

Of the other phenomena recorded I have no explanation to give, but only suggest that the veil between the seen and what we call the unseen is of thinnest gossamer, and that ever and again we have glimpses of what lies outside our mortal vision.

PIRATES

FOR MANY YEARS THIS PROJECT OF SOMETIME BUYING BACK the house had simmered in Peter Graham's mind, but whenever he actually went into the idea with practical intention, stubborn reasons had presented themselves to deter him. In the first place it was very far off from his work, down in the heart of Cornwall, and it would be impossible to think of going there just for week-ends, and if he established himself there for longer periods what on earth would he do with himself in that soft remote Lotus-land? He was a busy man who, when at work, liked the diversion of his club and of the theatres in the evening, but he allowed himself few holidays away from the City, and those were spent on salmon river or golf links with some small party of solid and like-minded friends. Looked at in these lights, the project bristled with objections.

Yet through all these years, forty of them now, which had ticked away so imperceptibly, the desire to be at home again at Lescop had always persisted, and from time to time it gave him shrewd little unexpected tugs, when his conscious mind was in no way concerned with it. This desire, he was well aware, was of a sentimental quality, and often he wondered at himself that he, who was so well-armoured in the general jostle of the world against that type of emotion, should have just this one joint in his harness. Not since he was sixteen had he set eyes on the place, but the memory of it was more vivid than that of any other scene of subsequent experience. He had married since then, he had lost his wife, and though for many months after that he had felt horribly lonely, the ache of that loneliness had ceased, and now, if he had ever asked himself the direct question, he would have confessed that bachelor existence was more suited to him than married life had ever been. It had not been a conspicuous success, and he never felt the least temptation to repeat the experiment.

But there was another loneliness which neither married life nor his keen interest in his business had ever extinguished, and this was directly connected with his desire for that house on the green slope of the hills above Truro. For only seven years had he lived there, the youngest but one of a family of five children, and now out of all that gay company he alone was left. One by one they had dropped off the stem of life, but as each in turn went into this silence, Peter had not missed them very much: his own life was too occupied to give him time really to miss anybody, and he was too vitally constituted to do otherwise than look forwards.

None of that brood of children except himself, and he childless, had married, and now when he was left without intimate tie of blood to any living being, a loneliness had gathered thickly round him. It was not in any sense a tragic or desperate loneliness: he had no wish to follow them on the unverified and unlikely chance of finding them all again. Also, he had no use for any disembodied existence: life meant to him flesh and blood and material interests and activities, and he could form no conception of life apart from such. But sometimes he ached with this dull gnawing ache of loneliness, which is worse than all others, when he thought of the stillness that lay congealed like clear ice over these young and joyful years when Lescop had been so noisy and alert and full of laughter, with its garden resounding with games, and the house with charades and hide-and-seek and multitudinous plans. Of course there had been rows and quarrels and disgraces, hot enough at the time, but now there was no one to quarrel with. 'You can't really quarrel with people whom you don't love,' thought Peter, 'because they don't matter.'... Yet it was ridiculous to feel lonely; it was even more than ridiculous, it was weak, and Peter had the kindly contempt of a successful and healthy and unemotional man for weaknesses of that kind. There were so many amusing and interesting things in the world, he had so many irons in the fire to be beaten, so to speak, into gold when he was working, and so many palatable diversions when he was not (for he still brought a boyish enthusiasm to work and play alike), that there was no excuse for indulging in sentimental sterilities. So, for months together, hardly a stray thought would drift towards the remote years lived in the house on the hill-side above Truro.

He had lately become chairman of the board of that new and highly promising company, the British Tin Syndicate. Their property included certain Cornish mines which had been previously abandoned as non-paying propositions, but a clever mineralogical chemist had recently invented a process by which the metal could be extracted far more cheaply than had hitherto been possible. The British Tin Syndicate had bought the patent, and having acquired these derelict Cornish mines was getting very good results from ore that had not been worth treating. Peter had very strong opinions as to the duty of a chairman to make himself familiar with the practical side of his concerns, and was now travelling down to Cornwall to make a personal inspection of the mines where this process was at work. He had with him certain technical reports which he had received to read during the uninterrupted hours of his journey, and it was not till his train had left Exeter behind that he finished his perusal of them, and, putting them back in his despatch-case, turned his eye at the swiftly passing panorama of travel. It was many years since he had been to the West Country, and now with the thrill of vivid recognition he found the red cliffs round Dawlish, interspersed between stretches of sunny sea-beach, startlingly familiar. Surely he must have seen them quite lately, he thought to himself, and then, ransacking his memory, he found it was forty years since he had looked at them, travelling back to Eton from his last holidays at Lescop. The intense sharp-cut impressions of youth!

His destination tonight was Penzance, and now, with a strangely keen sense of expectation, he remembered that just before reaching Truro station the house on the hill was visible from the train, for often on these journeys to and from school he had been all eyes to catch the first sight of it and the last. Trees perhaps would have grown up and intervened, but as they ran past the station before Truro he shifted across to the other side of the carriage, and once more looked out for that glimpse... There it was, a mile away across the valley, with its grey stone front and the big beech-tree screening one end of it, and his heart leaped as he saw it. Yet what use was the house to him now? It was not the stones and the bricks of it, nor the tall hay-fields below it, nor the tangled garden behind that he wanted, but the days when he had lived in it. Yet he leaned from the window till a cutting extinguished the view of it, feeling that he was looking at a photograph that recalled some living presence. All those who had made Lescop dear and still vivid had gone, but this record remained, like the image on the plate… And then he smiled at himself with a touch of contempt for his sentimentality.

The next three days were a whirl of enjoyable occupation: tin-mines in the concrete were new to Peter, and he absorbed himself in these, as in some new game or ingenious puzzle. He went down the shafts of mines which had been opened again, he inspected the new chemical process, seeing it at work and checking the results, he looked into running expenses, comparing them with the value of the metal recovered. Then, too, there was substantial traces of silver in some of these ores, and he went eagerly into the question as to whether it would pay to extract it. Certainly even the mines which had previously been closed down ought to yield a decent dividend with this process, while those where the lode was richer would vastly increase their profits. But economy, economy… Surely it would save in the end, though at a considerable capital expenditure now, to lay a light railway from the works to the rail-head instead of employing these motor-lorries. There was a piece of steep gradient, it was true, but a small detour, with a trestle-bridge over the stream, would avoid that.

He walked over the proposed route with the engineer and scrambled about the stream-bank to find a good take-off for his trestle-bridge. And all the time at the back of his head, in some almost subconscious region of thought, were passing endless pictures of the house and the hill, its rooms and passages, its fields and garden, and with them, like some accompanying tune, ran that ache of loneliness. He felt that he must prowl again about the place: the owner, no doubt, if he presented himself, would let him just stroll about alone for half an hour. Thus he would see it all altered and overscored by the life of strangers living there, and the photograph would fade into a mere blur and then blankness. Much better that it should.

It was in this intention that, having explored every avenue for dividends on behalf of his company, he left Penzance by an early morning train in order to spend a few hours in Truro and go up to London later in the day. Hardly had he emerged from the station when a crowd of memories, forty years old, but more vivid than any of those of the last day or two, flocked round him with welcome for his return. There was the level-crossing and the road leading down to the stream where his sister Sybil and he had caught a stickleback for their aquarium, and across the bridge over it was the lane sunk deep between high crumbling banks that led to a footpath across the fields to Lescop. He knew exactly where was that pool with long ribands of water-weed trailing and waving in it, which had yielded them that remarkable fish: he knew how campions red and white would be in flower on the lane-side, and in the fields the meadow-orchids. But it was more convenient to go first into the town, get his lunch at the hotel, and to make enquiries from a house-agent as to the present owner of Lescop; perhaps he would walk back to the station for his afternoon train by that short cut.

Thick now as flowers on the steppe when spring comes, memories bright and fragrant shot up round him. There was the shop where he had taken his canary to be stuffed (beautiful it looked!): and there was the shop of the 'undertaker and cabinet-maker,' still with the same name over the door, where on a memorable birthday, on which his amiable family had given him, by request, the tokens of their good-will in cash, he had ordered a cabinet with five drawers and two trays, varnished and smelling of newly cut wood, for his collection of shells… There was a small boy in jersey and flannel trousers looking in at the window now, and Peter suddenly said to himself, 'Good Lord, how like I used to be to that boy: same kit, too.' Strikingly like indeed he was, and Peter, curiously interested, started to cross the street to get a nearer look at him. But it was market-day, a drove of sheep delayed him, and when he got across the small boy had vanished among the passengers. Farther along was a dignified house-front with a flight of broad steps leading up to it, once the dreaded abode of Mr Tuck, dentist. There was a tall girl standing outside it now, and again Peter involuntarily said to himself, 'Why, that girl's wonderfully like Sybil!' But before he could get more than a glimpse of her, the door was opened and she passed in, and Peter was rather vexed to find that there was no longer a plate on the door indicating that Mr Tuck was still at his wheel… At the end of the street was the bridge over the Fal just below which they used so often to take a boat for a picnic on the river. There was a jolly family party setting off just now from the quay, three boys, he noticed, and a couple of girls, and a woman of young middle-age. Quickly they dropped downstream and went forth, and with half a sigh he said to himself, 'Just our number with Mamma.'

He went to the Red Lion for his lunch: that was new ground and uninteresting, for he could not recall having set foot in that hostelry before. But as he munched his cold beef there was some great fantastic business going on deep down in his brain: it was trying to join up (and it believed it could) that boy outside the cabinet-maker's, that girl on the threshold of the house once Mr Tuck's, and that family party starting for their picnic on the river. It was in vain that he told himself that neither the boy nor the girl nor the picnic-party could possibly have anything to do with him: as soon as his attention relaxed that burrowing underground chase, as of a ferret in a rabbit-hole, began again... And then Peter gave a gasp of sheer amazement, for he remembered with clear-cut distinctness how on the morning of that memorable birthday, he and Sybil started earlier than the rest from Lescop, he on the adorable errand of ordering his cabinet, she for a dolorous visit to Mr Tuck. The others followed half an hour later for a picnic on the Fal to celebrate the great fact that his age now required two figures (though one was a nought) for expression. 'It'll be ninety years, darling,' his mother had said, 'before you want a third one, so be careful of yourself.'

Peter was almost as excited when this momentous memory burst on him as he had been on the day itself. Not that it meant anything, he said to himself, as there's nothing for it to mean. But I call it odd. It's as if something from those days hung about here still...

He finished his lunch quickly after that, and went to the house agent's to make his enquiries. Nothing could be easier than that he should prowl about Lescop, for the house had been untenanted for the last two years. No card 'to view' was necessary, but here were the keys: their was no caretaker there.

'But the house will be going to rack and ruins,' said Peter indignantly. 'Such a jolly house, too. False economy not to put a caretaker in. But of course it's no business of mine. You shall have the keys back during the afternoon: I'll walk up there now.'

'Better take a taxi, sir,' said the man. 'A hot day, and a mile and a half up a steep hill.'

'Oh, nonsense,' said Peter. 'Barely a mile. Why, my brother and I used often to do it in ten minutes.'

It occurred to him that these athletic feats of forty years ago would probably not interest the modern world...

Pyder Street was as populous with small children as ever, and perhaps a little longer and steeper than it used to be. Then turning off to the right among strange new-built suburban villas he passed into the well-known lane, and in five minutes more had come to the gate leading into the short drive up to the house. It drooped on its hinges, he must lift it off the latch, sidle through and prop it in place again. Overgrown with grass and weeds was the drive, and with another spurt of indignation he saw that the stile to the pathway across the field was broken down and had dragged the wires of the fence with it. And then he came to the house itself, and the creepers trailed over the windows, and, unlocking the door, he stood in the hall with its discoloured ceiling and patches of mildew growing on the damp walls. Shabby and ashamed it looked, the paint perished from the window-sashes, the panes dirty, and in the air the sour smell of chambers long unventilated. And yet the spirit of the house was there still, though melancholy and reproachful, and it followed him wearily from room to room—'You are Peter, aren't you?' it seemed to say. 'You've just come to look at me, I see and not to stop. But I remember the jolly days just as well as you.'...From room to room he went, dining-room, drawing-room, his mother's sitting-room, his father's study: then upstairs to what had been the schoolroom in the days of governesses, and had then been turned over to the children for a play-room. Along the passage was the old nursery and the night-nursery, and above that attic-rooms, to one of which, as his own exclusive bedroom, he had been promoted when he went to school. The roof of it had leaked, there was a brown-edged stain on the sagging ceiling just above where his bed had been. 'A nice state to let my room get into,' muttered Peter. 'How am I to sleep underneath that drip from the roof? Too bad!'

The vividness of his own indignation rather startled him. He had really felt himself to be not a dual personality, but the same Peter Graham at different periods of his existence. One of them, the chairman of the British Tin Syndicate, had protested against young Peter Graham being put to sleep in so damp and dripping a room, and the other (oh, the ecstatic momentary glimpse of him!) was indeed young Peter back in his lovely attic again, just home from school and now looking round with eager eyes to convince himself of that blissful reality, before bouncing downstairs again to have tea in the children's room. What a lot of things to ask about! How were his rabbits, and how were Sybil's guinea-pigs, and had Violet learned that song 'Oh 'tis nothing but a shower,' and were the wood-pigeons building again in the lime-tree? All these topics were of the first importance...

Peter Graham the elder sat down on the window-seat. It overlooked the lawn, and just opposite was the lime-tree, a drooping lime making a green cave inside the skirt of its lower branches, but with those above growing straight, and he heard the chuckling coo of the wood-pigeons coming from it. They were building there again then: that question of young Peter's was answered.

'Very odd that I should just be thinking of that,' he said to himself: somehow there was no gap of years between him and young Peter, for his attic bridged over the decades which in the clumsy material reckoning of time intervened between them. Then Peter the elder seemed to take charge again.

The house was a sad affair, he thought: it gave him a stab of loneliness to see how decayed was the theatre of their joyful years, and no evidence of newer life, of the children of strangers and even of their children's children growing up here could have overscored the old sense of it so effectually. He went out of young Peter's room and paused on the landing: the stairs led down in two short flights to the storey below, and now for the moment he was young Peter again, reaching down with his hand along the banisters, and preparing to take the first flight in one leap. But then old Peter saw it was an impossible feat for his less supple joints.

Well, there was the garden to explore, and then he would go back to the agent's and return the keys. He no longer wanted to take that short cut down the steep hill to the station, passing the pool where Sybil and he had caught the stickleback, for his whole notion, sometimes so urgent, of coming back here, had wilted and withered. But he would just walk about the garden for ten minutes, and as he went with sedate step downstairs, memories of the garden, and of what they all did there began to invade him. There were trees to be climbed, and shrubberies—one thicket of syringa particularly where goldfinches built—to be searched for nests and moths, but above all there was that game they played there, far more exciting than lawn-tennis or cricket in the bumpy field (though that was exciting enough) called Pirates… There was a summer-house, tiled and roofed and of solid walls at the top of the garden, and that was "home" or "Plymouth Sound," and from there ships (children that is) set forth at the order of the Admiral to pick a trophy without being caught by the Pirates. There were two Pirates who hid anywhere in the garden and jumped out, and (counting the Admiral who, after giving his orders, became the flagship) three ships, which had to cruise to orchard or flower-bed or field and bring safely home a trophy culled from the ordained spot. Once, Peter remembered, he was flying up the winding path to the summer-house with a pirate close on his heels, when he fell flat down, and the humane pirate leaped over him for fear of treading on him, and fell down too. So Peter got home, because Dick had fallen on his face and his nose was bleeding…

'Good Lord, it might have happened yesterday,' thought Peter. 'And Harry called him a bloody pirate, and Papa heard and thought he was using shocking language till it was explained to him.'

The garden was even worse than the house, neglected utterly and rankly overgrown, and to find the winding path at all, Peter had to push through briar and thicket. But he persevered and came out into the rose-garden at the top, and there was Plymouth Sound with roof collapsed and walls bulging, and moss growing thick between the tiles of the floor.

'But it must be repaired at once,' said Peter aloud… 'What's that?' He whisked round towards the bushes through which he had pushed his way, for he had heard a voice, faint and far off coming from there, and the voice was familiar to him, though for thirty years it had been dumb. For it was Violet's voice which had spoken and she had said, 'Oh, Peter: *here* you are!'

He knew it was her voice, and he knew the utter impossibility of it. But it frightened him, and yet how absurd it was to be frightened, for it was only his imagination, kindled by old sights and memories, that had played him a trick. Indeed, how jolly even to have imagined that he had heard Violet's voice again.

'Vi!' he called aloud, but of course no one answered. The wood-pigeons were cooing in the lime, there was a hum of bees and a whisper of wind in the trees, and all round the soft enchanted Cornish air, laden with dream-stuff.

He sat down on the step of the summer-house, and demanded the presence of his own common sense. It had been an uncomfortable afternoon, he was vexed at this ruin of neglect into which the place had fallen, and he did not want to imagine these voices calling to him out of the past, or to see these odd glimpses which belonged to his boyhood. He did not belong any more to that epoch over which grasses waved and headstones presided, and he must be quit of all that evoked it, for, more than anything else, he was director of prosperous companies with big interests dependent on him. So he sat there for a calming five minutes, defying Violet, so to speak, to call to him again. And then, so unstable was his mood today, that presently he was listening for her. But Violet was always quick to see when she was not wanted, and she must have gone, to join the others...

He retraced his way, fixing his mind on material environments. The golden maple at the head of the walk, a sapling like himself when last he saw it, had become a stout-trunked tree, the shrub of bay a tall column of fragrant leaf, and just as he passed the syringa, a goldfinch dropped out of it with dipping flight. Then he was back at the house again where the climbing fuchsia trailed its sprays across the window of his mother's room and hot thick scent (how well-remembered!) spilled from the chalices of the great magnolia.

'A mad notion of mine to come and see the house again,' he said to himself. 'I won't think about it any more: it's finished. But it was wicked not to look after it.'

He went back into the town to return the keys to the house-agent.

'Much obliged to you,' he said. 'A pleasant house, when I knew it years ago. Why was it allowed to go to ruin like that?'

'Can't say, sir,' said the man. 'It has been let once or twice in the last ten years, but the tenants have never stopped long. The owner would be very pleased to sell it.'

An idea, fanciful, absurd, suddenly struck Peter.

'But why doesn't he live there?' he asked. 'Or why don't the tenants stop long? Was there something they didn't like about it? Haunted: anything of that sort? I'm not going to take it or purchase it: so that won't put me off.'

The man hesitated a moment.

'Well, there were stories,' he said, 'if I may speak confidentially. But all nonsense, of course.'

'Quite so,' said Peter. 'You and I don't believe in such rubbish. I wonder now: was it said that children's voices were heard calling in the garden?'

The discretion of a house-agent reasserted itself.

'I can't say, sir, I'm sure,' he said. 'All I know is that the house is to be had very cheap. Perhaps you would take our card'

Peter arrived back in London late that night. There was a tray of sandwiches and drinks waiting for him, and having refreshed himself, he sat smoking awhile thinking of his three days' work in Cornwall at the mines: there must be a directors' meeting as soon as possible to consider his suggestions... Then he found himself staring at the round rosewood table where his tray stood. It had been in his mother's sitting-room at Lescop, and the chair in which he sat, a fine Stuart piece, had been his father's chair at the dinner-table, and that book-case had stood in the hall, and his Chippendale card-table... he could not remember exactly where that had been. That set of Browning's poems had been Sybil's: it was from the shelves in the children's room. But it was time to go to bed, and he was glad he was not to sleep in young Peter's attic.

It is doubtful whether, if once an idea has really thrown out roots in a man's mind, he can ever extirpate it. He can cut off its sprouting suckers, he can nip off the buds it bears, or, if they come to maturity, destroy the seed, but the roots defy him. If he tugs at them something breaks, leaving a vital part still embedded, and it is not long before some fresh evidence of its vitality pushes up above the ground where he least expected it. It was so with Peter now: in the middle of some business-meeting, the face of one of his co-directors reminded him of that of the coachman at Lescop; if he went for a week-end of golf to the Dormy House at Rye, the bow-window of the billiard-room was in shape and size that of the drawing-room there, and the bank of gorse by the tenth green was no other than the clump below the tennis-court: almost he expected to find a tennis ball there when he had need to search it. Whatever he did, wherever he went, something called him from Lescop, and in the evening when he returned home, there was the furniture, more of it than he had realised, asking to be restored there: rugs and pictures and books, the silver on his table all joined in the mute appeal. But Peter stopped his ears to it: it was a senseless sentimentality, and a purely materialistic one to imagine that he could recapture the life over which so many years had flowed, and in which none of the actors but himself remained, by restoring to the house its old amenities and living there again. He would only emphasise his own loneliness by the visible contrast of the scene, once so alert and populous, with its present emptiness. And this 'butting-in' (so he expressed it) of materialistic sentimentality only confirmed his resolve to have done with Lescop. It had been a bitter sight but tonic, and now he would forget it.

Yet even as he sealed his resolution, there would come to him, blown as a careless breeze from the west, the memory of that boy and girl he had seen in the town, of the gay family starting for their river-picnic, of the faint welcoming call to him from the bushes in the garden, and, most of all, of the suspicion that the place was supposed to be haunted. It was just because it was haunted that he longed for it, and the more savagely and sensibly he assured himself of the folly of possessing it, the more he yearned after it, and constantly now it coloured his dreams. They were happy dreams; he was back there with the others, as in old days, children again in holiday time, and like himself they loved being at home there again, and they made much of Peter because it was he who had arranged it all. Often in these dreams he said to himself "I have dreamed this before, and then I woke and found myself elderly and lonely again, but this time it is real!"

The weeks passed on, busy and prosperous, growing into months, and one day in the autumn, on coming home from a day's golf, Peter fainted. He had not felt very well for some time, he had been languid and easily fatigued, but with his robust habit of mind he had labelled such symptoms as mere laziness, and had driven himself with the whip. But now it might be as well to get a medical overhauling just for the satisfaction of being told there was nothing the matter with him. The pronouncement was not quite that...

'But I simply can't,' he said. 'Bed for a month and a winter of loafing on the Riviera! Why, I've got my time filled up till close on Christmas, and then I've arranged to go with some friends for a short holiday. Besides, the Riviera's a pestilent hole. It can't be done. Supposing I go on just as usual: what will happen'?

Dr Dufflin made a mental summary of his wilful patient.

'You'll die, Mr Graham,' he said cheerfully. 'Your heart is not what it should be, and if you want it to do its work, which it will for many years yet, if you're sensible, you must give it rest. Of course, I don't insist on the Riviera: that was only a suggestion for I thought you would probably have friends there, who would help to pass the time for you. But I do insist on some mild climate, where you can loaf out of doors. London with its frosts and fogs would never do.'

Peter was silent for a moment.

'How about Cornwall?' he asked.

'Yes, if you like. Not the north coast of course.'

'I'll think it over,' said Peter. 'There's a month yet.'

Peter knew that there was no need for thinking it over. Events were conspiring irresistibly to drive him to that which he longed to do, but against which he had been struggling, so fantastic was it, so irrational. But now it was made easy for him to yield and his obstinate colours came down with a run. A few telegraphic exchanges with the house-agent made Lescop his, another gave him the address of a reliable builder and decorator, and with the plans of the house, though indeed there was little need of them, spread out on his counterpane, Peter issued urgent orders. All structural repairs, leaking roofs and dripping ceilings, rotted woodwork and crumbling plaster must be tackled at once, and when that was done, painting and papering followed. The drawing-room used to have a Morris-paper; there were spring flowers on it, blackthorn, violets, and fritillaries, a hateful wriggling paper, so he thought it, but none other would serve. The hall was painted duck-egg green, and his mother's room was pink, 'a beastly pink, tell them,' said Peter to his secretary, 'with a bit of blue in it: they must send me sample by return of post, big pieces, not snippets.'... Then there was furniture: all the furniture in the house here which had once been at Lescop must go back there. For the rest, he would send down some stuff from London, bedroom appurtenances, and linen and kitchen utensils: he would see to carpets when he got there. Spare bedrooms could wait; just four servants' rooms must be furnished, and also the attic which he had marked on the plan, and which he intended to occupy himself. But no one must touch the garden till he came: he would superintend that himself, but by the middle of next month there must be a couple of gardeners ready for him.

'And that's all,' said Peter, 'just for the present.' 'All?' he thought, as, rather bored with the direction of matters that usually ran themselves, he folded up his plans. 'Why, it's just the beginning: just underwriting.'

The month's rest-cure was pronounced a success, and with strict orders not to exert mind or body, but to lie fallow, out of doors whenever possible, with quiet strolls and copious restings, Peter was allowed to go to Lescop, and on a December evening he saw the door opened to him and the light of welcome stream out on to his entry. The moment he set foot inside he knew, as by some interior sense, that he had done right, for it was not only the warmth and the ordered comfort restored to the deserted house that greeted him, but the firm knowledge that they whose loss made his loneliness were greeting him... That came in a flash, fantastic and yet soberly convincing; it was fundamental, everything was based on it. The house had been restored to its old aspect, and though he had ventured to turn the small attic next door to young Peter's bedroom into a bathroom, 'after all,' he thought, 'it's my house, and I must make myself comfortable. They don't want bathrooms, but I do, and there it is.' There indeed it was, and there was electric light installed, and he dined, sitting in his father's chair, and then pottered from room to room, drinking in the old friendly atmosphere, which was round him wherever he went, for They were pleased. But neither voice nor vision manifested that, and perhaps it was only his own pleasure at being back that he attributed to them. But he would have loved a glimpse or a whisper, and from time to time, as he sat looking over some memoranda about the British Tin Syndicate, he peered into corners of the room, thinking that something moved there, and when a trail of creeper tapped against the window he got up and looked out. But nothing met his scrutiny but the dim starlight falling like dew on the neglected lawn. 'They're here, though,' he said to himself, as he let the curtain fall back.

The gardeners were ready for him next morning, and under his directions began the taming of the jungly wildness. And here was a pleasant thing, for one of them was the son of the cowman, Calloway, who had been here forty years ago, and he had childish memories still of the garden where with his father he used to come from the milking-shed to the house with the full pails. And he remembered that Sybil used to keep her guinea-pigs on the drying-ground at the back of the house. Now that he said that Peter remembered it too, and so the drying-ground all overgrown with brambles and rank herbage must be cleared.

'Iss, sure, nasty little vermin I thought them,' said Calloway the younger, 'but 'twas here Miss Sybil had their hutches and a wired run for 'em. And a rare fuss there was when my father's terrier got in and killed half of 'em, and the young lady crying over the corpses.'

That massacre of the innocents was dim to Peter; it must have happened in term-time when he was at school, and by the next holidays, to be sure, the prolific habits of her pets had gladdened Sybil's mourning.

So the drying-ground was cleared and the winding path up the shrubbery to the summer-house which had been home to the distressed vessels pursued by pirates. This was being rebuilt now, the roof timbered up, the walls rectified and whitewashed, and the steps leading to it and its tiled floor cleaned of the encroaching moss. It was soon finished, and Peter often sat there to rest and read the papers after a morning of prowling and supervising in the garden, for an hour or two on his feet oddly tired him, and he would doze in the sunny shelter. But now he never dreamed about coming back to Lescop or of the welcoming presences. 'Perhaps that's because I've come,' he thought, 'and those dreams were only meant to drive me. But I think they might show that they're pleased: I'm doing all I can.'

Yet he knew they were pleased, for as the work in the garden progressed, the sense of them and their delight hung about the cleared paths as surely as the smell of the damp earth and the uprooted bracken which had made such trespass. Every evening Calloway collected the gleanings of the day, piling it on the bonfire in the orchard. The bracken flared, and the damp hazel stems fizzed and broke into flame, and the scent of the wood smoke drifted across to the house. And after some three weeks' work all was done, and that afternoon Peter took no siesta in the summer-house, for he could not cease from walking through flower-garden and kitchen-garden and orchard now perfectly restored to their old order. A shower fell, and he sheltered under the lime where the pigeons built, and then the sun came out again, and in that gleam at the close of the winter day he took a final stroll to the bottom of the drive, where the gate now hung firm on even hinges. It used to take a long time in closing, if, as a boy, you let it swing, penduluming backwards and forwards with the latch of it clicking as it passed the hasp: and now he pulled it wide, and let go of it, and to and fro it went in lessening movement till at last it clicked and stayed. Somehow that pleased him immensely: he liked accuracy in details.

But there was no doubt he was very tired: he had an unpleasant sensation, too, as of a wire stretched tight across his heart, and of some thrumming going on against it. The wire dully ached, and this thrumming produced little stabs of sharp pain. All day he had been conscious of something of the sort, but he was too much taken up with the joy of the finished garden to heed little physical beckonings. A good long night would make him fit again, or, if not, he could stop in bed tomorrow. He went upstairs early, not the least anxious about himself, and instantly went to sleep. The soft night air pushed in at his open window, and the last sound that he heard was the tapping of the blind-tassel against the sash.

He woke very suddenly and completely, knowing that somebody had called him. The room was curiously bright, but not with the quality of moonlight; it was like a valley lying in shadow, while somewhere, a little way above it, shone some strong splendour of noon. And then he heard again his name called, and knew that the sound of the voice came in through the window. There was no doubt that Violet was calling him: she and the others were out in the garden.

'Yes, I'm coming,' he cried, and he jumped out of bed. He seemed—it was not odd—to be already dressed: he had on a jersey and flannel trousers, but his feet were bare and he slipped on a pair of shoes, and ran downstairs, taking the first short flight in one leap, like young Peter. The door of his mother's room was open, and he looked in, and there she was, of course, sitting at the table and writing letters.

'Oh, Peter, how lovely to have you home again,' she said. 'They're all out in the garden, and they've been calling you, darling. But come and see me soon, and have a talk.'

Out he ran along the walk below the windows, and up the winding path through the shrubbery to the summer-house, for he knew they were going to play Pirates. He must hurry, or the pirates would be abroad before he got there, and as he ran, he called out:

'Oh, do wait a second: I'm coming.'

He scudded past the golden maple and the bay tree, and there they all were in the summer-house which was home. And he took a flying leap up the steps and was among them.

It was there that Calloway found him next morning. He must indeed have run up the winding path like a boy, for the new-laid gravel was spurned at long intervals by the toe-prints of his shoes.

The following is a first-hand account of a haunting that Benson experienced directly at Lamb House in Rye. Despite what he says towards the end, the story that it inspired was published as 'The Flint Knife' and follows on straight after this account.

THE SECRET GARDEN

BEYOND THE WEST END OF THE GARDEN THERE LAY A SMALL square plot of ground surrounded by brick walls. Henry James, years ago, had heard that a local builder was casting a constructive eye on it, and a house on the site would annihilate any privacy in his garden, for the occupants could command his lawn at point-blank range, as they took tea at the open windows. I have no idea how imminent the danger was, but the rumoured hint was enough, and he bought it. This was merely a defensive measure, and he had then leased it to a neighbour in Mermaid Street, allowing him to make an entrance into it from his side, and incorporate it in his garden. This neighbour had now died, and since it belonged to the Lamb House estate, I opened a hole in the wall between it and my garden to see if I could do anything with it. I never saw a more dejected spot. There was an aged pear-tree against one wall, there was a gnarled ampelopsis against another, and a discouraged buddleia languished in a sunless corner. The rest had degenerated into rubbish heaps, with a weed-ridden path curving aimlessly among overgrown and flowerless beds.

This ghost of a garden was framed on all sides by old brick walls, and there is no plot of ground that, thus encompassed, cannot be fashioned into a gem of a garden, however small. I carted away the rubbish heaps, I cut down the atrocious ampelopsis, and gathered bushels of snails from the wall behind it. I transplanted the buddleia, and dug deeply over the rest. On the south the top windows of houses in Watchbell Street overlooked me, but a high close-meshed trellis on the top of the wall pulled down their blinds for them. On all other sides the walls gave complete seclusion, and there I was with this small square space, which I could design as I willed. At once I saw what could be made of it, a secret garden, and withal an outdoor sitting-room of which no inch was visible from the surface of the earth. There should be broad flower-beds below three of the walls with paths of crazy pavement in front of them and crazy pavement close along the fourth wall which faced north, leading to a roofed shelter in the corner with two sides open to the garden. The square thus enclosed should be turfed and a round flower-bed cut in the centre of it. I would build a short pillar of old bricks in the middle of the flower-bed and place thereon a marble bust of the young Augustus (a replica of that in the British Museum) which I had lately bought in Rye because I could not bear to leave it in the shop.

It was autumn, the right time for laying grass and planting out the spring garden. The turf arrived on a cart, like pieces of brown Swiss roll with green jam, Augustus was placed on his pillar, and a *fond* of forget-me-nots planted round him with Darwin tulips star-scattered among them. In the other beds I planted the common flowers of spring, more tulips and daffodils and narcissi and scarlet anemones and wallflowers with borders of aubrietia in front and summer perennials against the wall. The crazy pavement was laid down along the wall facing north with pockets in it for the clematises (Jackmanii and Miss Bateman) that hate the sun. In the corner I built the shelter, twelve feet square with tiled floor and wooden walls; open on two sides to the garden. Against the sunny walls I planted Mermaid roses, for I knew how the cream-coloured flowers and varnished leaves would look against the mellow brick. There was nothing of the slightest interest or rarity, for this garden was not intended to be one where the owner, with difficulty deciphering a metal label solemnly introduces the visitor to a minute mouse-coloured blossom, and tells him that never before has this species flowered in Sussex... How I long, on such occasions, to stamp on the mouse, passionately exclaiming 'And it shan't go on flowering in Sussex now...'

As soon as there were signs of summer in the succeeding years I furnished my outdoor study, laying rugs on the tiled floor and hanging pictures on its two walls. By the side of my writing-table I put an oblong mirror, so that sitting at work, I could see the reflection of the garden framed in it. Out of doors the eye wanders, but by this device it is forced to concentrate on what is framed and the picture of the sunlit beds seen in the shadowed mirror glowed with an added brilliance. The luxuriance with which everything grew there was uncanny: a pool of unbroken blue surrounded Augustus, the aubretias encroached on to the crazy pavement, and the web of wallflower scent spread like gossamer over the beds. The Mermaid roses threw out long, sappy shoots against the wall, and the Jackmanii, covered with purple stars, shot up to the top of the trellis and entangled itself in the pear-tree. We had week after week of sunny days, and every morning I trundled down a small wheeled table, such as they use in hospitals for bedside dressings, laden with the books I wanted for my work, bolted the door that led from the other garden, sunbathed in the secluded heat, and wrote in the shelter.

Gabriel never saw the secret garden. He was eighty-six now and bedridden, smacking his lips still over his glass of port with his dinner, but dozing most of the day. Then came the time when he could no longer be looked after in the house where he lodged, for he required more nursing than could be given him there, and he was moved into the infirmary at the workhouse. Then a dismal little tragedy happened, wounding to the sentimentally inclined. His long beard could not be kept clean; the doctor said it must be cut off, and Gabriel cried.

Many quite unimaginative folk are conscious, in certain houses or in rooms in those houses, of a quality in the atmosphere which seems independent of the physical environment. It may be happy or unhappy, peaceful or troubled, it does not vary with their moods and it is as evident to some inner sense as the odour of wood-smoke from the winter fires of six months before. It clings to the place faint but persistent. The secret garden soon developed some such atmosphere quite unconnected, it would seem, with Augustus or the flower-beds with sun or cloud or with the associations that gathered in it. I enjoyed my sun-baths and the new version of Charlotte Brontë at which I was working and the frequent presence of friends. Francis Yeats-Brown sprawled on the grass busy with *Bengal Lancer*, and refreshed himself with Yoga postures and deep breathing: Dame Ethel Smyth recalled some strangely erroneous impressions she had formed about my father and mother for her sequel to her enthralling *Impressions That Remained*: Clare Sheridan came over from Brede Place, and we discussed reincarnation (for which doctrine I had no use): the place was impregnated with the commerce and conversation of many friends. But it was not they who made this atmosphere: it was as if something out of the past, some condition of life long vanished, was leaking through into the present, and at least half a dozen of these friends perceived it. Then—it is next to impossible to describe this—this atmosphere became more personal: there was somebody there. The presence was in no way perilous or malign, like the presences in the enchanted woods of Ware, nor was it friendly: it was entirely indifferent. Suddenly a curious thing happened. Whether or no it betokened a visible manifestation of the haunting presence, I have no idea.

One windless summer day two friends, of whom the Vicar of Rye was one, were lunching with me, and afterwards we strolled down to the secret garden. It was a brilliant, broiling day and we seated ourselves in a strip of shade close to the door in the wall which communicated with the other garden. This door was open: two of our chairs, the Vicar's and mine, faced it, the other had its back to it... And I saw the figure of a man walk past this open doorway. He was dressed in black and he wore a cape the right wing of which, as he passed, he threw across his chest, over his left shoulder. His head was turned away and I did not see his face. The glimpse I got of him was very short, for two steps took him past the open doorway, and the wall behind the poplars hid him again. Simultaneously the Vicar jumped out of his chair, exclaiming: 'Who on earth was that?' It was only a step to the open door, and there, beyond, the garden lay, basking in the sun and empty of any human presence. He told me what he had seen: it was exactly what I had seen, except that our visitor had worn hose, which I had not noticed.

Now the odd feature about this meaningless apparition is that the first time this visitor appeared he was seen simultaneously by two people whose impressions as to his general mien and his gesture with his cloak completely tallied with each other. There was no legend about such an appearance which could have predisposed either of them to have imagined that he saw anything at all, and the broad sunlight certainly did not lend itself to any conjuring up of a black moving figure. Not long afterwards it was seen again in broad daylight by the Vicar at the same spot; just a glimpse and then it vanished. I was with him but I saw nothing. Since then I think I have seen it once in the evening on the lawn near the garden-room, but it was dusk, and I may have construed some fleeting composition of light and shadow into the same figure.

Now ghost stories, which go back into the earliest folktales, are a branch of literature at which I have often tried my hand. By a selection of disturbing details it is not very difficult to induce in the reader an uneasy frame of mind which, carefully worked up, paves the way for terror. The narrator, I think, must succeed in frightening himself before he can hope to frighten his readers, and, as a matter of fact, this man in black had not occasioned me the smallest qualms. However, I worked myself up and wrote my ghost story, describing how there developed an atmosphere of horror in my secret garden, how when I took Taffy there he cowered whining at my heels, how at night a faint stale luminance hovered over the enclosing walls, and so led up after due preparation for the appearance of the spectre. Then, for explanation, I described how I found in the archives at the Town Hall an account of the execution three hundred years ago of the then owner of that piece of land who had practised nameless infamies there, and how the skeletons of children, hideously maimed, were found below the bed over which Augustus reigned. I took a great deal of trouble over this piece, and having read it through I treated it as I had treated the first draft of Charlotte Brontë, and tore it up. What had actually happened (for I have no doubt whatever that the Vicar and I saw something that had no existence in the material world) made a far better ghost story than any embroidered version, and so I have here set it down unadorned and unexplained.

THE FLINT KNIFE

We were philosophising about gardens, Harry Pershore and I, as we sat one warm, serene June evening on the lawn outside his house, and the text of our observations was the scene in which we talked. The Pershore house, at which I had arrived that afternoon, was set in the very centre of a little country-town: its Georgian front looked out on to the main street, but at the back was this unsuspected acre of green lawn and flower beds, surrounded on all sides by high walls of mellow brick, over which peered the roofs and chimneys of the neighbouring houses. To me, weary of the heat and roar of London, it was indescribably delightful to sit, cool and at ease, in this green place, which to the inward sense seemed soaked in some peculiar tranquillity.

Just as old houses have their 'atmosphere' which has been distilled from the thoughts and the personalities of those who have inhabited them, so this garden seemed to me to have absorbed into the very soul of it the leisure of the generations whose retreat it had been. It was, I said, as if the spirit of that leisure had soaked into the darkling garden where we sat...

Harry was not encouraging about these mild sentimentalities.

'Very pretty indeed,' he said, 'but for myself I find your theory too fanciful.'

'Have it your own way,' I retorted. 'But I refuse to give up my theory that the inhabitants of houses create a special atmosphere in them. Walls and floors get soaked with them, and why not lawns and flower-beds?'

He rose from his seat and came to me.

'I don't believe a word of it,' he said, 'How can wood and stone receive qualities other than their own? But your remarks, though erroneous, are *à propos*, for we shall have an opportunity of testing their truth. There'll be a new atmosphere let into this garden tomorrow, and we shall see if it has any disturbing effect. Come across the lawn with me, and I'll show you what I mean to do.'

The lawn lay on a gentle slope, and to the west, where it declined down the side of a hill, there ran one of those tall brick walls which gave the garden so delightful a privacy. Harry set a ladder against this, and bade me mount it and look over.

'You won't be peering into the privacy of any neighbour of mine,' he said, so up I went and leaned my elbows on the top of the wall.

I found myself looking down into a small square plot, some eighty feet across, of wild uncultivated ground. It was thickly overgrown with weeds and wild flowers and rank seeding grasses, and though it lay on the slope of the hill, it instantly struck one that it must once have been levelled, for it was perfectly flat. All around its four sides ran high brick walls as tall as that over which I was now looking, with never a doorway or means of access in any of them: the square was completely sealed on every side. It had been grilled, of course, all day in the blaze of the sun, with not a breeze to stir the enclosed atmosphere, and now it was like leaning over a furnace, so heated was the air that met my face. Though the place lay naked to the sky, this warmth was not like that of the open; there was some indefinable taint about it, as of a room long shut up.

'But what is it?' I asked as I descended again. 'Why is it entirely closed?'

'Rather an odd affair,' he said. 'Only last week I was grubbing about in a box of old papers which I ought long ago to have sorted out, and I came across a diary of my mother's, written in faded ink and treating of faded topics. It began more than fifty years ago, soon after my birth. I did little more than glance at it, for it seemed to be occupied with the mere trivial chronicle of the days; how she walked one day, and hunted on another, and so forth.

'There were records of the arrival of visitors who came to stay with her and my father, and of their departure; and then I came across an entry which puzzled and interested me. She spoke of the building of a wall in the garden here, something to this effect: "I am sure it was only wise to have had it done," she wrote "and though it looks rather unsightly at present, it will soon get covered with creepers."

'That struck me as odd: I couldn't understand to what wall she referred.'

We had strolled back to the house as he spoke, and had entered his sitting-room. A shabby calf-bound volume lay on the table, and he pointed to it.

'There's the book,' he said. 'You might like to look at it, as it is most atmospheric. But I must finish my story: By one of those odd coincidences which mean nothing, on the very day on which I found and glanced at that diary, there was one of those summer gales which detached a big shoot of a climbing rose from the wall over which you have just been looking. My gardener had already gone home when I noticed it, and so I got a ladder and secured it again.

'Naturally,' he went on, 'one doesn't climb up walls and peer into one's neighbour's garden and I had always supposed that the garden of the next house to mine lay behind that section. But since I was already at the top of the wall, I looked over, and there saw what you have just seen—a little square overgrown plot with high walls and no access whatever to it from any side. At that, what I had read in my mother's diary about the building of a wall occurred to me, and later I found in the same box in which I had found the book, an old plan of this house and garden. This made it quite clear that the square plot had once been part of the garden, for there was no indication on the plan of the wall that now separates it.

'So next I called in my builder to examine that section of the wall. He told me that it was certainly much later than the rest and had probably been built fifty or sixty years ago, for he found at either end of it the straight perpendicular line where it joined the older walls. The date therefore is correct, and no doubt that is the wall mentioned in my mother's diary. Finally I consulted my good friend, the Town Surveyor, and he agreed that the square plot is quite certainly part of my estate.'

'So you're going to throw it in again?' I asked. 'Is that the new influence you spoke of as entering your garden?'

'Yes, that's it,' he said, 'though I shan't demolish the wall altogether, but only cut an arched doorway through it. I shall make a little secret garden of the place; it is absolutely sheltered, tall walls on every side, and it must be a wonderful sun trap. I shall have a little grass lawn in the middle of it, and a path of crazy pavement running round that, and deep flower beds against the walls. It will be a perfect gem of a place, and the builder is to begin cutting the doorway tomorrow.'

I took up to bed that night the diary of Harry's mother, and feeling disinclined for sleep I read it for a considerable time. A very pleasant impression emerged of this lady who, in the early days of the seventies, had found life so absorbingly filled with small interests.

She was just eighteen when Harry, her only child was born, and his remarkable precocity soon became an almost daily entry. But then I began to pick out certain scattered sentences which somehow seemed to be connected with each other: 'A lovely morning, but something rather uncomfortable about the garden'... 'Baby cried dreadfully in the garden this morning, but he was as good as gold when Nannie took him out in his perambulator into the street'... 'I sat on the square little lawn in the sun, but wasn't very happy. The flies were horrible. They buzzed continually round me, and yet I couldn't see them'... 'Something drove me in from the garden this evening, such an odd feeling, as if there was something looking at me from the little square lawn, and yet there was nobody there. Dick says it is all nonsense, but it isn't quite...'

Then after some interval was recorded the building of the wall, and following that came the entry which Harry had told me of, saying that she was sure it was wise. After that there was no more mention of the new wall, or of trouble in the garden. By this time I was drowsy with the deciphering of those faded lines, and I put out my light and went to sleep.

Now dreams are, of course, only a nonsensical medley of impressions lately received, or of those which in some stirring of the subconscious mind break like bubbles on the surface of the sleeping senses, so it was no wonder that I had vague and disquieting adventures in the garden, after I had fallen asleep. I seemed to be out there alone in some cloudy twilight; the wall over which I had peered that evening was gone, and in the centre of the small lawn that lay beyond was standing a tall upright figure toward which my steps were drawn.

In this veiled dimness I could not make out whether it was a man or some columnar block of stone. But the terror that began to stir in me was mingled with a great curiosity, and very stealthily I advanced toward it. I stood absolutely still, and, whether stone or flesh and blood, it seemed to be waiting.

There was the sound of innumerable flies buzzing in the air close about me, and suddenly a cloud of them descended on me, settling on my eyes and ears and nostrils—foul to the smell and loathsomely unclean to the touch. The horror of them overpowered my caution, and in a frenzy I beat them off, still keeping my eye on that silent figure. But my movements disclosed its nature: it was no stone column that stood there, for it slowly raised an arm, and made passes and beckonings to me.

A stricture of impotence was closing in on me, but the panic of sheer nightmare broke in on my dreams, and suddenly I was sitting up in bed, panting and wet with terror. The room was peaceful and silent; the open window looking out on the garden let in an oblong of moonlight, and there by my bedside was the closed volume which no doubt had induced this unease.

Next day the work of cutting a door in the garden wall began, and by the afternoon we could squeeze in through the slit of aperture and examine more closely the aspect of the new plot. Thick grew the crop of weeds and grasses over it, but underneath the northerly and easterly walls there was mingled with the wild growth many degenerated descendants of cultivated plants, showing that one time (even as the diary had indicated) there had been flower beds there. But otherwise the wild growth was rank and triumphant, and a deep digging over the soil would be necessary before the plot could be reclaimed.

Sun trap indeed it was: the place was a stew of heat, and though on the outer lawn close by it had been pleasant enough to sit out in the unshaded blaze of the day, thanks to the steady north-easterly breeze, here no faintest stir of moving air freshened the sultriness. Coming from that ventilated warmth outside, there was something deadly and oppressive about this hot torpor; the air was stagnant as the heart of some jungle, and there hung about it a faint odour of decay like that which broods in deep woodlands. I thought, too, that I heard the murmur of large flies, but that perhaps was an imagination born of the pages which I had read last night, and which had already worked themselves up into a most vivid and unpleasant dream.

I had not mentioned that to Harry, nor, in returning the diary to him, had I alluded to those curious entries I had found there. I had my own reason for this, for it was clear that his mother had felt there was something queer and uncanny about the spot where we now stood, and I did not want any suggestion of that from outside to enter Harry's mind.

Evidently there was nothing further from his thoughts at present, for he was charmed with this derelict little plot.

'Marvellously sheltered,' he said. 'No east wind can get near it; it will pass right over it. One could grow anything here. And so perfectly private; not a roof or a chimney looks over the walls—nothing but sky. I love a secret place like this! I shall have a door fitted with a bolt inside, and no one can disturb me. As for the rest, it is all in my head, ready to be realised. Beds, deep flower beds where the old ones have been, a square of grass, and a round bed in the centre. I can see it; it will turn out precisely as I want it.'

Next morning, while the bricklayers were finishing the doorway, Harry got in a couple of men in addition to his gardener, and all day barrowfuls of weeds and grasses were carted away for burning. The position of the flower beds was staked out, and that of the path, but all had to be deeply dug in order to get rid of the burrowing roots of the old vegetation, before the crazy pavement and the turfs of the lawn could be laid down. That afternoon as I lazed in the hot sun, Harry came out from his labours, hot and grimed, and beckoned to me.

'Come here!' he called, 'We've hit upon an odd thing, and I don't know what it is. Bring your archaeological knowledge to bear.'

It was indeed rather an odd thing: a square column of black granite, some four feet high and about eighteen inches across. In shape it somewhat resembled one of those altars which are not uncommonly seen in collections of Roman remains. But this was certainly not Roman; it was of far ruder workmanship, and looked far more like some Druidical piece. Then suddenly I remembered having seen, in some Museum of early British remains, something exactly like it: it was described as an altar of sacrifice from an ancient British temple. Indeed there could be no reasonable doubt that this stone was of the same nature.

Harry was delighted with this find.

'Just what I want for the centre of my flower bed in the middle of the lawn,' he said. 'I've got the place marked; let's haul it into position at once. I'll have a sundial on the top of it, I think.'

I was strolling that evening in the garden waiting for Harry to come out. The sun had just set behind a bank of stormy red clouds in the west, and as I came opposite the yet doorless archway into the new plot, it looked exactly as if it was lit by some illumination of its own. The tall black altar now in place glowed like a lump of red-hot iron, and as I stood there in the doorway, wondering at this lurid brightness, I felt something brush by me, just touching my shoulder and left side in its passage.

This was startling, but there was nothing visible, and immediately I heard—this time without any doubt whatever—the sonorous hum of many flies. That certainly came from the new garden, and yet in the air there was no sign of them.

And simultaneously with both these invisible impressions, there came to me a sudden shrinking and shuddering of the spirit, as if I were in the presence of some evil and malignant power. That came and went: it lasted no longer than the soft touch of the invisible thing that had pushed by me in the doorway, or that drone of hovering flies.

Then Harry appeared, coming out of the house and calling me to our usual diversion of piquet which we both enjoyed playing.

The laying of the lawn and the replanting of the old beds went on with great expedition: strips of turf from the downland were plastered onto the fresh-turned soil and rolled and watered, while against the walls for autumnal flowering Harry planted sunflowers, dahlias and Michaelmas daisies, and in the bed around the black column a company of well-grown young salvias.

A couple of days sufficed for this, and one evening we strolled down there in the dusk, marvelling at how well the turf was taking, and how vigorous and upstanding were the young plants.

There were heavy showers that night; blinks of lightning glared through my panes; distant thunder reverberated, and later, in the hot hours of darkness, I had to get up to close the window, for the rain was spattering on the carpet within. Having shut it, I stood there for a few moments looking out on the shrouded dimness and listening to the hiss of the thick shower on the shrubs outside. And then I saw something that curiously disquieted me.

The door into the new garden had been fitted that day, but it had been left open. The archway was thus visible from my windows, and now it stood out in the darkness as if there was light within. Then a very vivid flash zig-zagged across the sky, and I saw that in the doorway there was standing a black-draped figure.

It seemed hardly credible that a human being had got into the garden: why should a cloaked and living man be standing out there in the storm? If he was a burglar why should he be waiting out there, for the house had long been wrapped in quiet? And yet, supposing that in the morning it was found that someone had broken into the house, I should cut a very foolish figure if, having seen him before any damage was done, I went tranquilly back to bed again without investigation.

But I know that I did not really believe this was a man at all. What then was to be done? I decided that I would not wake Harry until I had carried my investigations a little further by myself, and I started to go downstairs. But as I passed Harry's door, I saw a chink of light underneath it, then a loose board creaked under my foot, and next moment he came out.

'What is it?' he asked. 'Did you see it too? Someone coming across the lawn from the new garden? Look here: I'll go out by the back door into the garden and you go through the dining room. Then he'll be between us. Take a poker or a big stick with you.'

I waited till he had time to get around to the back, and then, pulling aside the curtain in the dining-room, I unlocked the door that led into the garden. The rain had ceased and now through the thunder-laden canopy overhead there shone the faint light of a cloud-beleaguered moon. There in the centre of the lawn stood the figure I had seen in the archway, and on the moment I heard the click of the lock of the back-door.

Was it after all only a living man who now stood within ten yards of me? Had he heard the unlocking of the two doors? At any rate he moved—and that swiftly—across the lawn toward the archway where I had first seen him. Then I heard Harry's voice:

'Quick; we've got him now!' he cried, and while he took the path, I ran across the lawn toward the doorway through which the figure had disappeared. There was light enough to see, when we got there, that it stood in the centre of the garden; it was as if the altar was one with it. Then a near and vivid flash of lightning burst from the pall overhead, and showed every corner of the high-walled plot. It was absolutely empty, but the stillness was now broken by the buzzing of innumerable flies. Then the rain began, first a few large hot drops, then the sluices of heaven were opened, and before we could regain the house we were drenched.

Of all the men I have ever known, Harry Pershore has the profoundest disbelief in 'the unseen and the aware', and in the few minutes of his talk before we turned in again, and at breakfast next morning he was still absolutely convinced that what we had both seen was real and material, not ghostly.

'It must have been a man,' he said, 'because there's nothing else for it to be; and after all, the walls are not unscaleable for an active fellow. Certainly we both thought we saw him in the centre of the garden. But the light was dim and confusing, and I haven't the slightest doubt that we were both staring at the altar while he was shinning it up the wall. Come down and look.'

We went out. The garden was still dripping with the rain of the night, but the vigorous salvias planted yesterday in the bed around the altar were scorched, as if a flame had passed over them. Withered, too, though not so sorely burned, was the new-laid grass, and the sunflowers and Michaelmas daisies were drooping and yellow of leaf. It was as if some tropic day, instead of a warm night with copious showers of rain, had passed over them; or rather as if from the altar had emanated some withering ray, completely scorching all that lay nearest to it. But all this only stiffened Harry into an angry stubbornness when I asked him what explanation he offered.

'Good Lord, I can't tell you,' he said, 'but you've got to find the connection between a man who popped over the wall and my poor withered plants. I'll tell you what I'll do. I'll bring out a ground-sheet and a rug and sleep here tonight, and we'll see if anyone comes round with a warming-pan again. No, don't be alarmed; I'm not going to ask you to keep me company. That would spoil it all, for you might somehow infect me with your nonsense. I prefer a revolver. You think there's something occult and frightful at work. So let's have it; bring it out. What's your explanation?'

'I can't explain it any more than you,' I said. 'But I believe there is something here in this garden, some power connected, I imagine, with that altar you found. Your mother also believed there was something queer, and had the place walled-up. You've opened it again, and set the thing free, and I expect it's vastly intensified by your having disinterred that which lay buried.'

He laughed.

'I see,' he said. 'An instance of your theory that material objects can absorb and give out force they have derived from living folk—'

'Or years ago, from the dead,' said I.

He laughed again.

'I really think we won't talk about it,' he said. 'I can't argue about such monstrous nonsense. It isn't worth that much to me.'

During the day I made several efforts to dissuade him from his scheme, but it was perfectly fruitless. Indeed I began myself to wonder whether I was not the prey of ridiculous imaginings; whether my mind was not reverting to the bygone beliefs and superstitions of primitive man.

A lump of stone like that altar was just a lump of stone. How could it possess properties and powers such as those which I was disposed to attribute to it. Certainly that figure which we had both seen was difficult of rational explanation; so, too, was that withering and scorching flame that had passed over the garden. But it was a flight of conjecture, wholly unsupported, to suppose that a rough-hewn block of granite had any connection with them.

My fears and forebodings receded and dwindled till they lay back in my mind, cloaked with the darkness that common sense spread round them, and became no more than a tiny spark smouldering there. And so it came about that when, about eleven that night, Harry went forth from the house with his pillows and blanket and ground-sheet, revolver in hand, to spend the night on the new-laid lawn, I soon went up to bed.

The door from the dining-room into the garden Harry had left unlocked, for again the night was thickly over-clouded, threatening rain, and he laughingly said that though he would gaily face the fires of the powers of darkness, a downpour of common rain would certainly rout him and send him running for shelter. Throwing open my window, I leaned out into the night, and in the stillness heard Harry shut and bolt the door into the little garden.

I went to sleep at once, and from dreamlessness awoke suddenly to a consciousness of terror and imminent peril. Without waiting to put on a coat or slippers I ran downstairs and across the lawn towards the door in the wall.

I stopped outside it, listening and wondering why I had rushed out like that, for all was perfectly still. Then, while I stood there, I heard a voice—not Harry's—from within. I could not distinguish any words at all, and the tones of it were level, as if it were chanting some prayer, and as I listened I saw above the wall a dim red glow gradually brightening.

All of this happened in a moment, and with some swift onrush of panic I called aloud to Harry, and wrestled with the handle of the door. But he had bolted it from within. Once more I rattled at it and shouted—and still only that chanting voice answered. Then, exerting my full strength and weight, I hurled myself against the door: it creaked, the bolt snapped and it gave way, falling inward. There met me a buffet of hot air tainted with some rank smell; and round me was the roar of hosts of flies.

Harry, stripped to the waist, was kneeling in front of the altar. By his side stood a figure robed in black; one of its hands grasped his hair, bending his head back, the other, stretched out, brandished aloft some implement. Before the stroke fell, I found my voice.

'By the power of God Almighty!' I yelled, and in the air I traced the sign of the Cross.

I heard the chink of something falling on the altar; the red light faded into the dusk of earliest dawn, and Harry and I were alone. He swayed and fell sideways on the grass, and without more ado I picked him up and carried him out past the shattered door and through the archway, not knowing yet if he was alive or dead. But he breathed still, he sighed and stirred like one coming out of deep trance, and then he saw me.

'You!' he said. 'But what's been happening? Why am I here? I went to sleep, and I dreamed something terrible. A priest, a sacrifice... What was it?'

I never told him what had happened beyond that I had felt uneasy about him, had come out and called him, and getting no answer had burst in the door and found him lying on the grass. He knew no more than that; but for some reason he took a dislike to the altar which had pleased him so much. Somewhere in the dim recesses of his subconsciousness, I imagine, he connected it with the very terrible 'dream' which he could only vaguely recall, and he said he would have it buried again: it was an ugly thing. As we looked at it next morning, talking of this, he took up from it something that lay on the top of it.

'How on earth did that get here?' he said. 'It's one of those early flint knives, isn't it?'

THE BATH-CHAIR

EDMUND FARADAY, AT THE AGE OF FIFTY, HAD EVERY REASON to be satisfied with life: he had got all he really wanted, and plenty of it. Health was among the chief causes of his content, and he often reflected that the medical profession would have a very thin time of it, if everyone was as fortunate as he. His apprecia-tion of his good fortune was apt at times to be a little trying: he ate freely, he absorbed large (but in no way excessive) quantities of mixed alcoholic liquors, pleasantly alluding to his immunity from any disagreeable effects, and he let it be widely known that he had a cold bath in the morning, spent ten minutes before an open window doing jerks and flexings, and had a fine appetite for breakfast. Not quite so popular was his faint contempt for those who had to be careful of themselves. It was not expressed in contemptuous terms, indeed he was jovially sympathetic with men perhaps ten years younger than himself who found it more prudent to be abstemious. 'Such a bore for you, old man,' he would comment, 'but I expect you're wise.'

In addition to these physical advantages, he was master of a very considerable income, derived from shares in a very sound company of general stores, which he himself had founded, and of which he was chairman: this and his accumulated savings enabled him to live precisely as he pleased. He had a house near Ascot, where he spent most week-ends from Friday to Monday, playing golf all day, and another in Massington Square, conveniently close to his business. He might reasonably look forward to a robust and prosperous traverse of that tableland of life which with healthy men continues till well after they have passed their seventieth year. In London he was accustomed to have a couple of hours' bridge at his club before he went back to his bachelor home where his sister kept house for him, and from morning to night his life was spent in enjoying or providing for his own pleasures.

Alice Faraday was, in her own department, one of the clues of his prosperous existence, for it was she who ran his domestic affairs for him. He saw little of her, for he always breakfasted by himself, and encountered her in the morning only for a moment when he came downstairs to set out for his office, and told her whether there would be some of his friends to dinner, or whether he would be out; she would then interview the cook and telephone to the tradesmen, and make her tour of the house to see that all was tidy and speckless. At the end of the day again it was but seldom that they spent a domestic evening together: either he dined out leaving her alone, or three friends or perhaps seven were his guests and made up a table or two tables of bridge. On these occasions Alice was never of the party. She was no card player, she was rather deaf, she was silent and by no means decorative, and she was best respresented by the admirable meal she had provided for him and his friends. At the house at Ascot she performed a similar role, finding her way there by train on Friday morning, so as to have the house ready for him when he motored down later in the day.

Sometimes he wondered whether he would not be more comfortable if he married and gave Alice a modest home of her own with an income to correspond, for, though he saw her but seldom, her presence was slightly repugnant to him. But marriage was something of a risk, especially for a man of his age who had kept out of it so long, and he might find himself with a wife who had a will of her own, and who did not understand, as Alice certainly did, that the whole reason of her existence was to make him comfortable. Again he wondered whether perfectly-trained servants like his would not run the house as efficiently as his sister, in which case she would be better away; he would, indefinably, be more at his ease if she were not under his roof. But then his cook might leave, or his housemaid do her work badly, and there would be bills to go through, and wages to be paid, and catering to be thought of. Alice did all that, and his only concern was to draw her a monthly cheque, with a grumble at the total. As for his occasional evenings with her, though it was a bore to dine with this rather deaf, this uncouth and bony creature, such evenings were rare, and when dinner was over, he retired to his own den, and spent a tolerable hour or two over a book or a crossword puzzle. What she did with herself he had no idea, nor did he care, provided she did not intrude on him. Probably she read those gruesome books about the subconscious mind and occult powers which interested her. For him the conscious mind was sufficient, and she had little place in it. A secret unsavoury woman: it was odd that he, so spick and span and robust, should be of the same blood as she.

This regime, the most comfortable that he could devise for himself, had been practically forced on Alice. Up till her father's death she had kept house for him, and in his old age he had fallen on evil days. He had gambled away in stupid speculation on the Stock Exchange a very decent capital, and for the last five years of his life he had been entirely dependent on his son, who housed them both in a dingy little flat just around the corner from Massington Square. Then the old man had had a stroke and was partially paralysed, and Edmund, always contemptuous of the sick and the inefficient, had grudged every penny of the few hundred pounds which he annually allowed him. At the same time he admired the powers of management and economy that his sister manifested in contriving to make her father comfortable on his meagre pittance. For instance, she even got him a second-hand bath-chair, shabby and shiny with much usage, and on warm days she used to have him wheeled up and down the garden in Massington Square, or sit there reading to him. Certainly she had a good idea of how to use money, and so, on her father's death, since she had to be provided for somehow, he offered her a hundred pounds a year, with board and lodging, to come and keep house for him. If she did not accept this munificence she would have to look out for herself, and as she was otherwise penniless, it was not in her power to refuse. She brought the bath-chair with her, and it was stored away in a big shed in the garden behind her brother's house. It might come into use again some day.

Edmund Faraday was an exceedingly shrewd man, but he never guessed that there was any psychical reason, beyond the material necessity, why Alice so eagerly accepted his offer. Briefly, this reason was that his sister regarded him with a hatred that prospered and burned bright in his presence. She hugged it to her, she cherished and fed it, and for that she must be with him: otherwise it might die down and grow cold. To hear him come in of an evening thrilled her with the sense of his nearness, to sit with him in silence at their rare solitary meals, to watch him, to serve him was a feast to her. She had no definite personal desire to injure him, even if that had been possible, but she must be near him, waiting for some inconjecturable doom, which, long though it might tarry, would surely overtake him, provided only that she kept the dynamo of her hatred ceaselessly at work. All vivid emotion, she knew, was a force in the world, and sooner or later it worked out its fulfilment. In her solitary hours, when her housekeeping work was accomplished, she directed her mind on him like a searchlight, she studied books of magic and occult lore that revealed or hinted at the powers which concentration can give. Witches and sorcerers, in the old days, ignorant of the underlying cause, made spells and incantations, they fashioned images of wax to represent their victims, and bound and stabbed them with needles in order to induce physical illness and torturing pains, but all this was child's play, dealing with symbols: the driving force behind them, which was much better left alone to do its will in its own way without interference, was hate. And it was no use being impatient: it was patience that did its perfect work. Perhaps when the doom began to shape itself, a little assistance might be given: fears might be encouraged, despair might be helped to grow, but nothing more than that. Just the unwearied waiting, the still intense desire, the black unquenchable flame…

Often she felt that her father's spirit was in touch with her, for he, too, had loathed his son and when he lay paralysed, without power of speech, she used to make up stories about Edmund for his amusement, how he would lose all his money, how he would be detected in some gross dishonesty in his business, how his vaunted health would fail him, and how cancer or some crippling ailment would grip him; and then the old man's eyes would brighten with merriment, and he cackled wordlessly in his beard and twitched with pleasure. Since her father's death, Alice had no sense that he had gone from her, his spirit was near her, and its malevolence was undiminished. She made him partner of her thoughts: sometimes Edmund was late returning from his work, and as the minutes slipped by and still he did not come, it was as if she still made stories for her father, and told him that the telephone bell would soon ring, and she would find that she was being rung up from some hospital where Edmund had been carried after a street accident. But then she would check her thoughts; she must not allow herself to get too definite or even to suggest anything to the force that was brewing and working round him. And though at present all seemed well with him, and the passing months seemed but to endow him with new prosperities, she never doubted that fulfilment would fail, if she was patient and did her part in keeping the dynamo of hate at work.

Edmund Faraday had only lately moved into the house he now occupied. Previously he had lived in another in the same square, a dozen doors off, but he had always wanted this house: it was more spacious, and it had behind it a considerable plot of garden, lawn and flower-beds, with a high brick wall surrounding it. But the other house was still unlet, and the house agent's board on it was an eyesore to him: there was money unrealised while it stood empty. But tonight, as he approached it, walking briskly back from his office, he saw that there was a man standing on the balcony outside the drawing-room windows: evidently then there was someone seeing over it. As he drew nearer, the man turned, took a few steps towards the long open window and passed inside. Faraday noticed that he limped heavily, leaning on a stick and swaying his body forward as he advanced his left leg, as if the joint was locked. But that was no concern of his, and he was pleased to think that somebody had come to inspect his vacant property. Next morning on his way to business he looked in at the agent's, in whose hands was the disposal of the house, and asked who had been enquiring about it. The agent knew nothing of it: he had not given the keys to anyone.

'But I saw a man standing on the balcony last night,' said Faraday. 'He must have got hold of the keys.'

But the keys were in their proper place, and the agent promised to send round at once to make sure that the house was duly locked up. Faraday took the trouble to call again on his way home, only to learn that all was in order, front door locked, and back door and area gate locked, nor was there any sign that the house had been burglariously entered.

Somehow this trumpery incident stuck in Faraday's mind, and more than once that week it was oddly recalled to him. One morning he saw in the street a little ahead of him a man who limped and leaned on his stick, and instantly he bethought himself of that visitor to the empty house for his build and his movement were the same, and he quickened his step to have a look at him. But the pavement was crowded, and before he could catch him up the man had stepped into the roadway, and dodged through the thick traffic, and Edmund lost sight of him. Once again, as he was coming up the Square to his own house, he was sure that he saw him walking in the opposite direction, down the other side of the Square, and now he turned back in order to come round the end of the garden and meet him face to face. But by the time he had got to the opposite pavement there was no sign of him.

He looked up and down the street beyond; surely that limping crippled walk would have been visible a long way off. A big man, broad-shouldered and burly in make: it should have been easy to pick him out. Faraday felt certain he was not a householder in the Square, or surely he must have noticed him before. And what had he been doing in his locked house: and why, suddenly, should he himself now catch sight of him almost every day? Quite irrationally, he felt that this obtrusive and yet elusive stranger had got something to do with him.

He was going down to Ascot tomorrow, and tonight was one of those rare occasions when he dined alone with his sister. He had little appetite, he found fault with the food, and presently the usual silence descended. Suddenly she gave her little bleating laugh. 'Oh, I forgot to tell you,' she said. 'There was a man who called today—didn't give any name—who wished to see you about the letting of the other house. I said it was in the agent's hands: I gave him the address. Was that right, Edmund?'

'What was he like?' he rapped out.

'I never saw his face clearly at all. He was standing in the hall with his back to the window, when I came down. But a big man, like you in build, but crippled. Very lame, leaning heavily on his stick.'

'What time was this?'

'A few minutes only before you came in.'

'And then?'

'Well, when I told him to apply to the agent, he turned and went out, and, as I say, I never saw his face. It was odd somehow. I watched him from the window, and he walked round the top of the Square and down the other side. A few minutes afterwards I heard you come in.'

She watched him as she spoke, and saw trouble in his face.

'I can't make out who the fellow is,' he said. 'From your description he seems like a man I saw a week ago, standing on the balcony of the other house. Yet when I enquired at the agent's, no one had asked for the keys, and the house was locked up all right. I've seen him several times since, but never close. Why didn't you ask his name, or get his address?'

'I declare I never thought of it,' she said.

'Don't forget, if he calls again. Now if you've finished you can be off. You'll go down to Ascot tomorrow morning, and let us have something fit to eat. Three men coming down for the week-end.'

Faraday went out to his morning round of golf on Saturday in high good spirits: he had won largely at bridge the night before, and he felt brisk and clear-eyed. The morning was very hot, the sun blazed, but a bastion of black cloud coppery at the edges was pushing up the sky from the east, threatening a downpour, and it was annoying to have to wait at one of the short holes while the couple in front delved among the bunkers that guarded the green. Eventually they holed out, and Faraday waiting for them to quit saw that there was watching them a big man, leaning on a stick, and limping heavily as he moved. 'That's he,' he thought to himself, 'so now I'll get a look at him.' But when he arrived at the green the stranger had gone, and there was no sign of him anywhere. However, he knew the couple who were in front, and he could ask them when he got to the club-house who their friend was. Presently the rain began, short in duration but violent, and his partner went to change his clothes when they got in. Faraday scorned any such precaution: he never caught cold, and never yet in his life had he had a twinge of rheumatism, and while he waited for his less robust partner he made enquiries of the couple who had been playing in front of him as to who their lame companion was. But they knew nothing of him: neither of them had seen him.

Somehow this took the edge off his sense of wellbeing, for indeed it was a queer thing. But Sunday dawned, bright and sparkling, and waking early he jumped out of bed with the intention of a walk in the garden before his bath. But instantly he had to clutch at a chair to save himself a fall. His left leg had given way under his weight, and a stabbing pain shot through his hip-joint. Very annoying: perhaps he should have changed his wet clothes yesterday. He dressed with difficulty, and limped downstairs. Alice was there arranging fresh flowers for the table.

'Why, Edmund, what's the matter?' she asked.

'Touch of rheumatism,' he said. 'Moving about will put it right.'

But moving about was not so easy: golf was out of the question, and he sat all day in the garden, cursing this unwonted affliction, and all day the thought of the lame man, in build like himself, scratched about underground in his brain, like a burrowing mole.

Arrived back in London Faraday saw a reliable doctor, who, learning of his cold baths and his undisciplined use of the pleasures of the cellar and the table, put him on a regime which was a bitter humiliation to him, for he had joined the contemptible army of the careful. 'Moderation, my dear sir,' said his adviser. 'No more cold baths or port for you, and a curb on your admirable appetite. A little more quiet exercise, too, during the week, and a good deal less on your week-ends. Do your work and play your games and see your friends. But moderation, and we'll soon have you all right.'

It was in accordance with this distasteful advice that Faraday took to walking home if he had been dining out in the neighbourhood, or, if at home, took a couple of turns round the Square before going to bed. Contrary to use, he was without guests several nights this week, and on the last of them, before going down into the country again, he limped out about eleven o'clock feeling ill at ease and strangely apprehensive of the future. Though the violence of his attack had abated, walking was painful and difficult, and his halting steps, he felt sure, must arrest a contemptuous compassion in all who knew what a brisk, strong mover he had been. The night was cloudy and sweltering hot, there was a tenseness and an oppression in the air that matched his mood. All pleasure had been sucked out of life for him by this indisposition, and he felt with some inward and quaking certainty that it was but the shadow of some more dire visitant who was drawing near. All this week, too, there had been something strange about Alice. She seemed to be expecting something, and that expectation filled her with a secret glee. She watched him, she took note, she was alert...

He had made the complete circuit of the Square, and now was on his second round, after which he would turn in. A hundred yards of pavement lay between him and his own house, and it and the roadway were absolutely empty. Then, as he neared his own door, he saw that a figure was advancing in his direction; like him it limped and leaned on a stick. But though a week ago he had wanted to meet this man face to face, something in his mind had shifted, and now the prospect of the encounter filled him with some quaking terror. A meeting, however, was not to be avoided, unless he turned back again, and the thought of being followed by him was even more intolerable than the encounter. Then, while he was still a dozen yards off, he saw that the other had paused opposite his door, as if waiting for him.

Faraday held his latchkey in his hand ready to let himself in. He would not look at the fellow at all, but pass him with averted head. When he was now within a foot or two of him, the other put out his hand with a detaining gesture, and involuntarily Faraday turned. The man was standing close to the street lamp, and his face was in vivid light. And that face was Faraday's own: it was as if he beheld his own image in a looking-glass... With a gulping breath he let himself into his house, and banged the door. There was Alice standing close within, waiting for him surely.

'Edmund,' she said—and just as surely her voice trembled with some secret suppressed glee—'I went to post a letter just now, and that man who called about the other house was loitering outside. So odd.'

He wiped the cold dews from his forehead.

'Did you get a look at him?' he asked. 'What was he like?'

She gave her bleating laugh, and her eyes were merry.

'A most extraordinary thing!' she said. 'He was so like you that I actually spoke to him before I saw my mistake. His walk, his build, his face: everything. Most extraordinary! Well, I'll go up to bed now. It's late for me, but I thought you would like to know that he was about, in case you wanted to speak to him. I wonder who he is, and what he wants. Sleep well!'

In spite of her good wishes, Faraday slept far from well. According to his usual custom, he had thrown the windows wide before he got into bed, and he was just dozing off, when he heard from outside an uneven tread and the tap of a stick on the pavement, his own tread he would have thought, and the tap of his own stick. Up and down it went, in a short patrol, in front of his house. Sometimes it ceased for a while, but no sooner did sleep hover near him than it began again. Should he look out, he asked himself, and see if there was anyone there? He recoiled from that, for the thought of looking again on himself, his own face and figure, brought the sweat to his forehead. At last, unable to bear this haunted vigil any longer, he went to the window. From end to end, as far as he could see, the Square was empty, but for a policeman moving noiselessly on his rounds, and flashing his light into areas.

Dr Inglis visited him next morning. Since seeing him last, he had examined the X-ray photograph of the troublesome joint, and he could give him good news about that. There was no sign of arthritis; a muscular rheumatism, which no doubt would yield to treatment and care, was all that ailed him. So off went Faraday to his work, and the doctor remained to have a talk to Alice, for, jovially and encouragingly, he had told him that he suspected he was not a very obedient patient, and must tell his sister that his instructions as to food and tabloids must be obeyed.

'Physically there's nothing much wrong with him, Miss Faraday,' he said, 'but I want to consult you. I found him very nervous and I am sure he was wanting to tell me something, but couldn't manage it. He ought to have thrown off his rheumatism days ago, but there's something on his mind, sapping his vitality. Have you any idea—strict confidence, of course—what it is?'

She gave her little bleat of laughter.

'Wrong of me to laugh, I know, Dr Inglis,' she said, 'but it's such a relief to be told there's nothing really amiss with dear

Edmund. Yes: he has something on his mind—dear me, it's so ridiculous that I can hardly speak of it.'

'But I want to know.'

'Well, it's a lame man, whom he has seen several times. I've seen him, too, and the odd thing is he is exactly like Edmund. Last night he met him just outside the house, and he came in, well, really looking like death.'

'And when did he see him first? After this lameness came upon him, I'll be bound.'

'No: before. We both saw him before. It was as if—such nonsense it sounds!—it was as if this sort of double of himself showed what was going to happen to him.'

There was glee and gusto in her voice. And how slovenly and uncouth she was with that lock of grey hair loose across her forehead, and her uncared-for hands. Dr Inglis felt a distaste for her: he wondered if she was quite right in the head.

She clasped one knee in her long bony fingers.

'That's what troubles him—oh, I understand him so well,' she said. 'Edmund's terrified of this man. He doesn't know *what* he is. Not *who* he is, but *what* he is.'

'But what is there to be afraid about?' asked the doctor. 'This lame fellow, so like him, is no disordered fancy of his own brain, since you've seen him too. He's an ordinary living human being.'

She laughed again, she clapped her hands like a pleased child. 'Why, of course, that must be so!' she said. 'So there's nothing for him to be afraid of. That's splendid! I must tell Edmund that. What a relief! Now about the rules you've laid down for him, his food and all that. I will be very strict with him. I will see that he does what you tell him. I will be quite relentless.'

For a week or two Faraday saw no more of this unwelcome visitor, but he did not forget him, and somewhere deep down in his brain there remained that little cold focus of fear. Then came an evening when he had been dining out with friends: the food and the wine were excellent, they chaffed him about his abstemiousness, and loosening his restrictions he made a jolly evening of it, like one of the old days. He seemed to himself to have escaped out of the shadow that had lain on him, and he walked home in high good humour, limping and leaning on his stick, but far more brisk than was his wont. He must be up betimes in the morning, for the annual general meeting of his company was soon coming on, and tomorrow he must finish writing his speech to, the shareholders. He would be giving them a pleasant half-hour; twelve per cent free of tax and a five per cent bonus was what he had to tell them about Faraday's Stores.

He had taken a short cut through the dingy little thoroughfare where his father had lived during his last stricken years, and his thoughts flitted back, with the sense of a burden gone, to the last time he had seen him alive, sitting in his bath-chair in the garden of the Square, with Alice reading to him. Edmund had stepped into the garden to have a word with him, but his father only looked at him malevolently from his sunken eyes, mumbling and muttering in his beard. He was like an old monkey, Edmund thought, toothless and angry and feeble, and then suddenly he had struck out at him with the hand that still had free movement. Edmund had given him the rough side of his tongue for that; told him he must behave more prettily unless he wanted his allowance cut down. A nice way to behave to a son who gave him every penny he had!

Thus pleasantly musing he came out of this mean alley, and crossed into the Square. There were people about tonight, motors were moving this way and that, and a taxi was standing at the house next his, obstructing any further view of the road. Passing it, he saw that directly under the lamp-post opposite his own door there was drawn up an empty bath-chair. Just behind it, as if waiting to push it, when its occupant was ready, there was standing an old man with a straggling white beard. Peering at him Edmund saw his sunken eyes and his mumbling mouth, and instantly came recognition. His latchkey slipped from his hand, and without waiting to pick it up, he stumbled up the steps, and, in an access of uncontrollable panic, was plying bell and knocker and beating with his hands on the panel of his door. He heard a step within, and there was Alice, and he pushed by her collapsing on to a chair in the hall. Before she closed the door and came to him, she smiled and kissed her hand to someone outside.

It was with difficulty that they got him up to his bedroom, for though just now he had been so brisk, all power seemed to have left him, his thigh-bones would scarce stir in their sockets, and he went up the stairs crab-wise or corkscrew-wise sidling and twisting as he mounted each step. At his direction, Alice closed and bolted his windows and drew the curtains across them; not a word did he say about what he had seen, but indeed there was no need for that.

Then leaving him she went to her own room, alert and eager, for who knew what might happen before day? How wise she had been to leave the working out of this in other hands: she had but concentrated and thought, and, behold, her thoughts and the force that lay behind them were taking shape of their own in the material world. Fear, too, that great engine of destruction, had Edmund in its grip, he was caught in its invisible machinery, and was being drawn in among the relentless wheels. And still she must not interfere: she must go on hating him and wishing him ill. That had been a wonderful moment when he battered at the door in a frenzy of terror, and when, opening it, she saw outside the shabby old bath-chair and her father standing behind it. She scarcely slept that night, but lay happy and nourished and tense, wondering if at any moment now the force might gather itself up for some stroke that would end all. But the short summer night brightened into day, and she went about her domestic duties again, so that everything should be comfortable for Edmund.

Presently his servant came down with his master's orders to ring up Dr Inglis. After the doctor had seen him, he again asked to speak to Alice. This repetition of his interview was lovely to her mind: it was like the re-entry of some musical motif in a symphony, and now it was decorated and amplified, for he took a much graver view of his patient. This sudden stiffening of his joints could not be accounted for by any physical cause, and there accompanied it a marked loss of power, which no bodily lesion explained. Certainly he had had some great shock, but of that he would not speak. Again the doctor asked her whether she knew anything of it, but all she could tell him was that he came in last night in a frightful state of terror and collapse. Then there was another thing. He was worrying himself over the speech he had to make at this general meeting. It was highly important that he should get some rest and sleep, and while that speech was on his mind, he evidently could not. He was therefore getting up, and would come down to his sitting-room where he had the necessary papers. With the help of his servant he could manage to get there, and when his job was done, he could rest quietly there, and Dr Inglis would come back during the afternoon to see him again: probably a week or two in a nursing home would be advisable. He told Alice to look in on him occasionally, and if anything alarmed her she must send for him. Soon he went upstairs again to help Edmund to come down, and there were the sounds of heavy treads, and the creaking of banisters, as if some dead weight was being moved. That brought back to Alice the memory of her father's funeral and the carrying of the coffin down the narrow stairs of the little house which his son's bounty had provided for him.

She went with her brother and the doctor into his sitting-room and established him at the table. The room looked out on to the high-walled garden at the back of the house, and a long French window, opening to the ground, communicated with it. A plane-tree in full summer foliage stood just outside, and on this sultry overcast morning the room was dim with the dusky green light that filters through a screen of leaves. His table was strewn with his papers, and he sat in a chair with its back to the window. In that curious and sombre light his face looked strangely colourless, and the movements of his hands among his papers seemed to falter and stumble.

Alice came back an hour later and there he sat still busy and without a word for her, and she turned on the electric light, for it had grown darker, and she closed the open window, for now rain fell heavily. As she fastened the bolts, she saw that the figure of her father was standing just outside, not a yard away. He smiled and nodded to her, he put his finger to his lips, as if enjoining silence; then he made a little gesture of dismissal to her, and she left the room, just looking back as she shut the door. Her brother was still busy with his work, and the figure outside had come close up to the window. She longed to stop, she longed to see with her own eyes what was coming, but it was best to obey that gesture and go. The hall outside was very dark, and she stood there a moment, listening intently. Then from the door which she had just shut there came, unmistakably, the click of a turned key, and again there was silence but for the drumming of the rain, and the splash of overflowing gutters. Something was imminent: would the silence be broken by some protest of mortal agony, or would the gutters continue to gurgle till all was over?

And then the silence within was shattered. There came the sound of Edmund's voice rising higher and more hoarse in some incoherent babble of entreaty, and suddenly, as it rose to a scream, it ceased as if a tap had been turned off. Inside there, something fell with a thump that shook the solid floor, and up the stairs from below came Edmund's servant.

'What was that, miss?' he said in a scared whisper, and he turned the handle of the door. 'Why, the master's locked himself in.'

'Yes, he's busy,' said Alice, 'perhaps he doesn't want to be disturbed. But I heard his voice, too, and then the sound of something falling. Tap at the door and see if he answers.'

The man tapped and paused, and tapped again. Then from inside came the click of a turned key, and they entered.

The room was empty. The light still burned on his table but the chair where she had left him five minutes before was pushed back, and the window she had bolted was wide. Alice looked out into the garden, and that was as empty as the room. But the door of the shed where her father's bath-chair was kept stood open, and she ran out into the rain and looked in. Edmund was lying in it with head lolling over the side.

THE DANCE

I

PHILIP HOPE HAD BEEN WATCHING WITH LITTLE NEIGHING giggles of laughter the battle between a spider and a wasp that had been caught in its web. Once or twice the wasp nearly broke free, it hung with one wing only entangled in the tough light threads and he feared it would escape. But its adversary was always too quick and too clever; it swarmed about on its silken ladders, lean and nimble, and, by some process too rapid for Philip to follow, wound a new coil round head or struggling leg.

'Why, it's noosing its neck I believe,' chuckled Philip, putting on his glasses, 'like a hangman at work at eight o'clock in the morning. And it's got grey tips to its paws, like a hangman's gloves. Adorable!'

Clever spider! Philip's sympathy was entirely with it: he backed brains and agility against the buzzing, clumsy creature which had that curved sting, one stroke of which, if it could find its due target in the fat, round, mottled body of the other, would put an end to the combat. And the spider seemed to know that there was death in that horny scimitar so furiously stabbing, and skirted round it, keeping out of striking distance, while it spun its gossamers round the less dangerous members of its prey. The other wing was neatly tied up now, and then suddenly the spider pounced on the thread-like waist that joined the striped body to the thorax, and appeared to tear or to bite it in half.

The body dropped from the web, and the spider made a parcel of the rest, and took it into the woven tunnel at the centre of its home. Never was anything more neat and cruel; and neatness and cruelty were admirable qualities. Philip left the bed of dahlias, where he had watched this enthralling little spectacle, and stood still a moment thinking of some fresh entertainment. In person he was notably small and slight, narrow-chested, with spindle arms and legs. He leaned on a stick as he walked, for one of his knees was permanently stiff, but he was quick and nimble in spite of his limping gait. His clothes were fantastic; he wore a bright mustard-coloured suit, a green silk tie, a pink, silk shirt, with a low collar, above which rose a rather long neck supporting his very small sharp-chinned face, quite hairless and looking as if no razor had ever plied across it. His eyes were steel grey, and had no lashes on either lid: whether they looked up or down, they gave the impression of a mocking and amused vigilance. They saw much and derived much entertainment. He was hatless, and the thick crop of auburn hair that covered his head could deceive nobody, nor indeed did he intend that it should.

Beyond the lawn where he stood, half-screened by a row of shrubs, was the *en tout cas* court where, half an hour ago, he had left his wife and his secretary, Julian Weston, playing tennis. In point of age he might have been the father of either of them, and their combined years, twenty-two and twenty-three, just equalled his own forty-five. He could not catch any glimpse of their darting white-clad figures through the interstices of the hedge, and he supposed they had finished their game. He had told them that he intended to go for a motor drive, and no doubt they thought that he had gone, but there was no reason why he should not have a peep at them, to see what they were doing; and he walked quietly up to the screening shrubs. There they were, silly fools, only a few yards from him, sitting one on each side of the summer house. Sybil bounced a tennis ball on the tiled floor in the open space between them; Julian caught it and bounced it back. It was worth while to watch them for a little, and see what they would do when they tired of that. Five or six times the ball passed between them and then Julian missed it, and it rolled away, disregarded, under the table in the corner. They sat there, looking at each other. Philip, crouching down, moved a little nearer still invisible to them. He wanted to hear as well as to see. His face, satyr-like with its sharp chin and prominent ears, was alight with some secret merriment, and his small white teeth closed on his lower lip to prevent his laughing outright.

For the last week he had watched those two young creatures falling in love with each other. They had made friends at once when Julian came here a month ago, with the frank attraction of the young for each other: they rode, they played games, they bathed together in light-hearted enjoyment. But very soon Philip had seen that behind this natural comradeship there was stirring something that both troubled and kindled them. Their eyes were alight in each other's presence, their ears listened for each other. Sometimes each feigned an unconsciousness of the other till some swift glance betrayed the silly pretence. They would soon be as helpless in the silken web that enwrapped them as the wasp he had been watching, and indeed he himself was like the clever spider; for he had certainly helped to spread the net for them, encouraging their comradeship for the very purpose that they should get entangled. All this amused Philip, and it would be amusing to begin petting and making love to his wife again; that would touch both of them up. He would be very neat and dainty in device.

Suddenly these agreeable plans faded from his mind, and he became intensely alert. Julian got up, and Sybil also, and they stood facing each other.

'Does he know? Does he guess, do you think?' he asked.

She gave no audible answer. Then, which of them moved first it was difficult to say, but next moment they were clasped to each other, and then as suddenly stood apart again.

Philip, shaking with laughter, stole quietly away, for he had no notion of disclosing himself; that would spoil it all. Something in the abruptness of what he had seen made him feel certain that they had never passionately kissed like that before; for, if so, they would not have leaped to it thus and then instantly have recoiled from what they had done. But the time was ripe for him to intervene, and he promised himself an amusing week or two. Intensely amusing, too, was Julian's question as to whether Sybil thought that he knew. Did the boy take him for an idiot?

'I'll answer that question in my own way,' thought Philip. 'It will be great sport.'

It was too late to go for his motor drive now, and, passing through the house, he went for a short stroll along the edge of the sand-cliffs that rose a hundred sheer feet above the sea. He had been married now for three years, having been over forty when first he met Sybil Mannering. At once he had determined that he must possess this golden girl of nineteen. He was not in the least in love with her, but her beauty and her child-like vitality nourished him: it would be delicious to have the right to pet and caress her.

She was poor, but he was rich, which was all to the good, for that made an ally of her mother. He made the appeal of the weak to the strong, of the pitiful little loving *crétin* (so he called himself) to the young Juno, and her compassion had aided his suit. Then, as she got to know him, there grew in her a horror of him, and that was pleasant; her fright and her horror were grand nourishment, for they fed his dainty sadism. He loaded her with jewels, he designed her dresses. He took her about everywhere, boring himself with parties and balls for the sake of seeing the admiration she excited. But when he had had enough he would go to his hostess and say, 'Such a charming evening, but Sybil will scold me if we stop any longer.'

Then as they drove home he would say to her, 'Loving little wifie, aren't I good to you, taking you out of the gutter and covering you with pearls? You must be good to me. Give me a kiss,' and he would burst out into his little goat-like laugh at the touch of her cold lips. Then he had tired of that sport, but today, as he limped perkily along the cliff-edge, he thought he would renew his caresses. She shuddered at them before, she would shudder now with a far more acute loathing, and Julian would be there to see. Then he must make some needful alterations in his will. The chances were a hundred to one that she would survive him, and though nothing could prevent her from marrying Julian, he must make it as disagreeable as he could; make her feel that he wasn't quite done with yet. 'I wonder if the dead can return,' he thought. 'What fun they might have!' He did not in the least contemplate dying for a long while yet, but in case anything happened to him he would get his lawyer to frame a codicil. That, however, was not so important as the neat little comedy that he was planning.

It was growing dark; the revolving beams from the Cromer lighthouse swept across the golf-links like the spokes of a luminous wheel, and shone where he walked and then passed on and scoured the sea. The house he had built here stood within a hundred yards of the cliff-edge, queer and rococo, with two sharp turrets like the pricked ears of some wary animal. A big hall-like sitting room with a gallery above running along the length of it, and communicating with the bedrooms, occupied the most of the ground floor. Out of it opened a small dining room hatched to the kitchen, and close to the front door was Philip's sitting-room where a tape-machine ticked out Stock Exchange prices and the news of the day. You could scarcely call him a gambler, so acute and so well-reasoned were his conclusions as to the effect of the news of the day on markets, and often he spent the entire evening here, making out what would be the effect of the latest news on the market next day, and selling or buying first thing in the morning.

But tonight he had a more amusing diversion; there was to be dancing. He had the furniture in the hall moved away to the sides of the room and the rugs rolled up, and the polished boards made a very decent floor for one couple. He sat himself by the gramophone with jazz records handy, and watched the two with little squeals of pleasure.

'You beautiful creatures,' he cried. 'Why, you're positively made for each other! Dance again! I'll find a more exciting tune. Hold her close, Julian. Bend your head down to her a little as if you wanted to kiss her. Forget that there's old hubby watching you. Look into his eyes, Sybil. Try to think that you're in love with him.'

He gave his little goat-like laugh.

'Now we'll have a contrast,' he cried. 'You shall dance with me, darling. I can hop round in spite of my poor stiff leg.'

He hugged her close to him, he skipped and capered round her, dragging her after him.

'Faster, more fire!' he cried. 'Aren't I grotesque, and isn't it fun? I'm sure you never guessed I could be so nimble. Good Lord, how hot it makes one! Wait a second, while I take off my wig.'

He threw it into a chair: his head was as hairless as an egg, and gleamed with sweat.

'Now come along again,' he said. 'You are kind to your poor little cripple!... Now have another turn with Julian, while I cool down. But give me a kiss first.'

He gave her half a dozen little butterfly kisses, then kissed her on the mouth, cackling with laughter to see her eyes grow stale.

Every day he made traps and tortures for them. One night he went to bed early, passing with his limping tread along the gallery above the hall that led to the bedrooms beyond, knowing that, in spite of his injunction that they should sit up and amuse themselves together, he had poisoned the hour for them. He was right, and it was but a few minutes later that he heard them come upstairs, and Sybil went into her room next door, and Julian's step passed on.

He went in to see her before long in his yellow silk dressing-gown, and sent her maid away, saying that he would brush her hair for her. He kissed the nape of her neck, he talked to her about Julian, the handsomest boy he had ever seen: did not she think so? But did she think he was well? Sometimes he seemed to have something on his mind...

The next morning it would be Julian's turn. Philip told him he must be getting married soon. Wasn't there some nice girl he was fond of? Then he consulted him about Sybil. He thought she had something on her mind. Julian must find out—they were such friends—what was it, and tell him, and whatever it was, it must be put right. Sybil mustn't worry over any secret disquietude. They would dance again tonight, and dress up for it. What should Julian wear? Could he not make a costume—Sybil and he would help—out of a couple of leopard skins? Julian should be a young Dionysus, and Sybil a Mænad, wearing that Grecian frock that he had designed for her. They would have dinner in the loggia in the walled garden, and dance on the grass, and Julian should chase his Mænad over the lawn through moonlight and shadow. He laughed to see the boy's eyes gleam and then grow cold with hate. He was on the rack and no wonder, and the levers could be pulled over a little farther yet.

Then he had other devices for a day or two; he never let them be alone together for a moment, to see if that suited them better. He kept Julian at work all morning, he took Sybil out with him all afternoon, and there were prospectuses for his secretary to read and report on when dinner was over. He nagged at Sybil; he made mock of her before the servants, and it was amusing to see the angry blood leap to Julian's face, and the whiteness come to hers. Rare sport: they would have killed him, he thought, if they had the spirit of a louse between them.

'What happy times we're having,' he said one day. 'We'll stop on here into October, for we're such a loving harmonious little party. Do put your mother off, Sybil; she will spoil our lovely little triangle. Yet we've both got reason to be grateful to her for bringing us together. What about your marrying Mother Mannering, Julian? It would be nice to have you in the family. She can't be more than sixty, and as tough as a guinea-fowl without the guineas.'

There they were then: they were bound on wheels for his breaking. He could wrench this one or that as he pleased, and the other could do nothing but look on impotently. For a day or two yet it was pleasant to make sport with them, but the edge was wearing off his enjoyment and it was time to make an end.

He took Julian for a stroll along the cliff one afternoon.

'I've got something to say to you, dear fellow,' he said. 'I hope it will meet with your approval, not that it matters very much. Now cudgel your clever brains, and see if you can guess what it is.'

'I've no idea, sir,' said Julian.

'Dull of you, sir. Not even if I give you three guesses?...Well, it's just this. I've had enough of you, and you can take yourself off tomorrow. A week's wages or a month's wages of course, whichever is right. My reason? Just that Sybil and I will be so very happy alone. That's all. What damned idiots you and she have been making of yourselves. So off you go, and there will be a little discipline for her. You must think of us dancing in the evening. So that's all pleasantly settled.'

He was walking on the very edge of the cliff, and, as he finished speaking, he turned and looked out seawards. A yard behind him there was an irregular zigzag crack in the turf, and now it ran this way and that, spreading and widening. Next moment the riband of earth on which he stood suddenly slipped down a foot or two, and with a shrill cry of fright he jumped for the solid. But the poised lump slid away altogether from him, and all he could do was to clutch with his fingers at the broken edge.

'Quick, get hold of my hands, you senseless ape,' he squealed.

Julian did not move. If he had thrown himself on the ground and grasped at the fingers which clutched the crumbling earth he might perhaps have saved him. But for that crucial second of time his body made no response: if it could have moved at all, it must have leaped and danced at the thought of what would presently befall, and he looked smiling and unwavering into those lashless, panic-stricken eyes. Next moment he was alone on the empty down. He felt no smallest pang of remorse; he told himself that by no possibility could he have saved him. But, soft as the fall of a single snowflake, fear settled on his heart and then melted.

A flock of sheep were feeding not far away, and they scattered before him as he ran back to the house to get the help which his heart rejoiced to know must be unavailing.

II

The house remained shut up for a year and the turrets pricked their ears in vain to hear the sounds of life returning to it. Philip, by the codicil he had executed the day before his death, had revoked his previous will, and had left to Sybil only certain marriage settlements which he had no power to touch and this house 'where' (so ran his phrase) 'we are now passing such loving and harmonious days.' During this year Julian's father had died, and their marriage took place in the autumn.

Today they came to spend here their month of honeymoon. Fenton Philip's butler, and his wife had been living here as caretakers, the garden had been well looked after, and all was exactly as it had been a year ago. But the shadow of the mocking malevolence had passed for ever from it, and the spring sunshine in their hearts was as tranquil as the autumn radiance that lay on the lawns. Everything, flower-beds and winding path and sun-steeped wall, was full of memories from which all bitterness was purged; it was sweet to remember what had been, in a babble of talk.

'And there's the tennis court,' said he, 'with the summer house where we sat—'

'Yes, and bounced a ball to and fro between us—' she interrupted.

'And then I missed it and it rolled away, and we thought no more about it. Then I asked you if you thought he had guessed, and we kissed.'

'Just here we stood,' she said.

'And it was on that day that he began to mock us,' he said. 'How he enjoyed it! It made sport for him.'

'I think he must have seen us,' she said. 'You could never tell what Philip saw. And he wove webs for us. Look, there's a wasp caught in a spider's web. I must let it free. I hate spiders. If ever I have a nightmare it's always about a spider. Oh, what a pity! The sunlight is fading. There's a sea fog coming up. How chilly it gets at once! Let's go indoors. And we won't talk about those things any more.'

The mist formed rapidly, and before they got in it had spread white and low-lying over the lawn. A fire of logs burned in the hall, and as they sat over them in the fading light, a hundred memories which now they left unspoken, began to move about in their minds, like sparks crawling about the ashes of burnt paper that has flared and seems consumed. There was the cabinet gramophone to which they had danced… there was the chair on to which Philip had thrown his wig; above, running the length of the hall, was the gallery along which his limping footstep had passed when he left them to go early to bed, bidding them stay up and divert themselves. How the sparks crawled about the thin crinkling ash! Presently it would all be consumed, and the past collapse into the grey nothingness of forgotten things.

Outside the mist had grown vastly denser, it beleaguered the house, and nothing was to be seen from the windows except a woolly whiteness. From the sea there came the mournful hooting of fog-horns.

'I like that,' said Sybil. 'It makes me feel comfortable. We're safe, we're at home, and we don't want anyone to know where we are, like those lost ships. But pull the curtains, it shuts us in more.'

As Julian rattled the rings across the rod he paused, listening.

'Telephone wasn't it?' he said.

'It can't have been,' said she. 'Why, it's standing close by my chair, and I heard nothing. It was the curtain-rings.'

'But there it is again,' said he. 'It isn't from this instrument, it sounds as if it came from the study. I think I'll go and see. The servants won't have heard it there.'

'If it's for me, say I'm in my bath,' said Sybil.

Julian went along the passage to the room that had been Philip's workroom close to the front door. It was dark now, and, as he fumbled for the switch by the door, the bell sounded again, rather faint, rather thin, as if the fog outside muffled it.

He took off the receiver.

'Hullo!' he said.

There came a little goat-like laugh, just audible, and then a voice.

'Settled in comfortably, dear boy?' it asked. 'I'll look in on you before long.'

'Who's speaking?' said Julian. He heard his voice crack as he asked.

Silence. Once more he asked and there came no reply.

Julian felt the snowflakes of fear settle on him again. But the notion that had flashed out of the darkness into his mind was surely the wildest nonsense. The laugh, the voice, had for that moment sounded unmistakable, but his sane self knew the absurdity of such an idea. He turned out the light and went back to Sybil.

'The telephone did ring, dear,' he said, 'but I couldn't make out who it was. Somebody is going to look in before long. Not at home, I think.'

The fog cleared during the night before a light wind from the sea, and a crystalline October morning awaited them. Sybil had some household businesses that claimed her attention, and Julian walked along the shore until she was ready to come out. Not half a mile away was the precise spot he wished to visit, namely, that belt of shingle at the base of the cliff where, a little more than a year ago, they had found the shattered body on its back with wide-open eyes. He had dreamed of the place last night; he thought that he came here, and that, as he looked, the shingle began to stir and formed itself into the figure of a man lying there, and the dreamer had watched this odd process with interest, wondering what would come next. Then skin began to grow like swiftly spreading grey lichen over the head, and eyes and mouth moulded themselves on a face that was coming to life again; the eyes turned and looked into his, the mouth moved, and Julian awoke in the grip of nightmare. Even when the night was over and the morning luminous the taste of that terror still lingered, and he had to come to the place and convince himself of the emptiness of his dream. There lay the shingle shining and wet from the recession of the tide, and the wholesome sunlight dwelt on it.

Dusk had already fallen when they got home from a motor-drive that afternoon. As she got out Sybil stepped on the side of her foot and gave a little cry of pain. But it was nothing, she said, just a bit of a wrench, and she hobbled into the house.

As Julian returned from taking the car to the garage he noticed that there was a light in Philip's room by the front door. Sybil perhaps had gone in there, but, when he entered, he found the room was empty. The fire had been lit, and was beginning to burn up. No doubt the housemaid had thought he meant to use the room, and after lighting the fire had forgotten to turn off the switch.

He went on into the hall. Sybil was not there and she must have gone upstairs to take off her cloak and fur tippet and veil. He sat down to look at the evening paper, got interested in a political article, and heard with only half an ear the opening of the door to the bedroom passage at the end of the gallery that crossed the hall. The floor of it was of polished oak boards, uncarpeted, and he heard her step coming along it, and she limped as she walked. Her ankle still hurts her, he thought, and went on with his reading. He wondered then what had happened to her, for she had crossed the gallery several minutes ago, and she had not yet appeared. He had made no doubt that that limping step was hers.

The door at the end of the hall into the kitchen-quarters opened and she came in. She was still in her cloak and furs.

'So sorry, dear,' she said, 'but there was a bit of a domestic upset. Fenton told the housemaid to light the fire in the study, and she came running back, rather hysterical, saying that as she was lighting it she saw a man outside in the dusk looking in at the window, and she was frightened.

'Perhaps she saw me looking in,' said Julian, 'When I came back from the garage I saw there was a light in the room.'

'No doubt that was it. But Fenton and the gardener have gone to have a look round.'

'And the foot?' he asked.

She stripped herself of her wrappings and threw them into a chair.

'Perfectly all right,' she said. 'It only lasted a minute.'

Motoring had made Julian sleepy, and when, after tea, Sybil gathered up her things and went upstairs he must have fallen into a doze. He did not appear to himself to have gone to sleep, for there was no change of consciousness or of scene, and he thought he was still looking into the fire, and wondering to himself, with an uneasiness that he would not admit, what that limping footstep had been. He had felt no doubt at the time that it was Sybil's, but she had not been upstairs, nor did she halt in her walk. And he thought of that nightmare of his about the shingle on which Philip had fallen, and of the voice that he had heard on the telephone, and the familiar laugh, and the promise that the speaker would soon be here. Was he here in some bodiless form? Was he giving token of his unseen presence? Then (in his dream) he reached out for the paper he had been reading to divert his thoughts. As he did so his eye fell on the chair from which Sybil had picked up the cloak and veil and fur tippet she had thrown there, but apparently she had forgotten to take the tippet. Then he looked more closely at it and saw it was a wig.

He woke: there was Fenton standing by him.

'The dressing-bell has gone a quarter of an hour ago, sir,' he said.

Julian looked at the chair beside him. There was nothing there: it was all a dream, but the dream had brought the sweat to his forehead.

'Has it really?' he said. 'I must have fallen asleep. 'Oh, by the way, you went to see if there was anyone hanging about in the garden. Did you find anything?'

'No, sir. All quite quiet,' said Fenton.

Sybil lingered behind in the dining-room after dinner to pour fresh water into the bowl of touzle-headed chrysanthemums that stood on the table, and Julian strolled on into the hall. The furniture was pushed aside from the centre of the room and the rugs rolled up, leaving the floor clear. Sybil had said nothing about that to him, but it would be fun to dance. Presently she followed him.

'Oh, Julian, what a good idea,' she said. 'How quick you've been. Turn on the gramophone. Why, it's a year since I have danced. Do you remember?...No, don't remember: forget it...'

Julian, standing with his back to her, picked out a record. Just as the first gay bars of the tune blared out, Sybil shrieked and shrieked again.

'Something's holding me,' she cried. 'Something's pressing against me. Something's laughing. Julian, come to me! Oh, my God, it's he!'

She was struggling in the grip of some invisible force. With her head craned back away from it, her hands wrestled furiously with the empty air, and, still violently resisting, her feet began to make steps on the floor, now tip-toeing in a straight line, now circling. Julian rushed to her, he felt the shape of the unseen horror, he tore at the head and the shoulders of it, but his hands slipped away as if on slime, and fear sucked his strength from him. Then, as if suddenly released, Sybil dropped to the ground, and he knew that all the hellish forces of the unseen was turned on him.

It played on him like a blast of fire or freezing, and he fled from the room, for that was its will. Down the passage he ran with it on his heels, and out into the moonlit night. He dodged this way and that, he tried to bolt back into the house again but it drove him where it would, past the tennis-court and the bed of dahlias, and out of the garden gate and on to the cliff, where the beams of the lighthouse swept across the downs. There was a flock of sheep which scattered as he rushed in among them. There were a boy and a girl, who, as he fled by them, called to him to beware of the cliff-edge that lay directly in front of him. The pencil of light swept across it now, and as he plunged over the edge he saw the line of ripple breaking on to the shingle a hundred feet below, where, one evening, he and the fisherfolk found the shattered body of Philip staring with lashless eyes into the sky.

BILLY COMES THROUGH

MRS DOROTHY YATES WAS SEATED IN FRONT OF HER TYPEwriter, the keys of which under her confident fingering were making busy music. Her dress indicated widowhood, her alert and comely face efficiency. Opposite her, on the other side of the square, spacious table at which she was working, stood a similar typewriter covered with a black japanned case: on the blotting pad in front of it, as if in sepulchral decoration, was a vase of flowers.

Occasionally she glanced at some sheets of blue foolscap paper covered with very legible notes and jottings, which lay on her left: occasionally paused for a moment of concentration with her hands raised above her typewriter as if in benediction, but the pauses were short and soon the nimble clacking of the keys began again.

A broadcasting cabinet, rightly termed 'handsome,' connected with an electric plug in the wall, had proclaimed the News Summary at 9-40 p.m., and at 10 p.m. the listeners had just been taken back to the Scala Theatre, at Milan, to hear the Second Act of *Aida* which was now in full blast. But had Mrs Yates been bidden, at point blank rifle range, to give a single item of the news which had been so lately announced or to state any impression which the Second Act of *Aida* was conveying to her musical perceptions, she would have been unable to recapture any sort of memory of these emphatic noises. They were altogether external to her: the strange SOS which had preceded the News Summary, the brilliant *coloratura* soprano with her shrill assaults on the auditory nerve had arrived, so to speak, at a *cul de sac* and had failed to make any impression on Dorothy's brain. Nor did the storm of applause, the cries of '*Brava!*' which hailed the conclusion of her great song penetrate any further.

All that these noises effected was to entrench Dorothy more securely in the inviolable citadel of her inner consciousness. A storm of brass instruments, it is true, had caused her to murmur to herself 'Trumpets,' but that was only because, at that precise moment, she was tapping out that identical word on her machine...

Then suddenly the electric light in the room went out, and the wireless was stricken dumb.

This plunge into darkness startled her, and the interruption to her work, when her brain was teeming with ideas that clamoured to be recorded, was extremely annoying. But one of her admirable servants would certainly bring candles in a few moments, and she sat with hands in readiness to resume. Then she remembered that she had given her household leave to see a notable film that was being shown in the little town on whose outskirts she lived, and that if she wanted candles she would have to fetch them for herself.

She groped as far as the head of the kitchen stairs, but that steep and murk descent daunted her, and she shuffled back to her room. Clearly there was nothing to be done but to wait for the restoration of the electric current or to sit idle till the household returned.

Her chair was opposite the window, which was open and uncurtained, for the night was very hot, and she looked out over the flat land intersected with drainage dykes that stretched southwards and seawards. Every now and then the lighthouse at Dungeness opened and shut a luminous eye, and more remote winkings from the Gris Nez light on the French coast, punctuated the overcast darkness.

How often had those untiring sentinels furnished her with poetical passages in the stories on which she was so incessantly engaged! No doubt they would often again serve to embellish her narratives, and she peered into the night for fresh impressions. She could just see grey blots where a flock of sheep were scattered over the rich marsh pasturage; one of the dykes, catching such light as there was, smouldered sombrely; a train crawled like a glow-worm across the dark. But all these phenomena had been noted many times before: she knew the nocturnal aspect from her window with much minuteness, and her thoughts took a retrospective turn.

Twenty years of very happy married life had been hers, and her childlessness had been compensated for by an unvarying congeniality of companionship. Her mind and her husband's had indeed been complementary halves of a very agreeable whole, and for all those years their main and never-failing occupation, which earned for them both great enjoyment and a steady income, had been the joint compilation of incessant *feuilletons* for the daily press.

Dorothy and William Yates had indeed worn a track of their own in ephemeral literature: no sooner was one story finished than they embarked on another for which a further contract had been long ago signed and waited fulfilment.

They first discussed the skeleton outline together, and together they made a very full synopsis of the chapters on blue foolscap paper. It was then Dorothy's province to compose and to type the narrative portions of the work, including descriptions of natural scenery and of the personages of the tale, and as chapter after chapter was done she passed it over to Billy who furnished it with those justly famous dialogues between lovers and bitter enemies and epigrammatic conversations at fashionable luncheon-parties. The tale was then retyped by Dorothy, who was far the speedier manipulator, to Billy's dictation, and very little adjustment and planning was needful before the inserted conversations fitted into their places like a well-cut jigsaw puzzle.

Each of them felt the most sincere admiration for the other's work. Billy would say, 'My dear, you have never done anything finer than that word-picture of the thunderstorm in Chapter Ten.' And Dorothy's eyes were moist as Billy read those pages of heart-to-heart talk which finally expunged all misunderstanding and brought the lovers together.

These tales generally treated of high life, but broke away from the old-fashioned tradition that the upper classes were, only too often, of idiotic or criminal temperament. Both collaborators believed that kind hearts were quite compatible with coronets and that even Marquises could be intelligent in mind and impeccable in morals. They endeared the British aristocracy to the middle classes and went bail for its respectability.

This harmony between the two extended to the conditions in which they found they could produce their best work. One evening the wireless had not been silenced when they sat down to their writing, and both found that their inventive minds functioned with unusual fluency. They tried the experiment next day with the same happy result, and thereafter Billy always turned on the wireless when they got to work. National, London Regional, West and Midland programmes were indifferently tapped or they sought their noises from overseas.

'I think, Billy,' hazarded Dorothy in explanation of this odd phenomenon, 'that the aural evidence that other folk, as well as we, in London or Hilversum or wherever, are busy over artistic production, subconsciously encourages us to concentrate on our work. Or perhaps mere noise instead of distracting our inventive powers drives them inward, makes them dive, so to speak, below the storm-vexed surface into deep subaqueous calm.'

What the character of these artistic productions was appeared not to matter in the least. Whether a famous critic was giving one of his thoughtful talks about books, or a French professor was conversing in his elegant native tongue; whether a Wagner opera was being relayed from Bayreuth or dance music from a hotel in Mayfair or matins from Westminster Abbey, the same tonic effect was produced on the authors' imaginative faculty. Neither of them was directly conscious of what was going on: the quiet flow of agreeable erudition, the Terpsichorean gaiety, the religious solemnity were unheard by them, and Dorothy's conjecture that the aural evidence of artists at work was sufficient to open the sluices of the mind seemed a reasonable suggestion.

Less accountable were some curious little phenomena connected with their work and the wireless, which occasionally occurred. One evening, for instance, Billy had been engaged in writing the libretto of that stirring scene in which Lady Selina Vere and the son of her ducal father's estate-agent knew that they loved each other, and exchanged their first chaste yet passionate kiss. She was a girl of the open air, winner of the ladies' golf and tennis championships in the summer, and, in the winter, an intrepid rider to her own pack of hounds: he a lover of wild life to whom the song of birds was almost articulate speech.

In the very hour at which Billy was pouring forth this ecstatic dialogue, the last act of the *Valkyrie* was coming through from Covent Garden, and Brünnhilde and Siegfried, those eternal types of elevated human nature, were bawling out their exultant duet on the mountain top before they crashed into each other's arms.

Again, when Dorothy happened to be describing the wedding of the young Duke of Wessex in Westminster Abbey (a marriage that turned out so speedily disastrous for that godlike bridegroom), the third act of *Lohengrin* was being performed at the Opera. Or again, when, in one of their rare historical romances, Billy was describing an imaginary meeting between George IV and Jane Austen, it was curious that a literary critic should have been devoting his illuminating quarter-of-an-hour to novelists only lightly appreciated in their own day, but subsequently acclaimed as classics.

Similar coincidences—if such they were—continued so to multiply that it became impossible not to suspect some physical connection, as yet undefinable, between the nature of the entertainment—opera or lecture or symphony—which the wireless was emitting and the subject on which the minds of the authors was engaged.

'I keep on puzzling over it,' said Billy one night, looking out of the window when work was over. 'Ah, the sea-mist has grown thick, the fog-horns are moaning, and not a ray comes through it from Dungeness—'

'If it did, there would be no need for fog-horns,' observed Dorothy.

'Quite. I was only telling you what the night was like. I've been puzzling over those odd coincidences. Perhaps it is fanciful to imagine there can be any connection between the wireless and our minds, but think what a series of fanciful notions have eventually become scientific truths. Telepathy, for instance. Or even wireless itself. Only fifty years ago some great scientist pronounced that wireless telegraphy was a contradiction of the established laws of nature. No, dear, I am not arguing with you; I am telling you. So it's not impossible that some power, undefined as yet, co-ordinates our minds with what is going on in the wireless programmes.'

'But our minds are not conscious of what the wireless is doing,' said Dorothy. 'It's only when we look up the programmes afterwards that we learn what it has been broad casting.'

'That's an argument for and not against my theory,' said Billy. 'It's our subconscious minds that have been in tune.'

Dorothy considered this. She was the more logical of the two partners, and sometimes in the sacred cause of probabilities she had to curb Billy's imaginative fantasies and clip his soaring wings.

'But let us be more definite, Billy,' she said. 'What's the function of this power? What's its range? Does it decree that, because we have planned to write a particular kind of scene on a particular evening, the directors of the B.B.C. shall broadcast a suitable accompaniment? It can't be that, you know, for their programmes have certainly been settled before we knew where we should have got to in our story on that night. Alternatively, does the fact that the B.B.C. has arranged to play the Wedding March out of *Lohengrin* cause us to have got to the Duke of Wessex's wedding just as the wireless is broadcasting it? It must be either one or the other if there is any connection, and both seem to me purely ludicrous. It's a pretty notion of yours, but it doesn't bear examination.'

'"There are more things in heaven and earth—"' began Billy.

'I know there are. Ever so many more. But which is this one? State it.'

'I can't tell you exactly, but it's one of them. After all, in our stories we have often suggested a connection or sympathy between inanimate Nature and our characters. It's not once or twice only that you've made a thunderstorm coincide with some violent crisis in their affairs. According to your reasoning—did Nature arrange that thunderstorm to synchronise with their crisis, or did they arrange their crisis to synchronise with the thunderstorm? Neither is logical, but we've both of us often felt that thunderstorms and crises go together. There's a harmony.'

'That's true,' said Dorothy. 'I should be sorry to give it up.'

'Well then, why should there not be a power that puts our minds in touch with wireless programmes?' said Billy. 'That's all that I postulate. One conceives of it, naturally, as acting from beyond the limits of humanity. And there's other evidence for something of the sort. I'm told that sounds come through occasionally that are quite unaccounted for.'

'Atmospherics,' said Dorothy.

'No, not atmospherics; music sometimes or an articulate voice, coming from none knows where. I've often thought we might use that some day in one of our stories…'

*

Tonight, waiting in the dark for the current to be restored and looking out over the marsh, Dorothy recalled that conversation with singular distinctness. Nothing to support Billy's theory had disclosed itself, but the coincidences went on.

A year afterwards he had been gripped by a deadly disease, and, mercifully, its very fierceness rendered his sufferings short. Since then, as had been agreed between them, she had undertaken the *feuilletons* alone, and, oddly enough, the conversations, the dialogues, those vivid vocal clashes of temperaments, which had been Billy's province and which she had been afraid she could never be able to write, had come quite easily to her from the first.

Mr Clark Eddis, the literary editor of the paper which had serialised so many of their joint productions, was amazed at the sureness with which she had caught Billy's note:

'I can hardly believe,' he wrote to her, 'that the superb quarrel-scene which I have just read was not from his pen.'

No one was more surprised than Dorothy. With the wireless to drive her thoughts inward, these passionate conversations streamed from her typewriter with the same fluency as thunderstorms and dainty descriptions of a heroine's loveliness. She had been engaged on a cut-and-thrust dialogue of tremendous significance just now, when the lights and the wireless were extinguished, and she felt that she had handled the situation as Billy would have done.

Then with startling suddenness the light leaped to the lamps again, and from the wireless came a man's voice speaking in a dramatic whisper.

'Can you hear me?' it said. 'Oh, can you hear me?'

Dorothy jumped to her feet. She knew that there was little individuality in a whisper, but there was something in it that reminded her of Billy's voice.

A woman answered:

'Yes, I can hear you, but only very faintly, like a whisper from one who sleeps.'

'That is because I speak from the Valley of Dreams.'

'Cannot you wake? Cannot you speak to me in the voice I know?'

'It is difficult, for dreams hang heavy about my eyelids and my throat, and they are thick as mists before morning. But wait; the wind of dawn is dispersing them.'

There was a pause and Dorothy held her breath to hear what the voice would be. Her reasonable self told her that her suspense was childish and ludicrous, but she could not help listening for it with tremulous eagerness. In a few seconds the man's voice came again, now clear and easily audible.

'It is always twilight here,' it said. 'It is twilight at noon and at midnight. And the sad rain falls without ceasing, from low clouds.'

Anything less like Billy's voice could not be imagined, nor anything less like his mode. Dorothy picked up the newspaper and saw that a short play by Granowitch was being broadcasted.

'Bah! What rubbish!' she cried.

In a fit of exasperation she switched on to another programme, and, to the sound of cheerful jazz music from the studio, resumed her work on the typewriter, which had been cut off half-an-hour ago by the failure of the current.

Brisk and metallic was the clack of the leaping keys, and never had she felt so full a flow of inspiration. This would be more to

Billy's mind than that anaemic melancholy of Granowitch. How he would enjoy the justly pitiless speech of the Reverend Lord Elderbridge as he exposed the trumpery lies of the adventuress who, but for his falcon pounce upon her, would have succeeded in wrecking his son's life! Dorothy was near the end now; two days' more steady work would bring the reader within sound of the wedding bells. She had got on famously tonight, after switching off Granowitch, and there was a straight run-in to the winning post.

As usual, when there was little left but the close of a story with the assembling of relations for a marriage, or the birth of the first-born (always a son) to carry on the line of a noble house, Dorothy began to plot out the ground for the next story. There was generally very little difficulty about this, for she had but to choose one out of two or three settings and then get out the boxes of familiar figures and stir them about in her mind, as with a spoon, till they assumed some grouping which fired her imagination.

Now, for the first time, they failed to do so. They remained stiff and wooden, like animals out of a child's Noah's Ark. Her sense of romance, which she had preserved undimmed into middle-age and widowhood, failed to respond. It sat like some ailing guest without appetite at the savoury board. Yet, in herself, she felt that the appetite was there if only something to its taste was presented to it. These viands had grown stale.

Dorothy sat in her garden one morning puzzling over the cause of her listlessness. The pergola—she and Billy always called it 'pegōla'—which had supplied the scene for so many romantic incidents, and which, clad in its full June beauty of climbing roses, had often before now sufficed to set her sense of romance at work, was barren of stimulus; the church at the top of the hill was as solemnly grey as ever, but equally void of suggestion, and the brilliant green levels of the marsh suggested nothing but grass.

'How disappointed Billy would be with me!' she thought. 'He used to say that I was like some fountain in Greece—yes, the Pierian spring, that was the name of it—that always bubbled with inspiration. I wish Billy was here to help me…'

Then, suddenly, the train of these depressing reflections was snipped clean off. She remembered once more those odd coincidences between the current subject of their work and what the wireless was broadcasting. Billy had thought that they contained the germ of a story about some power which came through the wireless and established a connection with the subconscious minds of those who were in tune with it. It had been a fanciful idea of his: he had not been able to answer her logical objections to it, nor had he outlined any framework which would bear the weight of a story. But now, when Dorothy recalled once more the memory of that conversation, her listlessness vanished.

She saw, too, how it was that the familiar figures had become indeed stale viands. Or was it not more true to say that they were nothing at all, altogether lacking reality? Perhaps Billy, when he suggested that new fantastic idea, had felt that also. There might prove to be more reality in it than there was in them. She bundled them back into their box, and contemplated her fresh adventure.

Authorities. Dorothy wanted authorities, guide-books to the unexplored country. She and Billy had soaked themselves in the daily life-technique of the British aristocracy till it had passed into their blood; they had imbibed the mother's milk of the middle-class from the works of an eminent novelist, they had walked in gardens with one popular author and trodden the pavements of the City with another. And they had shredded these herbs into the pot to make the base of their soup.

But where was she to gather stock for the new potion?

She gave a comprehensive order to her bookseller to send her any number of 'spookiform' volumes.

They arrived in vast quantities, and for a month she studied occult occurrences without very much result beyond that of frightening herself considerably when she read this or that blood-curdling tale at advanced hours of the night.

She bought, at a second-hand bookshop, various publications dealing with psychical research, and there, indeed, was material bearing on a cognate subject, for she learned how the practitioners of automatic script seemed to be receiving authentic messages from the further side of death in satisfactory quantities.

The messages were of a very abstruse kind and the explanatory comments were quite as difficult to understand as the messages themselves. Yet these were kindred experiences; through the pencils of automatic writers there were arriving communications that were not of this world. Some power, some discarnate intelligence was apparently in touch with living folk. That was parallel, anyhow, to Billy's notion of a power striving to communicate with them through the wireless and calling attention to itself, rather awkwardly, by those strange coincidences.

But, for all her study, Dorothy could get hold of nothing that could be hammered and fashioned into a tale. This was worrying, for it was a unique and very disconcerting experience to have a subject and yet not to be able to write about it. And never had a subject taken such hold of her before. She felt herself to be encompassed by it and soaking in it. It clung to her and penetrated her, but in some fluid form that would not solidify.

The Mermaid roses that clothed the pergola were aware of it: so was the summer breeze that rustled the leaves of her morning paper. It went with her on her shopping errands in the town and accompanied her on her daily walk on the field paths. Most vivid of all was its immanent presence when she turned on the wireless, and, to the sound of lecture or music, concentrated on the problem of how to embody it in narrative. Evening after evening, she sat by the window as dusk deepened over the marsh and the beam from the Dungeness lighthouse pierced it: always, now, she waited expectantly for that silent and illuminating moment. The realisation of what she sought, perhaps, would come to her like that sudden spear-head of light from afar.

But patiently though she waited, no faintest beam vouchsafed itself, and, at last, Dorothy determined to put the idea from her, discarding it as unrealisable, and to get to work on yet another combination of the old puppets. She had decided that they altogether lacked reality, but when she got to work she might delude herself with them again.

A broad-minded Bishop would be a pleasing and novel character. He should be a finished man of the world; he should have great house-parties at the Palace of Princesses and Dukes and other eminent persons and positively encourage them to play golf on Sunday afternoon, provided they carried their own clubs and attended morning and evening service in the Cathedral.

'Why should Your Royal Highness bore yourself by going for a walk instead of playing an amusing game just because it is Sunday?' he pertinently asked. 'His Grace the Duke of Southampton is longing for a game, and I should feel inclined to join you myself if I had not my sermon to meditate over.' He smoked a pipe as fully robed, he drove himself back in his car from a Confirmation. He was summoned for exceeding the speed-limit because he had been implored to come to the death-bed of a woman who in life had been of a professionally affectionate disposition: he paid his fine without pleading extenuating sacerdotal circumstances.

He invited all degrees of guests to his dinners: a Marquis might be bidden to give his arm to a female Major in the Salvation Army, a Countess to the verger of the Cathedral.

One day he found a man thrashing his dog with undue severity: the Bishop called him a damned scoundrel in a voice that resounded through the Close. He walked unattended into a slum where two gigantic navvies were fighting, and, having compelled them to shake hands, asked them to tea at the Palace.

The conception of such a character would, once, have filled Dorothy with the pure joy of creation. She would have had her meals brought to her writing-table sooner than interrupt the flow of inspired composition, and all day and far into the night the wireless programmes of the world would have been poured into her unheeding ear. But now, after a couple of days' work, the savour of it evaporated.

It was not that inspiration failed, for boiling in her brain and eager for transcription was a cauldron of episcopal magnificence.

Never had the ample notes which preceded typewriting been more sumptuous nor her invention more prolific. But her pen moved sluggishly over the sheets of blue foolscap, for it seemed hardly worth while to pour out the contents of the cauldron on to paper.

How Billy would once have delighted in the broad-minded Bishop! What a sermon he would have given him to preach from the Cathedral pulpit! But to Dorothy, the only begetter of these riches of the imagination, all seemed flat and unprofitable. She was not interested in the Bishop, and well she knew the reason. The story which she could not write and which she had tried to put out of her mind was the only thing that she yearned for. But she went on with her notes and eventually typed half-a-dozen glittering chapters.

She was in this condition of barrenness where she would fain be fruitful, and of luxuriant fertility where she was content to be fallow, when Mr Clark Eddis, on holiday in the neighbourhood, came to dine with her. He was a good-looking, middle-aged man, who, all unwittingly, had stood model for heroes and villains alike in the series of joint tales. A slight curl of the lip coupled with a shifty expression was all the disguise needed to give his otherwise noble features a truly sinister aspect.

Dorothy's last serial had been a signal success, and he was eager to know when the next would be ready. She had already sent him the six finished chapters, and he was loud in praise.

'The best commencement you ever made, Mrs Yates,' he said. 'The Bishop is a wonderful creation and quite new, surely. Bound to be most popular. A splendid scene, where he tackles the blackguard who has ill-treated his dog. I wonder if you could give me an approximate date for its completion. You work, I know, like a house on fire when you get going. I want to announce it well in advance.'

Dorothy shook her head.

'I haven't got going at all,' she said. 'To tell you the truth the Bishop bores me. I don't think it's worth while writing any more.'

'Then I most respectfully disagree,' said Eddis. 'And I may say that hundreds, thousands of your readers will be of my mind. A perfect beginning. I see so clearly where the clash of temperaments will come in. What can be the matter with you, dear lady, that you aren't thrilled over it yourself?'

'It's because my mind is taken up with something quite different. We once talked over, my husband and I, a totally new idea for a story. It seemed to me fantastic at the time, but, since his death, it has gripped me, and now I can think of nothing else.'

'Tell me about it,' said he.

'Well, the idea is this. Imagine that there's some power, not a human agency, that can get into touch through the wireless with human minds. Rather like automatic script. Billy and I, for instance, used always to do our writing with the wireless turned on, and odd coincidences often happened. We found that the National programme, if we switched on to that, broadcasted something directly connected with what we were working at. It was as if it was arranged for us, as if something was signalling to us. I'll turn it on now, and see if anything of the sort comes through.'

Just as she crossed the room the window leaped into illumination and a bump of thunder followed loud and quick on the lightning. She switched the current on, and a volley of cracks and rattlings answered.

'Those tiresome atmospherics!' she said. 'I wish they could find a way of eliminating them. Yes, there is somebody talking below all that fusillade. Look out the National programme Mr Eddis, if you please, and see what's going on.'

For a moment the crackling ceased and Dorothy, making a sign for silence, put her ear close to the speaker.

'Yes, I can catch something,' she said. 'I think I heard my name spoken in a very low voice. It said, "Can you hear me now?" Ah, those atmospherics have begun again. What is there in the National programme?'

Eddis turned it up and looked at his watch.

'There's nothing going on,' he said. 'There's an interlude. There'll be the second news in a moment. You must be on another station.'

She looked at the dials.

'No, I'm on the National,' she said. 'Didn't you hear the voice?'

'No, I heard nothing.'

Then the wireless spoke quite distinct and clear in spite of the disturbances.

'Before giving the second news,' it said, 'there's one S O S.'

'I told you so,' said Dorothy. 'I am on the National. Let us sit and listen, Mr Eddis, in case it comes again.'

In spite of her distaste, Dorothy, during the next few weeks, made gallant efforts to get on with the broad-minded Bishop who had roused such enthusiasm in Mr Eddis. But the ardour, which in old days had kindled her imagination, had cooled into grey ash and could set nothing a-fire.

Now, too, the wireless was useless as an instigator. Once, as she and Billy had known, it drove her thoughts inward, and, under its unheard inspiration, she dreamed dreams and saw visions. But today, so far from helping her to concentrate, to shut the door on all external distractions, it claimed her eager attention, for she was listening for the voice which, as she was becoming convinced, was striving to get into touch with her.

This adventure soon became an obsession with her. Not only did it prevent her writing, but it absorbed all her thoughts. Who or what, so she ceaselessly asked herself, was that communicator? Billy had suggested that some great story might be written on the theme that a discarnate intelligence was using the wireless for communications of its own. How fantastic!

Yet what marvel could be more fantastic than this scientific instrument itself which could transmute the silence of night or noon into a whole spectrum of voices? You turned a dial an imperceptible fraction of an inch and, instead of listening to some lecture in London, you were in a concert hall at Berlin; another fraction, and without the pause of a split second you had flown the Alps and were in Milan...

As the hot summer days went by, Dorothy began to sit, hour after hour, in her workroom with the unfinished story lying disregarded on her table, while she listened for a whisper, a muttering, to manifest itself below the advertised item. Sometimes a fragment of a voice was audible, and with held breath and straining ears she sat motionless and intent. If once she could definitely convince herself that some external intelligence was busy she felt that she could frame a story on the lines which Billy had suggested. But conviction was needed.

By degrees she became aware that what she hearkened for was no unidentified Ariel, but Billy's own voice: his spirit, discarnate but still individual, was trying as eagerly to be heard as she to hear. Whatever the impediment was that caused this failure to connect, she believed it to be weakening. Her desire on one side, his on the other, were wearing it down. Ah, if only the way could be clear!

She sat, now, all day, listening for what she felt sure was coming.

Dorothy found this long, torrid summer very tiring. The heat drained all energy out of her; her appetite failed; she lost flesh. Usually, in August, she went for a bracing month to the Norfolk coast while her servants took their holidays, but this year she sent them away singly and stayed on herself. She was more comfortable, she said, at home, but secretly she had a notion that Billy would find her more easily if she was here.

Day after day, the hot air from the south, enervating and relaxing, sauntered in at the window of her workroom, just fluttering the leaves of the unfinished manuscript which she had long abandoned. Sometimes she glanced at a chapter of it, wondering that she could have written anything so lacking in significance and reality. She had composed it with gusto, she had imagined Billy delighting in it, but now she knew better.

He was here, invisible but individual, and some development had come to him kindred to that which now caused her to regard with an amused indulgence this childish performance. He had the same indulgence for it, a tender kindliness as for children building sand-castles on the shore and seeing tragedy in the advancing tide that washed them away. It had been a waste of time and energy, but that did not matter now that time was taking on for her a new aspect, as of a veil wearing thin and presently to vanish like skeins of mist. Yet it was real as long as it lasted, just as hunger and thirst are real till they are assuaged.

For the present, also, this aching fatigue was real, and real were the lamentations of Mr Eddis that she could make nothing out of the story she had so brilliantly begun; and real were the warnings of her doctor that she had a very tired heart, and that if she valued life she must go to bed and rest.

But such considerations had only a temporary reality, and there was no permanence about them. The only permanent reality was this most illogical of fantasies for which there was as yet no true evidence.

She went to the window which overlooked the pergola. Full moon sharply outlined the shadows and the interspaces were ivory white. Never had the external world seemed so unconvincing, and, as in a dream, she saw the door of her workroom open and the anxious face of her maid framed there.

'It's very late, ma'am,' she said. 'It's close on midnight. Won't you be going to bed?'

Dorothy moved away from the window and sat down close to the blaring wireless.

'Yes, it's time to go,' she said. 'But what gay music, is it not? They must be dancing somewhere. We'll let them finish the dance.'

She increased the volume.

'So gay,' she murmured. 'But I wonder if it's real. Perhaps it's only the echo of something else. The world is so full of echoes and shadows; yet the shadows must be the shadows of something substantial, and the echoes, the echoes of real sounds.'

She sat there with closed eyes; then suddenly sprang to her feet.

'Ah, there's his voice clear at last!' she cried. 'Billy darling, I can hear you beautifully? Where are you speaking from?'

STORY SOURCES

'Dummy on a Dahabeah', first published in *The Weekly Welcome*, 1 June 1896 under the title 'Cherry Blossom', and collected in *The Flint Knife* (1988).

'A Winter Morning', first published in *Six Common Things* (1893).

'Between the Lights', first published in *The Lady's World*, December 1907 and collected in *The Room in the Tower* (1912).

'The Thing in the Hall', first published in *The Room in the Tower* (1912). Any previous serial publication unidentified.

'The Passenger', first published in *Pearson's Magazine*, March 1917 and collected in *The Flint Knife* (1988).

'The Light in the Garden', first published in *Eve*, 23 November 1921 and collected in *The Flint Knife* (1988).

'The Outcast', first published in *Hutchinson's Magazine*, April 1922 and collected in *Visible and Invisible* (1923).

'The Top Landing', first published in *Eve*, 7 June 1922 and collected in *Desirable Residences* (1991).

'The Face', first published in *Hutchinson's Magazine*, February 1924 and collected in *Spook Stories* (1928).

'The Corner House', first published in *Woman*, May 1926 and collected in *Spook Stories* (1928).

'By the Sluice', first published in *The Tatler*, 25 November 1927 and collected in *Fine Feathers* (1994).

'Pirates', first published in *Hutchinson's Magazine*, October 1928 and collected in *More Spook Stories* (1934).

'The Secret Garden', first published in *Final Edition* (1940).

'The Flint Knife', first published in *Hutchinson's Story Magazine*, December 1929 and collected in *The Flint Knife* (1988).

'The Bath-Chair', first published in *More Spook Stories* (1934). Any previous serial publication unidentified.

'The Dance', first published in *More Spook Stories* (1934). Any previous serial publication unidentified.

'Billy Comes Through', first published in *The Story-teller*, March 1936. Not previously collected.